A flight into danger. A portal to another world. Adventures, danger, a new beginning, and a romance that spans forever.

Carl Goodman, a Merchant Marine sailor during World War Two, is shipwrecked off the coast of China and a temporary visitor at an American airfield, finally scores a ride to India to ship out on another vessel. Accompanying him is Ruby Matthews, a black nurse with her own set of problems.

Bad weather forces their plane to crash on an escarpment high in the Himalayas. As the only survivors with minimal supplies, they take refuge inside a cave where they discover a portal that leads them into an almost Eden-like garden.

After starting at odds, Carl and Ruby come to an understanding, and romance builds over time. However, their peace is interrupted by the arrival of an alien called Norlok, who has an agenda of his own. Defeating him is only part of the problem.

When rescue finally arrives, they find that eighty-five years have passed, yet they've retained their youth—until they return to the US, where they begin to rapidly age. Getting back to their garden is of prime importance, but will they be in time?

This book is a work of fiction. Names, characters, places, and incidents either are products of the author's imagination or are used fictitiously. Any resemblance to actual events or locales or persons, living or dead, is entirely coincidental.

Here, Now, And Forever
Copyright © 2025 J.S. Frankel
ISBN: 978-1-4874-4308-5
Cover art by Martine Jardin

Published by Extasy Books Inc

Look for us online at:
www.extasybooks.com

# Here, Now, And Forever

## By

## J.S. Frankel

# Dedication

*To my wife, Akiko, our children, Kai and Ray, and to everyone who's supported me all these years. To Debbie Nygaard, who edited my novel and made it so much better. To fellow writers and readers Richard Correa, Gigi Sedlmayer, Joanne Van Leerdam, Eva Pasco, Helen Dunn (who served as my chief beta reader and is a talented writer in her own right) Sara Linnertz, Stephen Drake, and so many more.*

*And to my sister, Nancy Dana Frankel, gone but not forgotten, this one's for you, sis!*

# Chapter One: Shipping Out

Tsu-yang Airfield, Western China, 1943. Morning. March twenty-seventh.

*I*t was the cold that always woke me up. Dry, windy, and bone-rattling, it settled over my flesh like a blanket that had been dipped in water and hung in a snowstorm, seeping into my skin and causing it to crack. I'd been here only twelve days, and it was a miracle I hadn't caught pneumonia.

At night, sleep was almost impossible. The shack in which I lived was a hastily constructed wooden hut, really, and all the blankets in the world didn't help. Only decently thick walls would, along with heaters, and that simply wasn't going to happen. No money for thicker wood, no money for heaters…we had to make do with what we had, and that wasn't much.

*All right, the hell with it. Get up, Carl.* I opened my eyes, thinking about what time it was. The wind whipping through a half-open window and gray skies told me it was probably morning—probably.

With a groan, I got off my cot, slipped on a pair of boots that were cracked and broken, and slung a very worn jacket that someone had given me around my shoulders. It cut the

1

chill, but only a little.

"I hate winter," I muttered to no one in particular and rubbed my chest, then shook out my arms and legs, hoping to get a little circulation going. Warm weather would eventually come, but that wouldn't be for another two months, at least, and I'd probably go stark-raving mad in the interim.

I looked around. Naturally, the shack was empty. Ordinarily, some of the other pilots I bunked with would be there, but considering the base had lost three transports in the past week, it was pretty much a sure thing that they weren't coming back and that their bunks would be forever empty…until replacements came along. Hearing the heavy thrum of transport aircraft that had seemingly gone on all night reminded me that flights came in and went out at all hours.

Stretching offered some relief. I went over to the kerosene heater, picked up a match left on top of the heater, and started the thing. Five minutes later, the fuel ran out before I could get even half-warm, and the frigid cold returned. With a curse, I went back to my cot to sit and check out the time.

A watch on a box next to my cot showed it was nine-fifteen a.m. The watch had been left behind by a pilot named Jimmy Grogan, and he was one of the five fliers who'd gone down with his aircraft. Before he'd gone on his final mission, he'd said, "Hang onto this for me, pal. I'll be back to get it in a couple of days."

A pity Jimmy never returned to claim it.

As for the rest of the flyboys, they mourned Jimmy's loss, got drunk in his honor, and then went out the next day to deliver their supplies to other bases. Since no one claimed the watch, I took it.

That was how it went. Fliers got briefed and went off on their missions, knowing it might be their last time. Long story short, they either returned — or they didn't.

The clamor outside sounded like the crews were probably hard at work getting ready for another mission. Perhaps something big was going down. I'd have to ask the man in charge. No one ever told me anything. It was on a need-to-know basis — that was the most common phrase they used. And I didn't need to know.

I went to the bathroom, washed my face, combed my mop of dark brown hair to make myself look presentable, and stared at my reflection. "What now?"

Answer — nothing.

I'd been here the past two weeks, waiting for a chance to get out of this place, but so far, no luck. Since I had time to kill and my stomach grumbled, I figured I'd head to what was often called a mess hall, which was just another filthy shack. The idea of eating breakfast there made me want to gag — the food was *that* bad — but I had no other choice. I exited my sleeping quarters into harsh March winds, holding my jacket close to me to shut out the chill. It didn't help much.

Numerous Chinese as well as American soldiers patrolled the area on the lookout for members of the Japanese Imperial Army. Guns up, always alert. While there hadn't been any incursions on land, three Japanese Zeros had come in forty-eight hours ago to strafe our airfield. Fortunately, a few of our fighter planes from a nearby base arrived just in time to drive them off. So, this airfield was safe — for the moment.

While walking across the compound, I wondered for the umpteenth time whether Major Weatherly, AKA Major Pain in the Butt as most everyone else called him, would ever let me on a plane to fly out of this hellhole and get back to the US. Or at least a friendly country where I could possibly snag a position on another ship.

If the latter happened, it would call for stopovers in non-occupied Japanese territory, and if that meant having to stow away in a crate bound for a neutral country, I'd do it. I wanted to return to the sea in the worst way, although my upbringing had been anything but sea-related.

Born Carl Allen Goodman into a family with its feet firmly planted on the ground in a small community, I'd grown up feeling there was something more waiting for me…somewhere. My parents, both greengrocers, had come over from the old country, otherwise known as Russia. They'd put down roots in Bryer's Hill, Tennessee, a small community of less than four thousand people, located around thirty miles from Memphis.

Being the token Jews there, they'd experienced anti-Semitism at first, but by dint of hard work and keeping their mouths shut, they'd become accepted — more or less — into the largely Baptist community of bible-thumpers. Everyone needed groceries, and my father developed a reputation of being honest with his customers.

My mother often helped him, but my father did most of the work, and boy, he worked hard. Eighteen hours a day, running to the local market to make deals at six in the morning, bargaining, arguing, smoking, and chatting with the other greengrocers…it didn't leave my old man much time to give me, his only child.

A tall man—around six-two and lean—Dad had a prematurely lined face and grayish-white hair. He also hunched over and walked with a limp that was the result of a car accident he'd had fifteen years earlier. In short, he was old and weary before his time, beaten down by life.

I resembled him with my tall and lean build, and we both had gray eyes, but he was forty-two going on seventy. Although his life path had been thrust upon him, he'd accepted the role. I knew his life choice wasn't the one I wanted for myself.

"I don't want to sell fruits and vegetables the rest of my life," I told him shortly after I'd turned sixteen. "I've got a different plan."

Call it the ultimate act of defiance in my family. My old man lost it, slapping me across the face repeatedly until my mother intervened. Angry and ashamed, I knew I had to leave. I'd been on the fence about it before, but he'd made up my mind, and my course was set.

I turned on my heel, went to my room, and packed a small bag. The next day, I took off. After I'd bummed a ride into Memphis, I hocked a gold watch I'd been given when I was thirteen. I had some money saved, so I used the funds to pay for forged certificates, then took a cross-country bus to the Merchant Marine main office in New York. Shortly after, I was assigned to a ship.

At six-one and a skinny one-seventy soaking wet, I wasn't impressive, but being tall for my age, wearing a sweater under my uniform to make me look bigger, and having a serious-looking expression helped to make me look around five years older than I really was. Since the US needed soldiers and sailors, they took whoever enlisted and didn't ask questions. My ship was a Liberty-class cargo ship and a two-year veteran of the seas.

Life on board a ship wasn't easy, but I persevered. Keeping my head down and my mouth shut saved my butt from serious conflict most of the time. When that didn't work, it was time to man up and fight. Sure, I got my butt kicked at times, but I learned to give as good as I got, and eventually, the other seamen left me alone.

Unfortunately, a Japanese destroyer sank us off the western coast of China three weeks ago. Four torpedoes to the hull and the subsequent explosions sent me flying into the water, and then of one their shells hit square amidships. My ship blew up, while I was treading water.

In horror, I watched it sink. All those men I'd served with…it was too terrible to contemplate. But in the cold water, I couldn't afford to mourn. I was determined to survive, so I started swimming. A piece of wood from the ship served as a life raft. It took me over an hour of kicking in the frigid water to make it to shore, but eventually, I did. Only later did I learn that I was the sole survivor.

A group of Chinese resistance fighters found me more dead than alive and stuck me near a fire until I recovered. Once I was able to travel, they led me over the rough terrain and past Japanese patrols to Tsu-yang, where they unceremoniously dumped my butt and said the Yankee flyers could take care of me. I soon found out that none of the Americans there wanted me around, either.

The man in charge, Major Weatherly, was a no-nonsense sort, and he resented the intrusion of a, as he put it, a *punk kid* with no experience and little training. "Your ship got sunk. Congrats. You lived through it. Remember, kid, I'm doing you a favor by letting you stay here."

Staying at the air base meant wearing a soldier's uniform that someone had left behind. I wore it, as my seaman's togs had been torn to shreds. It meant living in a filthy shack with the rest of the fliers, doing all the Joe jobs like digging crap holes, hauling away garbage, and cleaning up the barracks as best I could.

And every single day, I had to listen to the flyboys brag about how great they were at flying and boast about sex with the local hookers. Someone had set up a shack for the girls about a mile from camp, which the fliers visited when they weren't on duty.

I also had to wave away the heavy smoke in the shack—all

my bunkmates were heavy smokers and drinkers—and hoped that no creepy-crawlies lived under my cot.

I put up with the big talk and the lousy food because the whole time I'd been there, I'd held onto the hope Weatherly would find a way to send me elsewhere. I asked him about it daily.

"I'm working on it, kid," was always his standard reply. "Don't you have some work to do around here?"

It felt like he was punishing me for surviving.

While waiting for the good word—or any word—I reflected on my life. So far, at almost eighteen—my birthday was in a week—I hadn't accomplished much. Call me the dutiful son. I'd helped my father in the grocery store every day and then studied late into the night. And what was my reward for wanting to go my own way? A vicious face-slapping...

I shut that memory down.

As for school, it hadn't been anything great, either. I excelled at English Literature. No book was safe, and I learned a lot from reading, beefing up my vocabulary so I sounded more intelligent than I actually was. Other than that, call me a B-student.

Among my classmates, I was considered the perennial foreigner, even though I was born in the US, which meant I never formed friendships with the guys. As for the girls...the possibility of dating one of them was nonexistent.

However, being at sea turned out to be a great adventure. I worked hard, learned the rules by heart, learned what to do in certain situations, read worn paperbacks the other men had discarded...I absorbed it all.

My formal education had stopped at sixteen, but my world education had increased tenfold. By the time my ship was sunk, I'd gone from being an apprentice seaman, grade seven, to seaman first class, grade five. My next goal was to become a Petty Officer, a huge step up in responsibility and pay.

Not that the money was a goal. It never had been. Seeing the world was, in addition to doing my bit to help the US win the war. On my ship, I felt like I was somebody…until my vessel was sunk.

And now, here I was, a nobody once again. *Here* meaning a supply base where Allied pilots flew supplies in and out of the base almost daily to places like Tibet, Nepal, and India, and they often flew over the Hump, as it was unaffectionately called by the Allies. To civilians, it was known as the Himalayas.

Supply pilots flew a C-46 Commando, a large aircraft that was slow, not very maneuverable, and easily shot down by the Japanese fighters. It was a tribute to the skill of the pilots that not as many fliers had been killed.

Still, from what the pilots told me, when your number was up, it was up. Bad weather had killed more men than the Japanese air force. Storms, unpredictable winds, fog, and rain often forced aircraft off course. Many of the aircraft also had design defects, and the engines sometimes caught fire due to poor wiring or poor craftsmanship—lots of reasons, really.

If the plane crashed and the crew was caught by Japanese soldiers, they'd be tortured for information and then killed. Such were the misfortunes of war.

Yet, the concept of dying had never scared me. Maybe it was because I was young and kind of dumb. I'd never really given it much thought. Maybe it was just plain luck. My shipmates hadn't been so lucky.

As I pondered the whys of war, I noticed Sam Johnson, a stocky, hard-drinking veteran flier in his early thirties, standing near the tarmac smoking a cigarette. When he saw me, he dropped his smoke, ground it underfoot, and waved me over. "Kid, I got some good news for you."

Kid…he always called me kid, which riled me, but I decided to let it go. After all, the man had mentioned good news. "What is it?"

Johnson coughed and hacked up a wad of mucus, pounding his chest and cursing the weather as he muttered something about feeling crappy. Knowing him, he probably had a hangover. He smelled of cheap booze and didn't often shower. "We're scheduled to go out soon. Have to talk to Weatherly first." He scratched the back of his neck, shivering in the cold and cursing the major this time, not his health. He didn't like Weatherly, either. "Let's go speak to the pain in the ass. I don't feel like waiting."

We walked out to the airfield to check on the aircraft we'd be flying on, which Johnson had nicknamed *Betty*. A couple of engineers were busily fixing up her dodgy tail fin, which had never worked right. Two other men were taking the seats off her. The airplanes could hold up to forty soldiers, but by taking out the seats, they could hold a lot more cargo.

From what the pilots had told me, *Betty* was an older model, one of the first models off the production line. She often broke down, but everyone spoke about her with respect. She'd never failed them, always getting them to their destination and back. That was an enviable record.

Major Weatherly stood at the edge of the airfield, watching the landing of one of the planes that had just returned from a mission. When a few of the ground personnel went over to unload the plane, he called out, "Put that stuff in *Betty*."

As the pilots disembarked, one of them went over to Weatherly to speak briefly to him. Afterward, Weatherly dismissed the pilot and waved his hands at the workers. "Haul ass, men. We got a flight going out soon!"

Weatherly was a tall, slim man in his late forties with a

pinched face, small, beady eyes, and the attitude of *do it my way or hit the highway*. He waited alongside a young woman dressed in an Army nurse's uniform.

I stopped when I saw her. I hadn't seen any women around this camp except those who worked in the bars the pilots dragged me to even though drinking held no interest for me. I'd tried it once and gotten sick.

As for the bar girls, they also didn't draw my interest. They slept with anyone willing. Even though I was just a punk kid, I understood what they were doing and didn't hold it against them. A war was going on, business was business, and money was money. People had to make a living.

Over here, prostitution wasn't against the law, but all the same, I wasn't interested in catching the clap. Penicillin didn't always work, and the idea of getting syphilis scared me.

However, this woman was different. About my age, she stood on the short side of five-four and wore a brown army uniform consisting of a dirty jacket, skirt, and cap that couldn't hide her slender figure. With a pert nose and long, permed hair, she was the nicest-looking woman I'd ever seen. She reminded me of Dorothy Dandridge, only prettier.

Her prettiness, though, was marred by Johnson's angry expression. "Colored girl," he muttered with distaste. "What the hell is she doing here?" The man had never been the tolerant sort.

"We'll find out," I said, feeling curious now. "C'mon."

When we reached Weatherly's position, Johnson saluted, which Weatherly barely acknowledged before saying, "Johnson, your radio man Etheridge will be ready in an hour, along with your co-pilot Morton. We had to move up the schedule to eleven hundred hours. Your last crewman isn't coming…he's tailing off a drunk." He curled his lip in disgust. "Your plane's being loaded now with some food supplies but

10

mostly machine parts for aircraft."

Johnson muttered something to the effect that the planes at Tsu-yang could use the parts. The major told him to keep his opinions to himself.

Johnson grimaced, but from the tone of his voice, maybe he'd decided to play nice and asked, "Where are we going?"

"Koirengei Airfield in India."

"Fine."

Major Weatherly turned to me. "Goodman, once you get to India, you'll catch a ride with some soldiers going down to the coast of Mumbai. I've been sending messages to any ship that could use a good crewman. A reply just came in. You'll be shipping out on an upgraded version of the old Liberty-class ships. Got it?"

My heart jumped a few beats. "Yes, sir."

The corners of Weatherly's mouth actually crooked upward. "Fine." He swung back to face Johnson. "You'll drop off the supplies, drop Goodman and her off, too, and then come back when your aircraft's been serviced. Any questions?"

A ship, I've got a ship, I thought, barely holding back a whoop of elation.

Johnson, though, clearly had something more immediate on his mind, asking, "What's with her? We don't transport colored cargo."

This time, I winced at his words. Johnson didn't like the Chinese, and he despised the Indians. Still, he had the rep of being a capable pilot and about to take me halfway to my destination, so I put aside my antipathy and turned to the woman. "Hi," I said. "I'm Carl. The bigot is Sam."

Johnson pulled a face and started to say something, but Weatherly cut him off. "Stow it, Johnson. This is Lieutenant Ruby Matthews. She's a nurse. She was serving with a nursing unit on Ledo Road, but the Japs overran the place, and they had to evacuate. The plane with the nurses came in last night, and the others shipped out at oh-four-hundred this morning."

I heard the sound of engines but was too busy trying to stay warm to think about who was coming in or going out. Flights always left and came in at odd times.

As for Johnson, his tone turned whiny, and he didn't bother to hide his distaste. "So, why didn't the other nurses take her along?"

The nurse had been shivering in the cold wind, but at Johnson's question, her head snapped up. Her expression showed anger, frustration, and a lifetime of being stepped on by society. "They don't take coloreds along for the ride, that's why," she snapped in a familiar Southern accent. She sounded like where I came from.

Her voice rose in anger as she continued. "When the Japanese army came in, we hid out with a colored brigade of engineers. A couple of days later, a plane came to evacuate us, and they made sure I got on with everyone else.

"But when we got here, our leader got me kicked out of her unit and off the flight back to the States. And I don't even have a jacket. You're all warm and toasty while I freeze. You got that?"

Her angry and defiant attitude caused Johnson to blink and back up a step.

Weatherly got a look of exasperation on his face and rubbed his temples as if massaging away a potential headache. "You've made your point, Lieutenant."

"I'm a Second Lieutenant, sir," she corrected softly.

"Fine." He then turned to Johnson and waved toward the *Betty*. "You're just transporting cargo this time. You'll have enough room on the plane for her and Goodman, along with the supplies. Those are your orders. As I said, you leave in an hour. Get your flight log ready."

Johnson saluted his superior, grimaced at the nurse, turned, and stalked off. Weatherly shook his head and headed for his office.

I turned to the woman. "Sorry about Sam. He's a jerk sometimes."

"Sometimes?"

I had to laugh. "All right, most of the time. But he's supposed to be a good pilot. C'mon, let's get settled inside. Uh, do you need to use the bathroom?"

"I already went, but I'm a little hungry."

She shivered again, so I took off my jacket and offered it to her. "Take it. You need to keep warm."

She gave me a look of doubt. "You sure?"

"Yeah."

After she donned it, she thanked me, and we headed toward the mess hall. Along the way, I thought that one problem was solved. All we had to do now was get to India, and I'd soon be back at sea.

"Well, that's the mess hall up ahead," I said, pointing to the shack. "Let's get something to eat."

# Chapter Two: Mess Hall

*T*he mess hall was another wooden structure with one small window on each wall that allowed a minimum of fresh air in. It also kept in the smells of food, cigarette smoke, and passed gas. A few pilots and mechanics sat at rickety wooden tables, plates of food in front of them. Mac, a pot-bellied man in his late thirties, called it *food*. We called it SOS—shit on a shingle.

"You'll eat it and like it," was his motto to anyone who complained.

We usually ate what Mac served and then threw up half of it. Everyone called our cook *Mac* because no one knew his real name. They knew about his food, though, and they hated it. In addition to carping about the grub, the enlisted men smoked, drank cheap beer on their off hours, groused about their upcoming work and flight details, played cards, or chased after the local prostitutes.

When the nurse and I entered, though, all activity stopped. One man's face formed a rictus of hate when he saw us, and he uttered a series of curses, finishing off with, "What the hell is this?"

His question wasn't taken up by the other men, but their glares were like the first man's—full of ignorance and outright unspoken bigotry. Hate was a better word. One of the pilots, a man named Wilson, got up and strode over to us.

My co-rider whispered that we should leave, but I told her to stay put. "What're you and she doin' here?" Wilson asked in an angry Texas drawl. "Y'all some sorta Lincoln man, Goodman?"

Lincoln man? Yeah…Wilson was a really enlightened sort. He didn't like anyone who wasn't white and Christian. I'd put up with jerks like him most of my life. Still, this wasn't a time to get into a scrap. "Getting something to eat," I answered, feeling my pulse race.

Wilson grimaced and shook his head. He was shorter than me but thickly set and always up for a brawl. I'd learned how to fight, but fighting could cost me a spot on the plane out of here.

Still… "Hey, Wilson, we're just here to get something to eat, then we're flying out."

"Is that so?" He thrust his face forward. "Goodman, just be a good li'l Jew-boy and take your darkie friend outta here. We don't serve her kind — or yours."

That was it. Insulting the nurse was one thing, but listening to someone spouting Jew hatred was another story. If there was one anti-Semitic expression I hated, which was guaranteed to start a fight, being called a Jew-boy was it. My pulse sped up, and icy coldness filled my veins. "Call me a Jew-boy again." I stepped forward, gently pushing the lieutenant out of the way. "I dare you, Tex."

"Jew —"

He didn't get out the second word because I head-butted him, knocking him down. Wilson got up a second later, though, shaking his head like a wounded bull. He touched his nose and recoiled. "You bastard," he said, sounding nasal. "You broke my nose!"

"Too bad."

Then we went at it while the other men watched. I got a

15

shot on my beak and felt the blood run down my upper lip, but then I tagged Wilson with a left hook that staggered him. He went down a second later, but not due to me. The nurse had grabbed a metal napkin container and bashed him on the back of his head. Wilson twitched, twisted over on his back, moaning and holding his head.

As for the nurse, she faced the rest of the men and yelled, "Someone else want to call me a darkie? Go ahead. I'll whip your butts, all of you."

One man moved in, and he got his face opened up by the metal. Another man pulled a switchblade from his pocket and flipped the blade out, but before he could use it, a shot from near the doorway shattered the angry mood.

While holding my bloody nose to stop everything from leaking out, I turned around. It was Weatherly, and from the purple coloration on his face, he was practically apoplectic. I'd read that word somewhere, looked up the definition, and always wondered how it would look on a person. Now, I knew.

"What in the hell is going on," Weatherly bellowed as he trained his gun on the man with the knife. He then glanced at me. "Goodman, you start this?"

*Oh, right, it's my fault.* I held back a swear word or six and said nothing.

However, Mr. Switchblade spoke up in a pseudo-friendly manner. "Just a disagreement, sir," he said while folding the blade back into the knife and tucking the weapon into his pocket. "Goodman, here, wanted to get something to eat, but Mac said the galley was closed."

Weatherly nodded and holstered his pistol. "Uh-huh. And why is one of my pilots on the ground and moaning like an old woman?" He stared at the downed man. "Get up, you piece of dirt."

"Yes, sir," Wilson said, groaning as he got to his feet and stood at attention, blood streaming down his face.

Weatherly addressed him. "All right, Wilson, we're open and above board here. What happened? Did Goodman start it, or was Mac involved? Tell me...and do it fast."

Wilson glanced at me and then spoke after wiping his face and leaving a red smear all over it. He could've sealed my and the nurse's fate by ratting us out, but he simply said, "Just a disagreement with Goodman, here, sir. No problem, sir."

"And what was the disagreement about?"

Wilson looked helplessly at the other men.

The man clearly couldn't think past his next sentence, so I helped him out. "Baseball, sir. I'm a huge Yankees fan, and Wilson, he likes the Dodgers. We both think they're going to meet in the World Series. Well, we, uh, stated our views, and—"

"Enough," Weatherly said to me while massaging his forehead. He then turned to the nurse. "I see that another man has a sliced-up face, and you're holding a napkin container with blood dripping from it. Did you have a disagreement with him on baseball, too?"

"Yes, sir," she said in all sincerity. "I'm a Cards fan. He likes Boston."

Mr. Sliced Face nodded, holding his hand to his ruined cheek. His blood leaked between his fingers and dripped on the floor. "That's what happened, sir."

Weatherly uttered a soft sigh. "Fine, we're all baseball fans here. Goodman, Matthews, outside. You have a flight to catch. I'll get something ready for you to eat on the plane."

Wordlessly, the nurse and I walked outside and into the wind.

When we were out of earshot of the others, she whispered, "Thanks for sticking up for me. People usually don't do that."

"Yeah." That was all I could think to say. I kept my hand to my nose, trying to staunch the bleeding. It didn't help.

"I can fix you up on the plane." She gently pried my hand away to look at my honker. She dug into her pocket and pulled out a handkerchief. "Use this."

I held it to my nose. "Thanks."

"It doesn't look too bad."

"You didn't get socked in the beak."

She uttered a brief laugh. "No, I didn't."

We continued walking in silence for a bit, and then she said, "I didn't know you were Jewish."

"Someone has to be."

\*

An hour later, inside our ride.

The nurse finished checking my nose, saying it was swollen but wasn't broken. I went to the door to toss away the bloody handkerchief at her command. Fortunately, a garbage can was nearby, and I made the shot. Things were looking up. My nose was safe, and soon, I'd be out of this place.

Another bit of news came when Weatherly delivered two plates of edible-looking food himself. "Courtesy of our cook," he said. "Goodman, I should report your sorry ass and yours, too, Lieutenant Matthews. I should also make both of you stay behind, but Mac came through for you."

Surprise, surprise. "He did?" I asked.

Weatherly's expression turned sour. "Yes, he did. He saw it all and told me what happened, and he vouched for you. Since you're both on this flight and will be out of my hair, and since we have a war to win, I'm letting that little altercation in the mess hall go."

Relief surged through me. "Thank you, sir."

He grunted. "You're lucky the other men didn't bring charges against you. Safe flight, both of you."

After he left, we ate our meals, and then I went forward to thank the pilots in the cockpit. Johnson sat in the pilot's seat, Morton, another pilot in his late twenties, occupied the co-pilot's seat, and Etheridge sat behind them, tuning the radio. It was chilly inside the metal tube, and it would get worse once we were at full altitude.

"Save your thanks for when we land in India," Johnson growled, massaging his chest. "Kid, lemme tell you, you got some set of balls on you. I know Wilson. He's a jerk, but if you ground another flyer, they could toss your ass in jail."

"You could try." I couldn't resist needling him.

He grunted. "Yeah, we could. Right now, it don't matter, so let's let that go. What I want you to do is get back to the cargo bay. Y'all feel comfortable with the dark cookie back there?"

Internally, I shook my head at Johnson's blatant bigotry. I'd never been into racism. Maybe it was because I'd grown up being the other in school. Or because I understood what being different meant, although I couldn't completely understand what that nurse might have gone through. Whatever the case, I snapped back with, "She's a person."

A mean laugh emanated from Johnson's belly, and he stopped his rubdown. "You sound like you're sweet on her. Not that you've had any experience."

There was no reply to that. I knew Johnson was into hookers. He'd bragged about bagging them often enough. Many of the other pilots were also into the nearby prostitutes. Even though I was young, I knew I had a choice, and I chose to be true to myself. "I'm waiting for the right one."

Another laugh came from Morton this time. "Then you're

going to wait a little longer, kid. Now, get on back and leave the flying to us."

I nodded and went back to where the nurse was. A few seconds later, our plane began to move, taxiing down the bumpy runway, gaining speed, and finally, taking to the air.

As for the nurse, she huddled between a box of airplane parts and a couple of cases of food. It wasn't frigid there yet, but it would be, so I asked, "Uh, are you okay, Lieutenant Matthews?"

She looked up at me with a wry expression and shivered. "Listen, I'm not much on calling people by rank. Call me Ruby. You want your jacket back?"

"Keep it for now," I answered, feeling the chill but trying not to shiver. "I'll, uh, make do with something else."

"I'm still cold."

Right. No sense in mentioning the cold again. "Hang on."

I hunted around, found five blankets, and offered three to her. "Wrap yourself up in these. It'll get colder later on. Use one blanket as a pillow. Try to rest, all right?"

I slung one blanket around my shoulders and turned to find my own place to sit, but Ruby called me back.

"Where are you from?" she asked. "You sound like you're from Tennessee. That's where I'm from."

I nodded and sat across from her. "From Bryer's Hill. It's about thirty miles outside Memphis."

"I'm from near Memphis. Nellis Point."

I knew that section of the state. It was a small town, but everyone in my area called it the colored compound. No white people lived there. "That's a small area."

"Yeah, around fifteen hundred people. Lots of farms and grain mills. I had to get out."

"Why?"

She shrugged. "I wanted to be a nurse, help out the war

effort…see the world." Her manner, guarded before, dropped, and she visibly relaxed against the hull of the aircraft. "I like taking care of people. Always took care of my pa. He had a stroke five years back, so I learned about helping him. Pa died two years ago, and my mama, she had a bad heart, passed on a year ago. I don't have any brothers or sisters, so I'm on my own." Her expression read sorrowful all the way.

"I'm sorry," I said, striving to keep up. I'd rarely spoken to women, and at that moment, I felt a bit tongue-tied. "My parents… I don't know what happened to them."

She arched her eyebrows. "You're an enlisted soldier, aren't you? I mean, I've seen soldier's uniforms before, and you're wearing one."

"I, uh, left home when I was sixteen. I'm eighteen." I felt comfortable lying somewhat about my age. "My folks and I didn't get along. Guess I wanted to see the world, too, do my bit for Uncle Sam, so I joined up with the Merchant Marines. Served on my ship until the enemy sank us. I ended up in Tsu-yang. They had no clothes for me except this uniform."

"Couple of orphans, huh?"

I chuckled. "I guess so." While I wasn't an orphan, not exactly, I didn't know what had happened to my parents. Maybe they'd worried, maybe not. Although I'd felt sort of guilty leaving them, I had to find my own way. And my path had led me here…

The plane flew on, the cabin got colder, and our teeth were soon chattering. There was only one way to keep warm. I found two more blankets, wrapped them around me and asked Ruby if she wanted some company. "I mean, to keep warm, you understand."

She nodded. "Sit with me. It's all right."

We sat together, swathed in the blankets, and all seemed

well until Johnson appeared in the cargo area. "While you and Miss Southern Pride were having your confab, the boys in Koirengei contacted us. Seems a storm's building near the mountain range, so you'd better get ready for a rough ride. We might have to divert to Kathmandu."

Ruby started to say something, but Johnson merely chuckled, turned around, and left. "Same as it always is," she muttered. "Knucklehead white men..." She stopped and looked at me. "Not you, just—"

"I get it. No problem." It wasn't worth getting angry over, and she happened to be right. Johnson was insensitive, bigoted, and stupid. What else could be said? Nothing, apparently.

As we spoke, I sensed a deep sadness in Ruby. Her anger was obvious, but the sadness, well, I figured that came with being what she was. "What'll you do when you get home?"

"Get a job, I guess," she replied. "I'm six months short of nineteen."

Nineteen? "Uh, I thought you were, you know, older. I mean, you're a nurse, aren't you?"

Ruby lowered her head and spoke quietly. I leaned over to catch her words. "I had to get out of where I was. No future there...so I lied about my age. I said I was eighteen when I signed up with the Army Nurse Corps. I was sixteen. I went through basic nursing training, so I can dress wounds, bandage people up, take blood, stick an IV in someone...it's easy. Then I got shipped out. I was supposed to be with a group of colored nurses, but they knew I wasn't a real nurse, so..." Her voice trailed off.

"So, you joined up with an all-white group of nurses, and the army sent you here?"

She nodded. "Yeah. The white girls treated me like trash. One of them, her name was Mary. She was from down south, roundabout Louisiana, I heard. She was the leader, and she was the worst. Hated colored people...hated anyone who wasn't white and Christian, just like that Wilson guy back at Tsu-yang. That's how she was, and that's how most of them were."

Ruby inhaled and puffed out a breath. "They thought I was garbage, but at least they didn't ask me any questions. Once they saw what I could do, they left me alone. That was the good part. The bad part...you already know."

I said nothing at first. I'd lied on my application as well. No one had come looking for me, but being white, I could probably get away with it. Call it a privilege of my race. This girl had no special privilege, so I asked again. "Uh, what are you going to do once you're back in the States?"

Ruby shrugged, lifting her hands in a what-can-you-do gesture. "Finish my training. There are some colored hospitals I can work at. I'll find something. You?"

I really had no idea. Going home didn't appeal to me. On the other hand, I'd already secured a spot on another Merchant Marine ship, so that was settled. Assuming my record of being underage didn't come up, all would be well. If it did...well, I'd cross that bridge when I came to it.

# Chapter Three: Escarpment

Hours later. Somewhere over the mountains. Perhaps Tibet, perhaps Nepal.

The storm hit roughly seven hours after we'd taken off. It began with a slight buffeting of our plane, sudden rises, followed by drops. My stomach lurched, and I hoped I wouldn't toss up the mystery meal Mac had prepared for us. While I felt queasy, Ruby had already turned green.

"I think…think I have to throw up," she said.

*Wonderful.* "There must be a bucket in the aft part."

She got up and ran unsteadily to the back of the plane. Despite the noise from the engines, I heard the most God-awful heaving noises. A few minutes and more buffeting later, she returned, weaving her way back to where I sat.

"Are you okay?" I asked.

Ruby's complexion had gone from green to ashen. Call it an improvement—maybe. "You were right. There was a bucket. I wrapped it up in a tarp and tied it off…it smelled bad. I'm sorry. Between the flying and that food…" She didn't finish her sentence, although she didn't have to.

I motioned to the spot between the crates. "Lie down if you can. I'll be back soon." I went forward to see who was flying.

Johnson was in charge, both hands gripping the yoke, guiding the plane in and around the air currents as a veteran

24

sea captain would guide his ship through rough waters. "Hard ride," he called out. "It's past midnight, and it ain't going to get any better."

"What's wrong?"

He gave a mirthless laugh and then coughed. "What isn't? High winds, we're off-course, and we got no radar. In short, we might make it to India—or not."

What could I say to that bit of wonderful news? Nothing, so I turned to Etheridge. "Did you hear anything more from Koirengei Airfield?"

"Nothing," the radio man replied. "Just static. Too much interference. I tried Nepal, also…got nothing."

The plane bucked, and I hung onto the bulkhead for support, feeling my stomach lurch and my heart jump. "Kid, go back and check on the cargo," Sam said, fighting the yoke. "Weather's going to get rougher. I don't want nothing busted up. Go strap everything down real good."

Naturally, he said nothing about our human cargo except to mutter that if things got bad and we had to eject the cargo, the nurse would be the first to get the old heave-ho.

That suggestion sickened me, and I thought that when we got to our destination—if we got there—I'd never get on another airplane again as long as I lived. Morton and Etheridge were all right, but Johnson was a hopeless case. Besides, the war couldn't go on that much longer, could it? I hoped not. In any case, I decided to report him when I reached India. People like him weren't part of the American ideal.

Once I reached the cargo area, some of the crates had broken free and were sliding back and forth. Ruby sat huddled against the wall. "You okay?" I called out.

"No."

That figured. I let her be and got to work, piling the boxes and crates on top of each other and then tying things down from the floor and to the hull.

"I'll help," Ruby said as she got up.

"Thanks."

While she started trying to lash things down, I caught the frightened look in her eyes. It probably mirrored mine, and it was a good thing I couldn't see my reflection. "Hey, don't worry," I said, trying to reassure her and keep my voice from shaking. "We'll make it. Sam's a first-rate pilot."

Call that a pile of bull, but she needed reassurance…and so did I. Ruby shivered, but I knew it wasn't from the cold, so after we finished getting everything secured, I repeated my earlier question as she sat on a crate. "You going to be okay?"

"No," she answered in a small voice. "I'm not."

Ruby's fear was obvious, so I grabbed the blankets and sat beside her as we wrapped ourselves up. Then, since I didn't know what else to do, I tentatively put my arm around her shoulder. "We're going to get through this. Count on it."

She didn't lean against me or pull away. "You think so?"

Her expression was one bereft of hope, and my heart went out to her. "Yeah, we will. Listen, uh, it might help if you tell me about yourself."

By asking that question, I hoped she'd forget about the danger, at least for a while.

Her story was simple. She'd grown up in her small community, and she and her family kept to themselves. They didn't speak to any white people unless they came around to collect taxes or talk about some of the government programs. "We always kept on the quiet. My mama always said to me, don't raise no trouble, be nice, listen up, and be nice a little more."

Now, her sarcasm mixed with bitterness came through. "Be nice. When white people called me names, when the other white nurses told me that I didn't have what it took to be a good nurse, my mama told me to be nice. Someone want to tell me why? Because I don't have an answer."

"I'm sorry," I replied. I'd had it bad in school, but Ruby had it far worse, and I could only imagine how rough a ride she'd had so far.

And speaking of rough rides, the plane shook more intensely, and Etheridge's frightened voice rang out. "We got a problem!"

*Now what?* "I'll be back soon," I said as I took my arm away from her shoulder. "Are you going to be all right?"

She offered a wan smile and gave me a thumbs-up.

When I reached the cockpit, Etheridge pointed at the pilot's seat. "He just gasped and fell over."

Oh, hell, I thought as I placed my finger on Johnson's neck. No pulse. "I don't think he's in the land of the living anymore."

Morton shot me a scornful look and then stared straight ahead at the swirling snow through the front window. "Yeah, no kidding. I figure he had a heart attack. Nothing we can do now. He's dead. We got no communications, and the damn storm is hitting us hard. We're also off-course."

A sudden boom on the starboard side had me leaning forward to look out the window. Something must've slammed into the right engine because it had caught fire.

Morton cursed and flicked some switches on the console. "Cutting fuel to the engine."

Our plane dipped sharply, and I hung onto the bulkhead for support.

Morton fought the yoke to steady the plane. "Etheridge, any com with India?"

"Negative, sir," Etheridge replied in a frightened voice. "Just static, no matter what frequency I try. Sir, where are we?"

"Somewhere over Nepal, near as I can tell."

"What're you going to do?" I asked and looked outside. The fire had gone out, but our altitude had dropped sharply. This was definitely a worst-case scenario come to life. We were going down.

As Morton tried to bring the plane under control, I thought I saw an escarpment through the swirling snow. I said so and pointed.

"I see it," Morton said as he pulled his harness tighter. "I'm aiming for the cliff. Kid, go back and tie yourself down with that girl."

"But—"

"Go." He swiveled his head around to nail me with an expression of determination combined with resignation. "Now. I'll handle this."

If we crashed, all the tying-down wouldn't be worth spit. Still, I went back anyway and found Ruby huddled in the corner. "Ruby, we have to tie ourselves down with something."

Her faint but terrified voice answered, "With what?"

"Anything!"

In desperation, I grabbed a couple of stray leather straps, wrapped them around Ruby's waist and my own, and secured them to the floor. It wasn't optimal, but it would have to do. "Hang on," I told her as she grabbed me around the waist. "Hang on."

Our descent continued, and just before we hit, I hoped that death would be kind to me.

*

Minutes or hours later.

I woke up to pain, feeling every inch of my body rebel. I remembered the past few moments of our stricken airplane, the buffeting from side to side, the up and down shocks, the thunder, then the screams from Ruby and probably my own.

"Uh." My grunt got me going, along with the cold that came in through the smashed port side of the fuselage. We'd landed on the escarpment. I gingerly got out of my lashings, pushed off some boxes that had fallen on me, and checked myself all over. I felt like a massive hematoma, but nothing seemed to be broken, so I moved up front to check on the pilots.

Johnson was already dead, but Etheridge...what about him? I turned around, only to find the radio operator twisted up like a pretzel. A piece of metal had pierced Morton's chest, and his eyes stared at nothing. Despair filled me, feeling alone, but then I heard a faint voice calling for help.

"Hey, someone want to get this off me?"

*Ruby.* I went back to search the fuselage and found her buried underneath boxes and blankets on the opposite side of the plane. Her lashings had broken, and it was a miracle she hadn't been killed. "I'm glad to see you," I said. She had a small bruise on her forehead, but she seemed alert. "Are you going to make it?"

"I think so."

I shivered in the cold. "Let's get out of here. I don't know where we landed, but we have to leave. If a fire starts, I'm not going to stick around."

She nodded. "What happened to the other men?"

"Dead. All of them."

Her jaw sagged, and then she clamped her lips together and followed me out. A biting cold wind greeted us, along with gusts of snow. Ruby started shivering, asking through chattering teeth, "Do you know where we are?"

Like I had an idea? Morton had said that maybe we'd been flying over Nepal. The only thing I knew was that it was still fairly light out, so I'd been unconscious for a long time, and my watch was smashed.

"I don't know. Maybe in Nepal." I breathed deeply...finding the air awfully thin. "And we're really high up." I turned back to the remains of the airplane. It teetered halfway over the cliff.

"What do we do?"

Right, like I was some kind of survival expert. I looked around, saw an opening in the mountainside, and pointed toward it. "I think there's a cave."

We made our way over. The snow continued, hard and heavy, but the cave hadn't been an illusion. It had an uneven stone floor and was empty. Although it provided refuge from the biting wind, it was still frigid. "Okay, we stay here for now," I said. "But we need the supplies from the airplane."

Ruby went with me to the wreckage. There was nothing I could do about the crew. With a sense of regret, I left them in their seats and went into the opening in the fuselage, taking baby steps so as not to upset the precarious balance. Fortunately, some of the lashings were still usable, so I tied them around my waist, tied a few others to add length, and tossed the other end to Ruby. "Listen, tie this onto a heavy rock somewhere."

"Is that plane safe?"

"No, so that's why I'm asking you to tie this off," I shot back, tired, sore, worried about not being able to inhale fully, and wondering if I was going to go down with the ship.

Ruby took the lashings, and a few seconds later, she called out, "Tied!"

Fine. I started to carefully unload whatever supplies I could. I found half-smashed crates that held cans of fruit, vegetables, canned meat, blankets, and a med kit…it seemed to go on forever. I gingerly made my way through the cargo area, taking out the materials and setting them on the ledge. Ruby helped by hauling the smaller boxes to the cave one at a time.

A sound of tearing metal forced me to stop, and then the plane began to teeter on a downward slope. *The hell with this.* When I stepped outside, the remains of the airplane plummeted from the cliff to the ground below, yet I heard no sound of it impacting. Between the snow and the cloud cover, I couldn't see a thing. I got out of my bindings, grateful I hadn't gone south.

"Hey, I'm back." Ruby had returned.

"Plane's gone," I said.

"I…I can see that," she gasped. "Hard to breathe…I'm already tired."

My lungs were rebelling as well. "Altitude sickness, maybe. We…have to wait."

After what seemed like an eternity, we got everything into the cave, managed to fold up the blankets, and rearranged the cases against the wall.

Ruby shivered and looked around the cave. "We need a fire."

Fires needed wood. I hadn't seen anything on the plateau, and we didn't have any paper, so in desperation, I smashed open a crate of canned food and broke the slats. "We'll use these. But I don't have any matches."

"I do," Ruby said, still breathing hard. "One of the girls in my unit smoked, and before we shipped out, she asked me to hold her cigarettes and matches for her." She pulled out a pack of Lucky Strikes and a box of matches from her pocket. "It's full," she added. "Do you smoke?"

"No." The cigarettes I didn't need, but the matches, yes.

Bless the heavens. I wasn't religious, but someone I knew used to say that, although I couldn't remember who it was. "Matches...that's what we need."

Overall, while the crates were made of wood, we'd probably have to use all of it or freeze. We built a base using smaller shards of wood but needed something fast-burning to start things off. Miracle of miracles, I found a case with ten unbroken bottles of whisky. I took one of them, unscrewed the top, poured it over the base, and lit the pile. Soon, we had a fire blazing merrily. "You warm?"

Ruby shook her head. "No." She shivered. "Cold."

I picked up a blanket and slung it around her shoulders. "Here. I'll grab one for me, too."

When I was about to move to the opposite side of the fire, she said, "Wait. Sit with me...please."

Fair enough. We huddled together, lost in our thoughts. Ruby broke the silence and asked the obvious question. "We're not going to be rescued, are we?"

I thought about what to say and then decided the truth was best. "In situations like this, Major Weatherly said that no rescue parties go out. Japanese troops patrol the ground below. They, uh, they don't take prisoners."

Oh, her eyes had gone wide and were filled with fear. They also contained lost hope. That was something we couldn't give up, so I hastily added, "Thing is, we're so far away, I doubt any of the enemy is going to come here."

She then asked the second most obvious question. "So, it's just us two?"

Despair threatened to overwhelm me, but it was time to show some courage. "Seems to be that way."

# Chapter Four: Truce

Initially, Ruby's sobbing worried me, but I shrugged it off. After all, it wasn't every day of the week that a person crashed into a mountainside and survived, only to find out they were permanently stranded. She seemed overwhelmed, and despite feeling overwhelmed myself, someone had to do something. That task fell to me, even though I couldn't do it without her help.

"Hey." I turned to her, and after hesitating a moment, I grasped her shoulders. Although I felt weak, I just had to ride it out. "We survived, okay? We're still here. That crash would've killed most other people, so we're the lucky ones."

She didn't relax, but at least she didn't draw back. "I don't feel so lucky," she murmured, knuckling away her tears. "I'm stuck here…I don't know what to do."

I gazed around the cave. "Well, we already stacked things. That's a positive. And…and we didn't get hurt so badly, so that's also a positive. We're out of the wind and got a fire going, and that's because you had the matches. So, that's another positive."

I then took my hands off her shoulders, reasoning she probably didn't want to be touched. "You know, since we're still alive, maybe we should eat something."

Ruby finished drying her eyes. "You got a can opener?"

Right. Bashing the cans on the ground or the wall wasn't a

great idea. I searched the cases of cans, and…voila, I found a can opener along with forks, spoons, and knives that someone back at the base had tossed in. I also found a compass and five sticks of dynamite. A compass, yes, but dynamite on a plane? Too late to worry about that now. "Yeah. What do you want to eat?"

"Anything."

"Coming up."

Dinner consisted of two cans of Spam, along with a can of vegetables. Carefully, I opened everything, handed her half of the food, a spoon, a fork, and a knife, and I took the rest. We ate quietly, and once we were finished, I took her cans, crushed them, and put them by the side wall. "Well, that was a decent meal."

In truth, no, it wasn't. It'd tasted slimy, but a full stomach helped to fight off the cold, if only for a short time. I'd read somewhere that people who lived in cold climates and did physical work had to eat more because the body burned more calories…or something like that.

Ruby gave me a wan smile. "My mama was a churchgoer. She always used to say that any meal is a blessing, and every meal eaten with a friend is a double blessing. I like that saying."

Her reply surprised me. "Uh, are you saying that we're friends?"

"I haven't decided yet," was her blunt reply. "I've been disappointed a lot, if you know what I mean."

I guessed it was probably due to the color barrier, so I tried to tone things down. "Well, if it means anything to you, I, uh, didn't have so many friends in school, either. I didn't finish high school, to be honest…joined the service. But I read whenever I could to improve myself. You know, fill in my education. Sea life doesn't leave you too much free time, but

I got my reading in."

"Yeah, I never had much free time, either," she replied, and her mood turned reflective. "My mama used to say that an education could do wonders for a person's life, so I read whatever I could. She never had much money, but she saved and paid for my lessons."

"Lessons?"

"Elocution lessons," Ruby answered while checking her fingers before returning her attention to me. "My mama said that speaking well without a drawl would help me in life. She had a drawl as thick as molasses."

Well, Ruby did speak well, better than I did, actually. "Anything else? Got any favorites?"

"Favorites?" she repeated. "Like what?"

"Uh, favorite color, favorite food…that kind of thing."

She put her fist under her chin with a faraway expression like she was contemplating the universe. "Favorite color—yellow. Favorite food—dry rub ribs…you put the sauce on it while cooking the meat. Favorite singer…I got two, Lena Horne and Billie Holliday."

I gave her mine. Color—dark blue. Food—brisket and pasta. And singers… "Yeah, I like Lena Horne, too. Dinah Shore's also fine. Uh, and also Benny Goodman. Big band always swings."

She nodded in appreciation, and then she brightened. "I forgot one thing. Reading. My mama always said that books could take me places. And here we are."

That comment, made so seriously and with a straight face, made me laugh, even though our situation wasn't funny at all. "Yeah, here we are. Who did you read?"

"You're going to think I'm silly."

Now I was curious. "No, any book is good for me."

Ruby named a few before adding, "*Grapes of Wrath* meant

something to me. I mean, everyone in the book was white, but they were poor. I could relate to people being poor. My family wasn't rich. Even when I went to Memphis to meet my mama at the cotton factory where she worked, the other white families I'd see weren't rich. They were farmers and factory workers, just trying to get by. That's how it was." She shrugged as if to say the truth was self-evident.

I'd been lucky, in a way. I'd had a middle-class upbringing, but at the same time, I was aware of how poor people like Ruby lived. Black and white were two separate races, and never the twain would meet. Equal but separate. Maybe there was a saying like that. Now, though, we were in the same boat, or on the same train...or something.

"I liked *Of Mice and Men*," I said, struggling to keep the conversation going. "*The Good Earth* was hard reading, though. I don't know much about China, even though I lived there for a short time. I mean, at the airfield."

She laughed a small laugh, but a laugh, nonetheless. "I don't know anything about it. I got there with the other nurses, and we were only on the Ledo Road for two weeks before the enemy overran us. We escaped with some colored engineers and had to keep moving all the time. Then more soldiers came, and those nurses and I got sent to the airfield where you were."

She fell silent for a time before she spoke again. "Back in the US, I was stuck in Tennessee. Reading books is one thing, but I never got out of my town when I was younger. Never even visited another state. Joining the nursing corps was my ticket out."

What to say? My conversational skills were like my love life—nonexistent. "Yeah, I dig it. I shipped out when I was sixteen but didn't see much of the other countries we visited. Just a day or two of shore leave here and there...never did much except try out the food in the local restaurants. Did some sightseeing, though. That was fun."

"Nothing else?" She arched her eyebrows. "Flyboys and sailors have a rep...they're not saints, if you know what I mean."

A wave of embarrassment hit. I knew what she was referring to and stammered my reply with a shrug. "I, uh, never went to those places. Just wasn't interested."

Ruby simply stared at me with a twinkle in her eyes. "Is that right?"

Heat flashed through my body. She'd busted me. "I'm... Well...never mind."

She chuckled. "Me, too. No problem."

*Well, that went well.* Then I also laughed. Losing one's virginity was a priority with guys my age, but I'd never met any girl I'd liked enough. Not one.

"So, what do we do now?" she asked, inhaling deeply and slowly exhaling. It seemed difficult for her.

Breathing was difficult for me, too. "We have to rest. We're way up high... The air's too thin, so we have to acclimate. And we have to keep the fire going. All we have are blankets, and unless we find some clothes in the crates, we'll eventually freeze."

Ruby got up slowly, dropping her blanket near me. "We should search, right? I mean, just in case."

It made sense, so we went through the remaining crates one by one. Besides the one I'd smashed earlier for firewood, two more held cans of food, and another had more bottles of whisky. Most of the other crates held machine parts, but we also found some tools—a hammer, a pair of pliers, and some nails—but not much else.

Ruby pried the lid off one of the smaller crates with a hammer and gave a cry of surprise. "Look!"

I peered inside and saw two bomber jackets and two army uniforms. "Probably for some servicemen. They're different sizes." I took out the jackets and handed the smaller one to Ruby.

She slipped it on and hugged her body. "I'm a lot warmer now," she said with a distinct lack of joy. "It's big, but, yeah, it's just fine. Thanks."

After her somewhat hostile response, she said nothing else. What was going on? I thought we'd been getting along, and now, my cave partner had gone colder than an ice cube in the North Pole. Shock, maybe? That was all I could think of.

Still, things were looking up. My jacket fit me like a glove. I swung my arms around, enjoying the warmth of the wool lining and the freedom it provided. "My jacket's perfect. This is a lot better."

We went back to tending the fire, neither of us speaking, and then Ruby yawned. I checked outside and saw the darkness rapidly closing in. The snow had stopped falling, but the wind was still biting, even though it had died down in intensity. With night quickly approaching, it would get colder.

Ruby yawned again, so I decided to try the be-nice approach. "Listen, sleep is the best thing right now. It'll help you get used to the altitude."

"What about you?"

"I'll watch the fire and stand guard."

"Are you sure?"

"Sure. Go ahead."

Without another word, Ruby grabbed a couple of blankets and curled up by the fire. Soon, she was asleep, but a fitful kind of sleep that had her tossing and turning, muttering something about owing money to someone. At one point, she came perilously close to the fire but twisted away at the last second. Finally, she fell silent, but occasionally, her hands twitched.

I watched her for a while and then took up a position near the fire, feeding it more wood shards to keep it going while turning my attention to the outside. It was quiet, cold, and yet somehow very peaceful.

Thoughts of my past, the sinking of the ship, the people I knew…they all hit, and while the images were vivid and made me cringe, that was all in the past. I had to concentrate on the now, and that meant staying alive. I kept guard, walking back and forth to keep my blood flowing, swinging my arms and shaking my legs.

Finally, though, the exhaustion and the altitude got to me, and I found myself curling up by the fire. Sleep…just what I needed…

\*

A day later.

While I could breathe easier and didn't feel sick anymore. Ruby's attitude hadn't improved. In fact, it seemed she'd gone backward. Silent and sullen were the only words I could think of to describe her mood.

During breakfast, she said nothing, only muttering something about going outside to relieve herself, and she asked if we had any toilet paper. I searched the crates but found only a few handkerchiefs.

"They'll do," she said and walked outside into the biting wind.

When she returned, she sat by the fire and stared into its heart as if drawing strength from it. Since I didn't want to bother her, I took care of my own needs with some clean rags

I'd found. When I returned, I asked her what she wanted to eat later.

"I didn't realize we were in some fancy restaurant," she snapped, which got my temper hot. "It's not like I ever ate in one…because I didn't."

Still, I kept a cool head and said nothing. I set about cleaning up the empty cans as best I could, stamping them flat underfoot and then stacking them off to the side.

At lunch, which consisted of a can of beans that didn't taste like anything, I snuck a look at my companion. She ate quietly, not volunteering anything, and I finally got a little tired of her attitude. "Hey, you know, I'm not your enemy."

She looked up from her meal. "Is that so?"

Oh, I did not need this, not now. She'd been nice enough on the flight out, but now, it was like cowboys versus Indians…or something like that. "Yeah, it is. Look, we're both stuck here. I wanted to go to India and ship out, and you wanted to go home. We didn't get what we wanted, so we have to make the best of it."

Her response, when it came, contained elements of hostility combined with vulnerability. "Make the best of it? What kind of fool talk is that?"

"Survival talk. I'm being honest. Don't snap your cap when I'm trying to be nice."

She flared, her eyes shooting off danger signals. "Being honest? Trying to be nice?" she repeated. "Honestly, you got no idea what it's like for me. None. I'm not saying you're the problem. But I see you… You're the only white man here, and every time I see white, I see my folks being talked down to. I see my pa treated like a slave. I see my mama working hard in a white-owned cotton factory, working like a slave. I see my neighbors being treated like…like…"

"Slaves?"

Thin-lipped, she spat out her answer. "Yeah, like slaves. Lincoln may've freed us, but tell that to the Tennessee City Council. Tell that to the zoning men, the tax collectors…tell that to the nurses who treated me like dirt. Tell me all that, and then tell me you're on my side."

Rant over, she tossed her half-empty can into the fire. The smell of beans and spices drifted through the air. What could I say that would assuage her anger? Nothing, but I'd try, anyway. "Listen, I told you the truth before, and I'm telling you the same now. I can't completely understand where you're coming from. I…I can't understand because I'm not…colored.

"But I'm not the one keeping you down. I'm not the one collecting taxes on your house or treating your parents badly. I'm just me, the guy you're stranded with, so either we work together, or else we'll split the cave in half. I'm not sure how that's going to work, though."

Ruby said nothing for a few seconds, but then she drew an imaginary line with her finger down the center of the cave. "You want the left side or the right side?"

It was sort of funny, but I didn't laugh, as I didn't want to set her off again. "Let's sleep on it."

She grunted. "Sleep. I can't sleep, not well."

"I saw."

Her eyes widened, and her tone turned accusatory. "What in the Sam Hill? You were watching me?"

*Uh-oh…not good.* The last thing I wanted was another argument, so I stuttered out my answer and hoped she'd accept it. "Well, we both had altitude sickness. And…and considering there's nothing else to do here, yeah, I watched you. You were twisting and turning, and I was worried you'd roll into the fire by accident. You were muttering something about a debt… That's all I got."

Ruby grimaced. "My folks, they owed the landowner monthly rent. After my pa died, it was harder to make ends meet. Took my earnings plus my mother's earnings to keep things going. We managed, but the owner always wanted more. He shoved the knife in and wanted to twist it a bit harder. Then my mama died, so that was more salt in my wound."

"I'm sorry." What else could I say? Nothing, so apologizing seemed the best I could do.

She bit her lip, heaved in a deep breath, then forcefully blew it out. Her expression held remorse, and I could see the open wounds of what she'd been forced to endure manifest themselves.

"I'm sorry, too," she muttered. "You didn't do anything wrong. You wanted to get on your ship, I wanted to go home...but we're here. This is our home now."

From the slightly softer tone in her voice, perhaps there was room for friendship. But when the food supplies ran low, things could change...and I wasn't looking forward to that day.

# Chapter Five: Discovery

Although Ruby and I had reached a truce, our communication wavered between little and none. For me, thoughts of my earlier days growing up in Tennessee came back. I'd always wondered why my parents had chosen to put down roots in the south.

Traditionally, immigrants of my faith who came from Russia, Poland, and Germany tended to stay in the northern states and larger cities where more of our people existed. Safety in numbers and all that. Those places also had greater opportunities for employment. It was the pattern of most immigrants to find their own and settle in the same cities.

And then there was the matter of the same language…the same culture…the same shared values… But I had none of that during my childhood. As a little kid, I played with the other kids. We ran around, played stickball, went swimming in a nearby river, and there was never any trouble.

However, at the end of elementary school, those friendships simply dried up. I later learned that the parents of the kids I thought were friends told their kids not to play with the *immigrant kid* because it was *wrong*.

I was the son of immigrants, born in the US, but try telling them that, so friendships were out. Just how it was. And if someone had asked me about finding a girlfriend in junior high or high school, my response would've been a grunt of resignation. It simply wasn't going to happen.

Maybe my parents knew what I was going through, and maybe not. They'd had an arranged marriage, but that wasn't what I wanted. Stuff like that was from the old country. This was the US, and I let them know my feelings.

"Old is old," I told my mother. "The old ways are fine — for you. I want to do this on my own."

Naturally, they ignored me and did their best to try to find me a girlfriend — once. They didn't ask me. They just told me one Saturday night as we were having dinner. It was summer, so there was no school, and I was happy to stay home and read books and help my father in his store.

As we were filling our plates, my mother casually announced the date. "You're going to meet a nice girl tomorrow for lunch at her parent's house."

Sudden? Yes. And my first thought was that they should've asked me about it before setting things up. After thinking it over, I asked the most obvious question. "Don't I get a say in this?"

My father paused his eating. He never spoke during dinner. However, this time, he did. "You're going. End of story."

A *shidduch,* they called it. An arranged meeting, which in turn was supposed to lead to marriage somewhere down the line. I was fifteen, too young, but my parents urged me to meet this girl.

The next day, I put on my only suit, combed my hair, and tried to look presentable. My father drove us into Memphis, and we parked outside a large, stately home with a huge, neatly trimmed front lawn and a magnificent garden full of flowers bordering the front porch. It made our house look like a hovel.

As we got out of the car, my mother filled me in on the

details. "The girl's name is Ellen Silverman. Her father is a big-time lawyer in Memphis. Her mother's a teacher."

"They must be rich."

"They are."

Armed with these facts, we walked to the front door, and my father knocked. Mrs. Silverman greeted us cordially, invited us in, and introduced Ellen. She was also fifteen, short, slender, with dark, probing eyes and a witty manner. In fact, she was almost too perfect, and I wondered why she'd agreed to meet me. I was a skinny kid then, and nothing special to look at.

Her parents obviously felt the same way, as Ellen's mother felt free to express her feelings about me. "Well, he is a bit on the slender side, but a few more good meals will help him fill out a bit. Maybe some exercise, too."

Right, insult my mother. It wasn't as if she wasn't a great cook. She was, but Mrs. Silverman didn't seem to think so.

While my mother and Mrs. Silverman went into the kitchen to get lunch ready, I took that time to excuse myself when Ellen motioned to the backyard where a large flowerbed lay. We went outside, and she and I walked to the end of the garden.

Once out of earshot, she turned to me. "I have to tell you something. This is my fifth time doing this."

"A shidduch?"

She nodded, and her voice rang with a sense of grievance. "My mother matches me with everyone. Nothing against you, but my mother is always about matching me with someone from our community, and…"

"And you're not interested," I finished for her.

Ellen ducked her head and whispered, "I'm not interested in men. Does that answer your question?"

Initially, her statement went over my head, and then the

light bulb went off. "Do your parents know, that you're, uh, well—"

"Homosexual?" Ellen picked her head up, displaying a faintly mocking smile. "Lesbian. Queer. My father hasn't figured it out yet, but my mother knows. She thinks that having a boyfriend will straighten me out." She chuckled at her own joke. "It doesn't work that way."

Although I should've felt disappointed, I wasn't. In fact, I felt relieved. None of the girls at school had ever interested me, and even though I was with someone of my own heritage, I'd experienced no attraction to Ellen. Just as well.

We never went back to the Silvermans, my parents never mentioned the lunch to me, and life went on... Until the day I took off and joined the Merchant Marine. I wondered if my parents missed me or if they'd contacted anyone. I doubted it. No one had ever mentioned it while I was on my old vessel.

Still, I felt a sense of guilt over leaving my parents. We'd parted on bad terms, and it was too late to change that, but I vowed to write to them once I got settled on my new ship.

My thoughts of the past got interrupted when Ruby returned from her morning clean-up ritual. We had no water, but the snow served just as well for washing. It also helped with cooking, mainly boiling water for tea and coffee, which we found in one of the crates. I didn't drink liquor, and neither did my unwilling partner in solitude, so we used the alcohol to fuel the fire.

"How are you feeling?" I asked once she sat down.

Her face betrayed nothing, but her eyes held regret. She heaved in a deep breath and then let it out slowly. "Better. I, uh, I wanted to say that I'm sorry for...for acting like I did. I know I apologized before, but I figured I had to tell you again."

"Tell me what?"

"Us—you and me. I mean, it's not your fault. My mama said that having hate makes you dark inside, but sometimes, I can't help it. I see what others did to my parents, and I get so angry I can't breathe. But I know you're not bad. I...I feel you're good."

Her comment made me smile. "Nice to know. So are you."

Once again, peace reigned between us, but so did the bitter cold. And another cold reality entered. Once the food ran out, that would be the end.

*

Forty-eight hours later.

The cold weather hadn't let up, and neither had the wind or the snow. As for our situation, it remained unchanged. I'd done the night guard shift, and after I'd passed out, I awoke to someone shaking me. For a moment, I thought we'd been rescued, but no. It was only Ruby.

"It's about ten in the morning," she said. "You were, uh, sleeping like a log."

Right. I got up, feeling stiff, but after shaking out my limbs to get the blood flowing, I felt better. "What is it?"

"I went outside. The wind's gone. So is the snow. It's still cold, but I found a trail. It was covered in snow before, but the wind blew it all away."

A trail? "Where?"

"I'll show you."

We went outside and took a quick left where Ruby pointed to crude steps. We climbed up about a hundred feet or so, bent over and holding onto the sides of the rock for support.

The steps ended at a trail that had been carved into the ground. I pulled out the compass I'd stuck in my pocket and discovered the trail stretched out north and south.

"I don't know how far this goes," Ruby said. "I turned left after I got to the top of the stairs and walked for a while but didn't see anything. Then I came back to see if you were up."

She'd gone north. I'd have to remember that. "Maybe it leads to another cave. Well, we can explore later. We have to take inventory first."

An uncertain look entered my companion's eyes, clearly knowing what it meant. She silently followed me to the steps, where we carefully climbed down. One slip, and we were history. Once back in the cave, we went through the supplies together.

After taking stock, I came to one conclusion. "Even if we ration things out, we've got about a month of food. After that..."

I left the sentence hanging but Ruby's shocked look told me she knew the rest. "I'm sorry," I added. "I can't lie to you. I mean, if I were alone, it would be one thing, but since you're here...I don't want to lie."

She started to cry. "I wish you had."

Like a child, she sobbed bitterly. I felt like crying as well, but this was one of those times when breaking down wouldn't help. The fire was almost out, so I fed it some more wood, watching it catch fire, turn black, and then turn to ash. That's when I noticed the silence. "Ruby...where'd you go?"

She wasn't in the cave, and I thought she'd done the worst thing possible. I ran outside only to find her staring at the entrance to the cave. No, not the entrance...she was looking at a carving at the left side of the entrance. Somehow, I'd missed it when we'd first taken shelter there.

"What is this?" she asked.

"I have no idea." It looked like an old pictograph. The image was faded, but I made out the picture of a crude tree with a cup on either side of it. How old it was, that was anyone's guess. "Someone was here, but why would they carve this?"

Ruby shook her head and wiped her eyes. She took in a deep, shuddering breath before saying, "You know…" She turned to me. "I got an idea. If someone lived here before, then maybe they left pictures in the cave. I mean, we still don't know what's at the back."

That much was true. Our main objective was survival. Exploration hadn't been on the menu, but I thought, why not? It would take our minds off our troubles. "Let's go look. I don't have a flashlight, but we can rig up some torches."

After building the fire up, I ripped off two of the boards from one of the crates, tore some strips off one blanket, then wrapped them around the makeshift staves and lit them. "Torches," I said. "Let's go."

The cave was deep and went back at least two hundred feet, but the ceiling was high enough for us to move around freely without having to stoop. We looked for any signs of a previous inhabitant, maybe bones from a traveler who'd expired long ago, but we found nothing. Or I found nothing.

Ruby, though, gave a cry of delight. "Hey, over here, Carl."

That was the first time she'd used my name. "What is it?"

I joined her at the back of the cave, and she pointed to the rock wall. "Look."

It was the same carving as the one outside. Without a word, we held our torches closer. Ruby's slender fingers slowly traced the outlines of a series of carefully carved cracks in the stone, spreading out, not unlike the branches of the tree symbol we'd seen outside, and then closing together at the base to form the trunk of the tree.

Once Ruby finished, she backed away, clearly anticipating a reaction, but nothing happened. She gave a huff of disappointment. "Well, that was a lot of nothing."

I asked her to wait and went outside to look at the carving again. When I came back, I knew what to do. "We have to do it together."

"Why?"

"Because when I double-checked, I saw a hand on either side of the tree symbol. Maybe I'm crazy, but it looked like hands on either side of the tree. I thought they were cups at first, but now, I think they're hands." I put my torch down and cupped my hands to demonstrate. "So, if I'm right, it means we have to do it together."

Ruby's expression was doubtful, but she shrugged. "Might as well try."

After she put down her torch, she took the left side of the figure, and I took the right. We slowly traced the outline of the tree in unison, and when we finished, we held our breaths and waited. This time, the wall began to quiver. Blue cracks appeared in the rock, and the quivering intensified.

"Uh-oh," I said as I grabbed our makeshift torches. "Back up."

We quickly moved back as the rumbling increased. Ruby turned to me with a mixture of fear and surprise, "What's happening? Did we do something wrong?"

A moment later, the rock turned to dust and fell away, revealing a kaleidoscopic opaque wall roughly seven feet in height by maybe ten feet wide. The colors of the rainbow shifted constantly, making me dizzy. Still, this had to be the find of the century.

"I don't think we did anything wrong," I said in wonder. "I think we did something right."

# Chapter Six: A New World

Call this…weird. A person didn't see pictographs every day, they didn't see walls turning into dust, and they didn't see gateways suddenly appear. It just didn't happen…yet I stared at the evidence. It had happened to us.

While thinking about how something like this could be possible, Ruby asked a more practical question. "Well, do we stay here or go see what's on the other side?" From her body language—and her shivering despite wearing her bomber jacket—she plainly wanted to get out of the cold.

I felt the same way, but my mind whirled with questions. Where did this gateway lead, and could we live on the other side? Was there oxygen? Were there monsters? Would we be shot into space or possibly a volcano? Every science fiction and fantasy story I'd read came back to me. My imagination ran wild, leaving me with no idea of what to do.

Still, anywhere was better than here.

I hesitated only a moment. I didn't want to stand around in the frigid air and turn into an ice cube. "I'm thinking that we should go through. Just for a minute or two. If the air's okay, we can walk around, but we'll stay close to the, uh, doorway."

Ruby agreed. She put her hand out, I did the same, and she

gripped mine firmly. "We go together," she stated.

"Together," I echoed, taking a deep breath as we stepped through the swirl, just in case…

*

Surprisingly, we emerged in a forest, something that wouldn't be out of place in Tennessee. Tall trees and lush green grass that went halfway up my thigh and soft to the touch. The smell of freshly cut hay wafted through the air, even though there was no hay to be seen and no breeze.

Ruby let go of my hand, turning in a circle and looking awed.

I let out the breath I'd been holding and sniffed the atmosphere, grateful I could breathe. "Hey, it's…it's real air. I mean, it's fresh." Then I took another deep breath, and a feeling of well-being filled me.

"It smells sweet," Ruby said. "Like being in the country, only better." She looked around at the scenery, then added in a dreamy voice, "It's like a dream. Is this heaven?"

"We're not dead," I reminded her.

She turned and gave me a look that made me feel dense. "How do you know that? We could've died in that crash, and…and our spirits were waiting around. Like, the cave was purgatory, and this is heaven."

Oh, maybe she was one of those bible thumpers. They sometimes came to our house preaching about Jesus and such. My mother always slammed the door in their faces. "Are you religious?"

Ruby shook her head. "No. I'm not much of a churchgoer. I mean, I sang in my church choir, but I'm not like a preacher man's daughter or anything. Still, this place… You know?"

She had a point. "Well, maybe it's, uh, our idea of heaven,

but I don't see any angels flying around or hear the voice of, uh…" I pointed upward. "The man upstairs."

Ruby chuckled. "You look so serious."

Well, she was the one who'd brought up the subject of heaven. "Okay, did you hear or see anything?"

Her good mood seemed to vanish as she gave her answer. "Honestly, no, but it's like what I read in books when I was little. That's all."

I couldn't disagree. The place *was* otherworldly. "Well, let's go with the we-survived-the-crash-and-this-is-a-different-world idea. And since we're here, we should explore a little."

Ruby waggled her head from side to side as if considering whether to toss my idea or accept it. Finally, she said, "It's a nice day for a walk, so why not?"

It was warm, so we shucked our jackets, leaving them near the gateway. The portal had closed, but the tree and cup symbols remained, which meant we could go back if something dangerous appeared. At least, I hoped the magic or science, or whatever it was, would hold. Still, all remained quiet as we slowly walked through the grass, taking note of the flora but not touching anything—yet.

"Might be poisonous," Ruby said, pointing at all the plants that resembled fungi and edible vegetables.

Red and purple flowers the size of my fist poked their heads out of bushes, and when I bent down to touch them, a pleasant smell of lavender emerged.

Ruby was also poking around, checking out the flora, and picking a few items to roll around in her hand. No swelling appeared, no disfigurement… She dropped them and moved on to another item. "My mama taught me what to look for in a forest, berries and mushrooms and such. We should boil anything we pick."

It made sense. "I'll go back and get some utensils and a

couple of pots." I attempted to open the barrier, only to have it not work. "What's going on here?" I asked in frustration.

Ruby came over, delivering the obvious answer. "Carl, we came in together, so…"

Right. I mentally smacked myself upside my head. "Together," I echoed with a nod.

We retraced the image, and the barrier opened. We joined hands and went through the gateway, emerging in the cave once more.

"Together," we repeated, grinning at each other before quickly gathering cooking utensils and bowls that we found in one of the crates.

Back we went to the other side, and no, it wasn't a dream.

We found a bush overflowing with blue berries the size of my thumbnail and another bearing green berries that were half the size and triangular-shaped. Further along, we found mushrooms — or what passed for mushrooms — growing at the base of a tree. Ruby added them to the large pot she carried.

The leaves of the trees were enormous five-pointed things and bluish-green, and the low-hanging branches were laden with orangey-colored fruit. I pulled one off, noting the lumps all over it, and it smelled like bread and butter. My astonishment was quickly moving toward acceptance, and Ruby seemed delighted at where we were.

We kept walking, and further along, we found a mini lake. I grabbed a nearby stick and tentatively stirred the water, but nothing surfaced. "I wonder if it's okay to drink."

"Boil first, then drink," Ruby reminded me.

Fine, I'd wait. We sat in the field, listening to the quiet around us and examining our take.

"I don't think the berries are poisonous," I said, trying one of the blue berries before she could stop me. It tasted sweet.

"How do you feel?" she asked after a couple of minutes had passed.

"Fine."

We waited, but after ten minutes, nothing happened, so she tried one, too, and nodded her appreciation.

"Oh, yes, these are good." She popped a handful of the berries in her mouth and mumbled, "Just fine."

It seemed as though all the fruit agreed with us. Nothing had any particular smell, so we had to go by taste. Well, except for the orangey fruit that had smelled like bread and butter and tasted just like it. After using the torches to build a fire, we boiled the mushrooms, and they tasted like bananas.

My stomach was almost full, but the green berries looked inviting. I took a couple, and while they tasted tart, they seemed to agree with me…until my bowels told me a different story.

"What is it?" Ruby asked. "You look like you—"

"Gotta go!" I ran off to the side, hid in a bush, dropped my pants, and everything poured out of me. Those green berries were a powerful purgative, and I kept going until my stomach was empty and aching. Leaves off a nearby bush served as toilet paper. I just hoped the bush wasn't like poison ivy.

When I returned, Ruby wore a grin a mile wide. "I told you we should've boiled those green ones."

Although the situation called for a sarcastic reply, I stifled it. "It's a little late for that."

A second later, my stomach told me it was time to go again, and with an air of resignation, I ran off to the side to answer nature's call. Live and learn, I told myself. Live and learn.

*

After my stomach felt normal again, we sat and discussed

the things we'd discovered so far. We came to a couple of conclusions. First, we were safe in this place, wherever it was. The fruit, outside of the green berries, also seemed safe. And while the water tasted like it had a high lead content, it was clean, so we wouldn't die of dehydration.

Conclusion number two was a little harder to digest.

"Okay, if this isn't heaven, then where are we? And who built that gateway?" Ruby wondered aloud. She seemed to have accepted my *we-survived-the-crash* argument.

I pointed to the sky, where a hot yellow sun hung high overhead, bathing us in a lovely yellow glow. It seemed as though this place was perfect for us. Hot but not too hot. Safe food and clean water. Just like paradise.

Ruby apparently picked up on my gesture. "Are you thinking what I'm thinking? I mean, li'l green men?"

"Maybe they're not green." I shrugged, trying to get used to the idea. "But you have to admit, humans didn't build that gateway. I don't think anyone could. I mean, there's a sun, so are we in a…a small universe someone built, or are we somewhere else? I got no idea, but I know that carving we saw and the carving on the wall that turned to dust…that portal…I don't think our science boys could come up with something like that."

Ruby gazed around the area. "I guess you're right. But why?"

I spread my hands wide, partially out of frustration because I didn't know what else to do. "I don't know. If someone built this place, then maybe they wanted a, I don't know, a vacation area. Maybe they just wanted to experiment and see what they could make. It doesn't matter. What matters is that we're here, and they're letting us use it."

After my speech, a question occurred to me. "You think they're watching us?"

Ruby's eyes grew round. "Y'mean, like we watch lab animals?"

I mentally winced at the implications. "Yeah, like lab animals. Or zoo animals."

Naturally, our gazes went to the sky. It was a beautiful blue devoid of clouds, and that yellow sun shined its glory on us. "Let's check the trees," I said.

So, we got up and checked around our immediate area, only to find...nothing. No cameras, no listening devices...nothing.

Once we regrouped, Ruby blew out a deep breath. "I guess they're not spying on us. I didn't see any cameras, did you?" Disappointment rang in her tone.

I felt sort of disappointed as well. It seemed that we were truly alone here. The unspoken question was, would someone return to this spot? If they did, what would they do? Even if no one showed up, I wondered what we'd do when night fell.

Ruby's voice interrupted my wayward thoughts. "Let's take a walk. I want to see more of this place."

Good idea.

We got up and walked around, going every which way, learning that we were indeed inside an enclosed space. Once we finished our trek, I was tired, but I figured we'd walked about a mile all around an almost perfect square. When we came to a wall west of our entry point, we found another carving identical to the one we'd already used.

"Another entrance and exit," I said.

"Nice to know we have another way to get out," Ruby replied. "But where does it lead?"

That was a question we'd have to explore later.

During our walk, we also found a stream with fast-running water that came out of the rock face. Where it came from was another mystery we couldn't answer, but we followed it to where it spilled into a good-sized pond.

I knew one thing for sure, and Ruby echoed it—when someone gave a person a gift, they should never turn it down.

Ruby glanced at me with curiosity shining in her eyes. "We should take a chance and check out that new portal," she said.

So we walked to the far wall, the one with the same tree symbol and two-hands symbol on it. We traced the outline of the pictograph, Ruby took my hand when a portal opened, and we stepped through. A blast of cold wind hit me, and I looked around, realizing we'd landed right back in our cave. The gateway stayed open for about seven seconds after we walked through and then snapped shut.

Still…coming out at the original entrance point? Call that a mind-bender. It was weird, and neither of us could explain it.

Ruby's expression filled with awe. "Some walk," she enthused as we reentered our garden. "This place isn't endless, but it's enough for us, don't you think?"

"Uh, yeah," I said, realizing that it was just for us, at least it seemed to be just for us. An old biblical story ran through my head, but it was too early to be thinking about the Garden of Eden. "Uh, I wonder when it gets dark here?"

She shrugged. "Maybe it doesn't."

We waited, and after our lunch and another walk, I felt tired, so I passed out under the shade of a tree. Ruby joined me, and when we awoke, the sun—artificial or otherwise—had shifted its position ever so slightly. In a few hours, it might get dark.

"We'd better think about where to sleep," I said. "I don't know if anything will come out at night. You know, insects, animals…that kind of thing."

"We haven't seen any," Ruby pointed out.

"Just because we haven't seen any doesn't mean there aren't any," I rejoined. "They may be better at hiding than we think. I don't know about you, but I don't want any creepy-crawlies getting inside my pants. Anyway, I have an idea. Let's pull some of the crates inside and try to get off the ground."

Ruby eyed me carefully. "You mean, build a treehouse?"

"You read my mind."

It took time, but we managed to get half of everything inside before darkness hit. I cracked off the tops of two crates and climbed a tree, where the branches spread out, offering a relatively flat area. With Ruby's help, I got the wooden tops nailed down and covered the boards with a few blankets, then I made makeshift pillows with two other blankets. "Come on up to our treehouse."

She climbed up quickly, and once atop our little nest, she lay down with a happy sigh. "Some interesting day." She glanced at me and patted the place beside her. "I, uh, guess it's okay if you sleep next to me. I mean, you don't want to sleep on the ground."

"Are you sure?"

"Yes."

I slipped in beside her and covered her with one of the blankets. "Just in case it gets cold."

The moon rose high and full in the heavens, and Ruby twisted around to look at it. "It's beautiful," she murmured drowsily.

I took a blanket for myself and felt the darkness creep in. But I looked at the moon, and it was a pretty sight. "Yeah, it's beautiful. Goodnight, Ruby."

"Night, Carl," she murmured.

And then sleep came up to catch me.

\*

The next morning.

My internal clock woke me. The sun was already up, and Ruby was still asleep beside me. I carefully climbed down the tree and stretched, then set off to check the walls. We'd originally landed facing north, and when I reached the east wall, I found another pictograph identical to the others we'd seen. I suspected the carving would take us back to our original cave like the west one had. However, without my companion — was she my companion, a friend, a fellow traveler…I wasn't sure — I wouldn't be able to check it out.

Not that I wanted to at that moment.

I wandered along the previous day's route, enjoying the sun's glorious heat. China's weather had been cold and windy, and we'd landed on an escarpment filled with snow and frigid temperatures. No one could live there for long.

However, this place provided a sharp contrast, as it had no insects, no animals — unless they were hiding — and the sun was hot and dry, but not overly so. Again, it almost felt like the environment had tailored itself to our needs…

"Silly," I said aloud. "Places like this don't think."

A moment later, I stopped. "Or do they?"

Maybe — and I felt ridiculous for thinking this in the first place — whoever or whatever had designed this place had given it a kind of…I struggled to find the right word… Wait, consciousness. Yes, that was the word. Consciousness, as in independent thought.

My stomach growled, interfering with my mental gymnastics of what-ifs and maybes. I picked a few berries, munching on them as I continued on the trail and made the journey back to the treehouse. Perhaps I could fix it up, although Ruby would probably want separate rooms.

It occurred to me that our situation wasn't usual. We were

together for survival, not companionship, yet I couldn't help but feel attracted to Ruby. Was that wrong? In my mind, no…

"Hi."

I whirled around, only to find Ruby in front of me. "Hi," I replied, suddenly at a loss for words. "Um, did you sleep okay?"

"Yeah." She still wore her uniform, but her hair was down, and her eyes sparkled. "I thought we could have breakfast together. You know, berries and stuff."

"Sounds good."

Breakfast consisted of some blue berries and the orangey bread-and-butter fruit. When we were done, Ruby let out a contented sigh and lay back, trailing her hands through the soft grass as though it was water. "That was nice. What should we do now?"

A lot of things came to mind, many of them unworkable. If only there was a door that took us back to the US, but I guessed that was too much to hope for. "Well, if we're going to live here, we should bring the rest of the supplies in. I mean, I'd rather live here than in that cave. Wouldn't you?"

She got up and made for the gateway. "Coming?"

*

An hour later.

Working hard certainly built up a sweat, and going from freezing temperatures to much more temperate ones played havoc with my body. Once we'd lugged, toted, and carried everything into our garden, we were both panting short and raspy breaths, and I collapsed on the nearest crate. "I don't know about you, but I'm hot, sore, tired" —I took a sniff of my body—"and I stink."

Ruby looked at me. "How about the lake?"

"How about...what?"

She pointed toward the lake, then herself, and then to me, smiling patiently. "How about we cool off in the lake? It's big enough to swim around in. I bet it's deep enough, so why don't we take a dip?"

"Uh..." Heat washed over me, but not from exertion. "I, um, I don't have a bathing suit." Call it a pitiful excuse, but it was the truth.

Her gaze was steady. "I don't either."

*Oh.* "Oh." That was all I could come up with. "Uh, so, how do we—"

"You turn around, close your eyes, and when you hear me yell, you walk in. I'll be in the water and promise not to look." A grin accompanied her statement.

It sounded reasonable enough, so I turned around. "Go ahead."

A minute later, I heard her feet running and then a splashing sound. "I'm ready!"

Maybe she was...but I wasn't sure about me. However, my need to get clean outweighed my modesty. I quickly stripped and dove into the water. It was cool, not cold, and the bottom was soft and silty. The water came up to my neck, and I immediately felt some of the sweat and dirt slough off my body.

"Hey," I called when I didn't see Ruby anywhere.

She suddenly bobbed to the surface and wiped her face. "It's dark down there."

Her nearness had me tongue-tied. "Uh, right. Did you feel anything?" *Oh, hell, that came out wrong.* "I mean, did you feel any fish, or maybe plants, or eels, or something like that?"

She shook her head, treading water. "Nothing. Isn't this special? I used to go swimming in a river near my mama's house, but the water there was always dirty. This is wonderful."

Ruby moved closer, and I became very aware of her presence. "Okay." Then I damned myself for not being wittier or cleverer...or something. "Uh, maybe we should get clean."

"How?"

I moved to the shore and found two small stones that were smooth all over. "Maybe these will do," I said when I swam back to her position.

Her eyebrows arched. "Good idea."

So, I turned around and scrubbed myself all over — carefully making circles on my skin. Once I was done, I swam to the shore and placed my rock next to three yellow flowers.

Ruby called out from nearby, "I'm clean. How about we swim to the other side and back?"

A quick turn in the water put me face-to-face with her. "You mean a race?"

"Yeah, why not?"

So, we had a friendly race in a front crawl only. Back crawl? I wasn't ready for that, and I doubted Ruby was either. We pushed each other but finished neck and neck. After the exertion, I was a little breathless, but otherwise, I'd never felt better in my life.

"Good race," Ruby said between panting breaths. "I could tell you weren't trying."

I had been trying but wanted to hear her reason for thinking otherwise. "How'd you know?"

"You're taller, and your pull is stronger."

That made sense.

Ruby ducked her head. "Anyway, thanks for the race. I'm going to get dressed."

"Fine, go ahead."

I focused on a tree and listened to her moving around until

she called out that she'd put on her clothes.

"Okay, hang on." I waded through the water to where my clothes were and shook the excess water off my body. The sun seemed to become a little stronger and quickly dried me off. I hastily donned my duds. "I'm done."

Ruby turned around, nodding. "Thanks again for the swim."

"Yeah, uh…you're welcome."

Nothing else came to mind, so after we let the sun dry our hair, we went for the exit, donned our jackets, and emerged into the cave.

"Why are we here?" Ruby asked.

"I want to check out the trail you showed me before. Maybe there are more caves like this one, maybe not, but since we have time, we should see what's there."

She agreed, so we climbed to the top, turned left, and started walking. It had gotten windy up there, with a light snow falling, but the trail was clearly marked, so we had no trouble following it. It went on for about a mile and ended in a series of steps that led to twelve other caves around the side of the mountain, spaced roughly twenty yards apart.

Ruby pointed to the first cave on our left, which had a different carving on the left side of the entrance. I couldn't figure out what it was, but she supplied the information. "It looks like a bunch of birds flying around a tree."

Staring at it, yeah, I saw her point. The tree symbol was the same, but there were simple bird carvings—two curved lines joined in the center and arcing upward, something a child would draw—on either side of the tree.

We ventured inside the cave and discovered it was three times the size of our cave with a much higher ceiling. We found the same carving at the far end, and after Ruby nodded, we traced the pattern of the trees and then the birds.

An odd rumbling sound came from the wall, and we stepped back.

"That isn't a good sound," Ruby said in a shaky voice. "Not a good sound at all."

No, it wasn't, but then it stopped, revealing a gateway. As we poked our heads through, I silently hoped nothing would bite them off. I immediately spotted something large and ugly flying our way, screeching madly. "Oh, hell," I said, pulling Ruby back out.

Not fast enough, though, as the bird swooped through the gateway at the same time we exited. Only it wasn't a bird, not exactly. It looked prehistoric with a wingspan of maybe six feet, brown, leathery skin, a pointy beak—two of them actually since it had two heads—and a raucous cry that sounded like a million crows clawing their way out of hell. It flew around the cave, screeching its rage.

Ruby ducked as the thing came at her, and it slammed into the wall. It dropped to the ground, screaming its rage, but after shaking its heads, it immediately took to the air again.

"What now?" she yelled.

I grabbed a large rock, and when that prehistoric monstrosity came at me again, I brained its left head. It fell to the ground. Ruby came over with her own large rock, and we smashed its heads to a pulp.

Once done, Ruby dropped her rock and panted, looking at the gateway fearfully as if expecting another denizen from hell to come through. "What…what the hell was that?"

"A critter," I said. Nothing else came to mind.

"What if there are more?"

It was a sensible question. I thought fast. "Blow up the portal. There's some dynamite with the supplies. I need three sticks and some fire."

"I'll go."

"We'll both go. The dynamite's inside the garden."

Ruby offered a sheepish smile. "I forgot."

She extended her hand, I took it, and we made our way back to our garden and gathered the supplies.

After about an hour of walking back and collecting what we needed, we were back inside the dangerous cave. "Okay," I said, placing two of the dynamite sticks on a small rock shelf above the portal. "I'll light these. Wait ten seconds, then light the stick you have. We have to throw it inside the gateway. Together, right?"

She nodded, and once I lit the sticks, I counted to five. The wicks gradually burned down. I waited…waited…then I grabbed Ruby's forearm. "Throw it!"

She tossed the stick inside, then we ran out of the cave and took shelter at the side. A moment later, the dynamite went off, and when I went back to check on things, the wall had reformed. Those creatures wouldn't be coming through again.

"Is everything good?" she asked once I'd rejoined her.

"It's not my idea of a second vacation home."

# Chapter Seven: Morlok

The days passed, and in order to keep track of the time, Ruby drew a calendar using a piece of paper and a pen that we found in one of the crates. "We've been here for...about twenty-nine days," she said one morning as she drew an X in one of the boxes. "Almost a month." She whistled softly as if in awe of our surviving for so long.

Survival, though, came at a price. I'd once read a story about a man who sold his soul for immortality. Things went fine for him, at least at first. He could eat whatever he wanted, drink a hundred bottles of liquor a day, and didn't exercise. He even jumped off cliffs and high buildings and always walked away unscathed.

However, there was a tradeoff. The man never aged, but all his friends and family did. They died, he continued on, and life soon became dull. By the time a century had passed, he wanted out of the deal, and it took another century of begging and pleading for the infernal one to appear.

When Satan finally arrived, so much time had passed that the man had grown extremely frustrated with life. He was too set in his old-fashioned ways and had never adapted to the modernity of the ages he'd lived through—couldn't get used to the changing attitudes of the people either.

Moreover, when Satan wouldn't give him back his

mortality, the man left society. He spent all his time in a cave, never eating or drinking or enjoying the company of anyone ever again. Perhaps he was still in his cave, weeping for his lost mortality and praying that death would take him.

I wondered if something like that would happen to us. Living here with Ruby was fun, but would we soon run out of topics to talk about? Food was a big thing—at least, at first.

"Do you like the fruit here?" Ruby had asked me on the third, or maybe the fifth or tenth day. I'd forgotten.

"Yeah, I got used to it." Back in the real world, I'd enjoyed steak or brisket, vegetables...ice cream, too. My mother had made all the foods she loved from the old country—borscht, kasha, knishes, and much more. But she'd adapted and learned to cook the foods that Southerners loved, though she still kept a kosher home.

Still, much as I'd liked my mother's old-world and Southern cooking, I'd lost my taste for it. The fruit here tasted like the food back home in some ways, but it had a unique flavor all its own.

Ruby got a semi-wistful look on her face. "Same here. I loved barbecue back home...grits...it was all good, but now, I don't miss it."

That was pretty much the extent of our conversation. Once we ran out of things to say, though, there was only the silence of the place to comfort us. It was quiet there, almost too quiet. No birds or insects...no life at all, except for the trees and other flora. It was idyllic but also kind of boring.

It wasn't as if I didn't like Ruby. I did. She was my age, pretty, and smart. She also knew a lot about books, and having someone of the opposite sex with me was neat—until the boredom set in.

Boredom led to us having a few set-tos. Spats, the novels called them. Nothing racial...they were always about privacy.

Ruby needed hers. At night, we'd discuss—okay, argue—over the sleeping arrangements. Finally, I got a little angry, grabbed a blanket, and said she could have the treehouse. "It's all yours. I'll take my chances on the ground. Maybe I'll build my own treehouse later."

A week later, I regretted saying what I'd said. Sleeping on the ground wasn't so bad. It was warm at night, I could look at the moon, and nothing bit or stung me. But it got lonely. My eighteenth birthday came and went, but it was hardly worth mentioning.

In fact, Ruby and I barely spoke and went our own ways during the day. If I went swimming, she waited until I got out. Same deal with eating and bathing.

I thought about apologizing to her. To argue over something so trivial was childish. When I started to say something on the fifth—or maybe the seventh—day, she snapped, "What?"

I shut my mouth and walked away.

A day later, when she came to me while I was eating lunch, looking like she wanted to talk, I barked, "What?" She turned and stalked off.

This went on for about fifteen days, until one night, slowly being lulled to sleep by the quiet and peacefulness, someone tapped me on the shoulder. Obviously, it was Ruby. Who else would it be? "What is it?" I mumbled.

"Come on up."

I turned over and saw the moonlight framing her face in a lovely halo. "Want to tell me why?"

When she answered, she sounded like I felt—lost. "I don't like sleeping alone…and I don't want to be alone."

Yeah, sleeping alone wasn't fun. I'd only been doing it every day since I was born. "Are you sure?"

"Yes."

Fine. I rose, shook out the blanket, and up in the treehouse, Ruby had rearranged things to make it a bit wider. "No line down the center," she said. "I saw this movie once where the man hung a blanket over a line to split the room in half and give the woman he was with some privacy. I don't want it to be that way between us."

"Neither do I."

It was all about trust. I suppose Ruby was frightened that I'd do something bad to her. I wasn't like that, but she didn't know me, so this was kind of a test.

We lay down together, and in a surprise move, Ruby grasped my hand and squeezed it briefly. "Night, Carl."

I didn't know how I felt about that. We'd held hands to get in and out of this garden, but this? Well, it wasn't bad — not at all. "G'night, Ruby."

*

Since we didn't want to have any more arguments, Ruby came up with the perfect solution. "We keep busy."

I agreed since it seemed like the thing to do. During the days, we improved the treehouse by adding another level and installing walls using more staves from the crates. We also shored up the flooring. Since I wanted to relax after a hard day's work, I made a rocking chair using more slats from the crates and a few nails I'd found with the hammer. My rocking chair looked rickety, but I figured it would hold together, and after I finished building it, I sat and gave my treehouse mate a jaunty thumbs-up.

A second later, the chair collapsed, and I fell flat on my butt, which got a giggle from Ruby. "Something funny?" I asked as my tailbone ached. "I'm going to be pulling splinters out of my rear end for the next week."

"Need some medical attention?" She had to be joshing, plain and simple.

"I'll live."

She continued laughing, and it was infectious, as I started laughing, too, and then rubbed my butt, ruefully reflecting on my lack of carpentry skills.

"I'll do that," she said when I started to make another chair.

"You know carpentry?"

"Some," she said as she started working.

More than some, it seemed. Ruby's hands were deft and sure, and a chair soon began to take shape. "I taught myself," she said while hammering in a nail. "Had to do something when my pa died. He used to take care of the fixing around the house, and since I don't have any brothers or sisters, I had to learn. Helped my mama, and now...we're here."

"Setting things up, just like home."

Ruby gave me a quick look and then went back to her task. "Yeah, just like home. Now, get."

She said that good-naturedly, so I obliged and walked around, trying to figure out how to improve this place. Then I decided that outside of fixing up our treehouse, there wasn't a need to fix this place, except maybe to construct an outhouse.

No shovel, but I found a few sharp pieces of metal among the spare aircraft part that would serve, and I got to digging. Once the pit was deep enough, I set about building the outhouse with longer planks from the crates. While working on my project, the concept of modernity came back to me. I'd read about the developers in some parts of California and other areas who had turned deserts or empty land into housing complexes or malls. It seemed that anytime people moved into a country area, they had this weird kind of need to build or, in their minds, improve it. They couldn't leave a place alone.

How could a person improve on perfection? They couldn't, and that was my opinion. This place, wherever it was, was pure and untouched, and outside of our treehouse, it needed to be left alone...

"Hey, I'm done."

I spun around to find Ruby standing in front of me, uniform on but sans cap. Her hair hung down, and she wore a pleasant smile. "All done," she repeated. "You finished?" She pointed to the outhouse.

It had taken about five days, by my estimation, but it was functional. Once the pit was full, though, I'd have to fill it in and dig another pit. "Yeah, all done. What do you think?"

Ruby appraised the structure and nodded. "It's...an outhouse. Er, how about taking a walk?"

Surprised by her suggestion, I replied. "Sure thing."

As we walked along our usual path, I pondered our little oasis. Our adopted home remained the same...uniform in all areas. The same trees, the same bushes, tall green grass, fresh air—which remained a mystery to me. How was the air circulated anyway? There weren't any vents here unless they were invisible.

When I'd served on my ship, I spent my off hours lying in bed, reading. The air was always foul because the vents were old and rusty. If I wanted fresh air, I'd have to go up to the top deck. Most of the other guys I bunked with felt the same way. Here, the air always smelled fresh and sweet. Perhaps it was best not to question things too much...

"What're you thinking about?"

"Huh?" Ruby's question surprised me. I had a bad habit of losing myself in my own world, just my thoughts and me, and her question broke my concentration.

"What are you thinking about?" she repeated.

"Nothing."

"Maybe a special someone." She flashed a quick smile.

Yeah, she was joshing me again, so it was time to set her straight. "Listen, there isn't anyone special. I mean, I never met anyone special. It was just...school, homework, no friends, and I helped my old man in his store after school and on the weekends for pocket change."

Ruby stopped walking and leaned against a tree, crossing her arms over her chest. "Sounds like you didn't like working for your pa."

She would have to bring up the past. "Honestly, no, I didn't. Customers didn't like dealing with me...said I didn't know squat about the products. Bull. I did. I just wanted to go my own way. So, my life was going nowhere. My parents were okay, but they didn't understand what I wanted to do. That was why I left."

My voice had gotten louder with each passing sentence, frustration packing each word. I sat on the ground, picking idly at the grass and regretting my outburst. I didn't want to tell Ruby too much, but since there was no one else who'd listen... Whatever. I'd already shot my big mouth off.

She uncrossed her arms and sat beside me, sounding surprisingly sympathetic when she said, "I never had anyone special, either. After his stroke, my pa needed help, and my mama needed help around the house. Nursing was always the thing I wanted to do. I wanted to be the one who'd help out, the one people would turn to if they needed help. It was important to me."

Being noticed, yeah, I could relate to that. "So, did anyone notice you? Turn to you for help?"

She uttered a soft laugh, followed by a headshake. "No," she finally answered. "At my school, all the other girls said I was foolish for always reading. *Why you readin'?* they'd asked.

*It ain't like you're going into politics or you're gonna be anyone famous. You just a broke-ass colored girl, same as us...* That's what they always said to me."

"And?"

Ruby turned to spear me with a glare. "And what? Colored folk have no options except to take a job that's lower than what others got. You're white. You can go anywhere. My road's blocked, if you know what I mean."

The sarcasm rang out in her voice, so I cautioned myself to listen. She continued, her anger dialed down a few notches. "Sorry, me and my mouth, I just run off sometimes."

Her mood then turned reflective. "I guess I'm like you. I had to get out of where I was. My mama pushed me to read. I didn't have much as a kid. No dolls or nice clothes, but my mama, she always brought me books to read. And I liked it. Like I said, reading took me places...made me think I could be someone." Her shoulders lifted in a sad shrug.

Perhaps she was thinking about the cruel reality of our world. I didn't know for sure. "So, uh, no one special?"

Ruby glanced at me and then looked away. She remained silent for a time and then uttered a laugh that sounded more like a sob. "No, no one. Some guys were sweet on me, but I didn't...I wasn't interested. They were always saying I was pretty, asking me if I had a date for that Saturday night...that kind of thing. But they weren't my type."

"What is your type?"

She turned to regard me, her eyes holding a glint of suspicion. "Are you funning with me?"

"No. I'd like to know."

She inhaled and then blew out a heavy breath. "All right, it's someone who's kind, who works hard, who sees me as a person, not just some dirt-poor colored girl from the colored area. But I...I always hoped that someone would be there for

74

me. That's all I want, really."

Her answer, so honest, made me think that I'd never fully embraced what life was all about. "Well, since we're not seeing anyone at the moment, how about we see each other?"

Her eyes widened. "Are you saying what I think you're saying? You're asking me...asking me on a date?"

My mind was made up, and I made an exaggerated motion of peering at the non-existent crowds behind her. "I don't see anyone else around, do you?"

"You're crazy."

Maybe I was. "It's no crazier than where we were and where we are now. And I think you're kind of neat, so...why not?"

Ruby rose and brushed off her skirt. "I...I don't know. I have to think this over."

She walked off, making a shooing motion behind her when I moved to follow. Right, leave her alone, so I got up and went back to the treehouse and lay down, hoping she didn't hate me for asking her a question I thought was only natural.

*

An hour later.

Ruby came back while I was still lying down, trying to take a nap but not getting anywhere. She sat beside me and didn't say a word at first, but after a few seconds of silence, she asked the question I'd hoped she'd ask. "What would we do on our date?"

Oh, maybe I had a chance. I turned to see her styling her hair, her slender fingers working overtime. "I was thinking I'd take you to the Hotel Spam, treat you to vegetables a la carte, which means eating them out of the can, top our dinner off with an orange-bread-and-butter dessert, then go for a walk in the garden. It's supposed to be beautiful at night."

It wasn't the best or most romantic answer around, but it made her smile. She stopped her makeshift hair improvement. "Does that include dancing in the moonlight?"

Dancing? I couldn't dance to save my life. "If you want."

"Then let's wait until it gets dark." She leaned forward and sniffed me, and then she sniffed her forearm. "Oh, and we'd better take a bath. If we're going dancing, then I don't want a smelly partner."

*

That night, after the sun sank and the moon rose beautiful and full, Ruby met me near the stream. I'd taken a bath in the lake earlier to clean off the sweat and grit. No need to scrub with the aid of a stone.

Plus, I'd been wrong about the water having no life in it. Tiny blue fish nipped at me as if eating the waste off my body. What else they fed on was a mystery, as was all the ecology of this place.

As for the water, it always appeared fresh and clean, although how that happened was beyond me. It had to have a drain somewhere, but where? For the life of me, I couldn't figure out how things worked here.

"I brought the Spam and some oranges." Ruby held out a burlap bag, startling me from my musing.

I really had to stop daydreaming. "Oh, right, dinner," I replied. "That's great."

Her hair hung loose, and she looked pretty. Outside of that shidduch with Ellen, I'd never had a date in my life, so without any special social skills, I took a chance and told her she looked nice.

"Thank you," she replied softly. "You're looking good."

I'd donned the uniform I'd found in the crate. It fit fairly well, and even though I was still skinny, I figured I'd grow into it—in time. "Thanks. Um, do you want to eat?"

She sat and patted the spot beside her. "Good idea."

Moonlight bathed us in a comforting glow, and after we finished eating, I stamped the tins flat and put them in the bag. "What now?" I asked.

"You promised me a walk."

Good idea. I put the bag down near a tree, reminding myself to place it with the other garbage we'd deposited in the cave outside later on. I didn't want to spoil the nature here with our trash.

We strolled through the garden, neither of us speaking, the grass crunching softly under our feet. My hand brushed hers by accident, and she gripped it quickly, then just as quickly let it go. All right, I thought, let's not push matters too much.

Our stroll continued in silence, the air warm and soft, and finally, as if on cue, we stopped at our treehouse. Ruby looked up at the moon. "So beautiful," she breathed. "It's just so beautiful."

"Yeah, it is. And the moon's been full every night since we got here."

That was another mystery we couldn't solve, but it didn't seem very important at that moment. Ruby turned to me, looking a bit shy. "Well, um, we had a nice walk, but you also promised me a dance."

Music…we didn't have any. "There's no band playing."

"Hum something,"

I thought for a moment, and then I hummed a horrible version of a love song I'd heard during my sailing days. I even sang the words I knew, and…

Ruby giggled, and I stopped. "What's wrong?"

"You sound, er, bad."

That stung. "Bad?"

She winced, spread her hands, and shrugged. "I'm sorry, but your singing...doesn't sound like singing."

"What does it sound like?"

"A stuck pig."

While I was trying to get over the mini-insult, Ruby proceeded to sing a better rendition of the love ballad and sing it well. I stood and listened, marveling at the clarity and range of her voice. Once she finished, I said, "Church choir?"

She giggled again. "How'd you guess?"

I shrugged. "You're good – and you already told me."

Ruby offered a modest bow and then asked me again for the dance.

Right, I'd forgotten. "I, uh, don't know how to dance," I admitted.

"I used to sneak into the movies. I'll show you," she said.

We clumsily linked hands, and she directed me to put my right arm around her waist. She pressed close to me, and I felt her warmth and strength. Then we danced – more like swayed, really – under the moonlight as she sang another song in a soft voice, something about finding the one you truly love.

We stopped, and she slowly disengaged herself from my grasp with a small smile. "That was...kind of intense. I never danced with a guy before."

"A white guy?"

She shook her head and laughed quietly. "Any guy. You're my first, and you're not so bad. I mean, as a dancer, you know?"

I did. "You're pretty good, too."

Silence descended like a blanket, and I couldn't figure out what to say. Ruby didn't help in that regard, either. We simply stared at each other, sort of like two animals not entirely sure of the other's intentions. We'd already established a friendly relationship, but this felt like we were taking it to another level. Was she ready for that? Moreover, was I? I wasn't sure, so I said nothing.

Ruby broke the silence first. "I'm, uh... Maybe we should call it a night?"

Why stop was my first thought, but it was her decision, not mine. "Well, it was fun. Thanks for dinner, and the walk, and, uh...you're a great dancer."

She'd already turned to start climbing the tree, but she stopped, jumped to the ground, and pivoted around to hug me. Her body was small but strong, and her grip fierce. I hugged her back, realizing how much I liked her. At that moment, I wanted to kiss her. Call it an over-the-moon moment, but I went with it. She lifted her head to let me kiss her, our faces drew closer, and...

*"Nkarra, dritta yar ni fu. Koii na gruiit?"*

What in the hell was that? The voice had come from off to our right. We spun around to see who it was, and there stood a strange figure, six-foot-plus, spindly, and clad in an orange jumpsuit with a band of what looked like silver around his left wrist that glinted in the moonlight.

Upon further examination, I noted the alien's bald head and tomato-red face that looked like a cross between a bulldog and a giraffe, with the floppy jowls of the canine and tubular ears that twitched. I guessed he was male by the sound of his voice, but definitely not human. "Who are you?" I asked.

In response to my question, he tapped the band on his wrist. A knifelike pain went through my head, but then it faded.

Ruby also held her head. "What in the Sam Hill was

that?"?"

"Ah, my translator is working," the alien replied in a raspy tone. "My name is Norlok. I am here, in this garden you inhabit. Are you mated?"

Mated? He meant…oh. "We're friends," I decided to say.

Ruby nudged me with her elbow. "Friends?" she hissed. "Is that all?"

No, it wasn't all, but we were in a weird situation, and I didn't think it was a good idea for this guy to find out my true feelings for her. "Okay, we're more than friends," I whispered back. "Can we talk this over later?"

"Sure," she responded. "We need to talk, and —"

"Ahem," the alien guy — Norlok — cut in. "I am still here."

I turned on him. "Fine, you're here. What do you want? How did you get here?"

A faint laugh came from him. It sounded like he was going to spit. "That is none of your concern," he stated in an arrogant tone. "As for what I want, I have need of servants. I have much to do, and since I am here and you are available, you are now my prisoners."

Ruby stepped in front of me. "Go to hell. I'm nobody's prisoner, and neither is Carl."

Norlok gazed at her with a bland expression. "I do not know much about humans, but others who have come to my world have told me about your species. They say that they have visited your world discreetly and lived among you. And what they say amuses me."

"Mind telling us how," I said.

A look that appeared to be condescension mixed with humor crossed Norlok's face. "They say that humans talk too much. They also say that humans pretend to act bravely, but when confronted, they are nothing except sheep."

I balled my fists. "Mister, you got a lot of brass coming here and saying that." I wanted to swear, but I figured Ruby wouldn't appreciate it.

Norlok favored me with the same bland expression he'd given Ruby. "By curling your fingers into your hands and speaking in that manner, is that your way of expressing defiance?"

"Yeah. Go ahead and do something about it."

The jerk actually yawned. "I grow weary of this conversation."

He reached behind him and pulled out what looked like a ray gun from the Buck Rogers comics. His finger twitched, and a charge of something green came out of the barrel in a blur. It hit Ruby square in the chest, and she collapsed, her arms and legs twitching.

"What did you do?" I yelled. "Did you kill her?"

Norlok grunted. "No. In case you were not listening before, I have need of servants to assist me. She will do nicely, and so will you."

I knelt to feel Ruby's neck. Her pulse was strong and steady. When I looked up, Norlok had already leveled his weapon at me. Well, my only plan was to show no fear. "Might as well do it, you rat bastard."

He looked surprised. "What is a rat?"

"Do you know what vermin means?"

That got his crap hot, and he glowered at me. "Yes. We have them on my world."

"Then that's you." I steeled myself for the shot. "Go ahead, rat."

"As you wish."

He fired, and I saw the universe, then…darkness.

# Chapter Eight: Trapped

Waking up to pain wasn't my idea of a good time. A headache that felt like a dozen hammers were playing the anvil chorus inside my skull, blurred vision…someone or something had worked me over like no one's business. I told myself to breathe. Deep breaths. In…out…in…out. After a while, my vision cleared.

This wasn't the garden. I was in a room big enough for maybe four people. It had no furniture, or color, or door. It was a solid white-on-white-on-white cube… Wait, I spotted a vertical line in the wall to my right. Maybe it was a doorway, although I couldn't be sure. Since we'd arrived in the garden, nothing was what it seemed.

Reality intruded when my aching muscles and head reminded me that I'd gotten hit with some kind of shock. Another part of reality hit when I realized that I'd peed myself. On my old ship, the wiring was bad, and one of the veterans said that if a person got a nasty electrical shock, they sometimes lost control of their bowels. Count me in as a part of that club. I smelled the air, and it was vile.

On the other hand, I was still alive. Fine and good, but where was Ruby?

"Uh…"

A groan to my left signaled that my companion was still with me. I slowly turned my head and saw Ruby lying on her back.

She stirred, groaned again, and then her eyes opened. "What...what happened? Where are we?"

"Your guess is as good as mine." My reply sounded like something I'd read in a pulp novel, but it fit the situation. "That guy, Norlok, he knocked us out and took us prisoner."

Ruby shook her head and then got up. She wavered on her feet and smacked her cheeks twice. I got to my feet and did the same. It helped to clear the dizziness.

"Are you okay?" we asked each other simultaneously.

I ducked my head. "I'm fine, just feeling banged up."

"Me, too. Listen, that friend thing I said before —"

"I know —"

She interrupted anything else I might have said by hugging me briefly. She then sniffed the air and wrinkled her nose in disgust. "Did you..."

Ruby didn't finish her question, but I knew what she was thinking. "Yeah," I admitted, shame heating my face. "I did. Sorry."

She shrugged. "Me, too."

To get my mind off my stink, I went over the door outline and searched for a way to open it, gently touching the panel and hoping not to get shocked. Lucky me — no electrical jolt. On the other hand, the door didn't open. We were locked in. "Norlok," I yelled. "If you stuck us in this jail, we'll get out. Somehow, we'll get out, and then I'll kick your —"

"No, you will not."

His voice came from all around, and a moment later, a shock ran through me from my toes to my head. I was riveted to the floor, shaking violently. *Aw, hell, he would shock us through the floor.* From the corner of my eye, I saw Ruby going through the same thing.

"Let. Us. Go." Ruby sounded savage. "Now!"

The shock — electrical or otherwise — didn't ease. In fact, it intensified. "I think not," Norlok said. "But if you will listen to what I have to say, I will turn off the charge."

Anything to stop the torture. "Fine, we'll listen," I grunted, feeling like every nerve in my body had turned to mush. My brain was starting to short out, too, and sure enough, I felt a stream of piss run down my leg. "Just turn it off. You hear me? Turn it off!"

A moment later, the pain stopped. I staggered over to Ruby's side and held her. It seemed like the right thing to do.

Norlok spoke again. "I have shown you a measure of mercy. Moreover, I will allow you out of your cell. You will need food and refreshment. We will talk. That is, I will talk, you will listen, and then…then you shall be ready to do my bidding."

I had to ask. "What if we say no? What are you going to do?"

Stupid question. Another shock hit, this one more severe, and I fell to the floor. My heart stopped for a moment. I couldn't breathe, and all of my muscle movement…gone. When the jolt stopped, I could breathe again, but that…that was painful.

Beside me, Ruby gasped for air, holding her chest. She whispered, "Carl, he's as crazy as a June bug. Don't push the mental case, okay?"

Me and my big mouth. "Got it."

We waited, listening for Norlok's mocking voice to come again, and sure enough, it did. "You have already seen what I can do. The shock you received the first time was a level one shock. That was enough to make you lose control of your bowels."

*Thanks for telling us.*

He continued speaking almost clinically. "The second

shock you received just now is considered level three. At level five, you will vomit and perhaps suffer internal damage to your organs. At level eight, your hearts will explode. Think that over, and ask yourselves if you really have a choice. To be brief, you do not."

Obviously not. We could say no, but it was a given that Norlok would shock us again, harder and heavier, and soon, one of us would die. I didn't want that for Ruby or for me. "Fine," I said, hating that I was about to agree. "Let us out. We need to eat anyway."

My muscles were still twitching from the shock. I had difficulty getting up. Walking took a great effort. Ruby said her body felt like it was on fire. But we were still alive, and that counted for everything.

A scraping sound to our right alerted me to something happening. I turned to see the line on the wall forming a door that slid to one side.

Norlok's voice came again. "I have furnished this other room with objects that you are familiar with. Be seated and refresh yourselves. I have gleaned the knowledge of what your species eats from your minds. The food will be palatable."

Through the doorway, I saw a table set with some squares of what might be food and two square cups made from some kind of transparent material. The table and two chairs were made from the same clear material. All of that was against a white background.

Ruby touched my arm. "We should go," she whispered. "Listen to this guy, and then maybe figure out what to do."

Common sense ruled...although a shower would've been nice. We went to the table, sat, and checked out the eats. I sniffed the liquid inside the cups, then took a cautious sip. It was water. As for the food, it looked like stacks of pancakes, though they were square, not round. I took one and tentatively bit into it. "Tastes like boiled eggs."

Ruby already had a slice of whatever-it-was in her hand. "Yeah," she replied after she'd taken a bite. "Just like eggs."

Once we finished eating, the empty plate and cups disappeared, and Norlok's voice came again from all points of the room. "Since you are now finished, I will explain things. You are primitive beings, but I will use simple words so that you may understand me clearly."

Simple words...what a jerk. "Fine."

Norlok didn't appear. Instead, his voice echoed around the room as he explained that he'd been born on a distant world. "My home is called Briina." It came out as Bree-ee-na, with the accent on the second syllable. He'd been a scientist on his world, known for many inventions. "The weapon I used on you is but one of them. Others form constructs such as these rooms. I also have a portal opener."

Ruby frowned. "A what?"

"It is a matter transportation device that allows me to move from world to world. However, it cannot bring me home."

I briefly wondered if he'd somehow gotten lost, but considering his actions against us — torture, really — I came up with another possible reason for his being here. "Did you break the law on your planet?"

A moment of silence ensued, followed by a dull, "Yes. You are quite intuitive for someone from a lesser species."

He *would* have to insult us — again.

Then Norlok continued with a note of grievance working overtime in his tone. "My crime was to search for knowledge. Because of my efforts, the leaders of my world exiled me to this world."

"You mean Earth?" I said. "We're from Earth."

My question apparently made him mad because he

suddenly appeared before us, gun in hand. "Yes, I am aware of where I am." He sniffed the air. "What is that horrible smell?"

*And he calls us ignorant.* "You shocked us, remember? We, um, couldn't hold it in."

His nose wrinkled, but he nodded. "Understood. Wait." He pressed something on his left wrist, disappeared, and returned a few seconds later. "Stand up and do not move."

He proceeded to toss a small metal ball in our direction. It landed at our feet and exploded, covering us with a fine white dust. A moment later, the dust worked its way through my clothes, then my pores. It took away the smell and the stains on my uniform, then the dust vanished.

Not quite the shower I wanted, but it worked. "Thanks." I sat back down, and Ruby followed my example.

"A small matter," Norlok replied. "Now, I want to know how you managed to get into that world where I found you."

Why not tell him the truth? "Do you know what an airplane is?"

"Yes. I have the knowledge from your minds. It is a primitive method of transport."

There he went with the primitive thing again. Fine. "All right, you know. Short version, there's a war going on in our world, our supply plane crashed, we ended up in the cave, figured out what the symbols meant, and got inside. That's where you found us. And now, we're here...wherever *here* is."

Norlok shook his head. "Ignorant savages, I am saddled with ignorant savages. I will tell you about this place. As I said before, it is a construct I have created. Call it a cell if you wish. It will hold you for however long I deem necessary. During that time, you shall serve me."

Serve him? Not likely.

"I'm no slave." Ruby literally growled the words. "Neither is Carl."

Norlok's throat-clearing laugh indicated that he didn't care. "Dark one, I do not care for your attitude. All I care about is your compliance. And you will comply."

What an arrogant moron. However, he had the gun and the gadgets, and we had nothing. "All right, answer me this," I said, rising from my chair and leaning on the table. "The place where you found us, who built it? Your people?"

He laughed again. "Ignorant. That is all you are. No, my people did not build it. There is only one race capable of creating that world you formerly inhabited. How you got there is called interdimensionalism, the capability of moving from one dimension to another or one world to another in the same dimension or universe. I use my portal opener, which operates on the same principle of adjusting your atomic structure to the environment it enters."

Most of what he said went over my head, but I shut my mouth and listened in case he told us something useful.

Norlok continued speaking, sounding like he was talking to children. "As for the garden I found you in? The race who constructed it has the ability to transform matter into anything they wish. I speak of the people known as the Settlers."

"The Settlers?" I echoed. "Why did they build that place? How does it work?"

He mulled over my question for about a minute. Did he know, or was he debating whether or not to tell us? I didn't see any harm in him telling us the truth...if he *could* tell the truth. I didn't trust him, but he had us where he wanted us, and we couldn't do a thing about it.

Finally, he walked over to lean against the door. "My information on the Settlers is limited. They are a very secretive group of people. Even we, the Briinan, do not know where their home world is. We do know that they are an extremely advanced group of people in the technological sense. They are somewhat humanoid, like you, but their mental capacity is much greater."

*Thanks for insulting us Earth people – for maybe the tenth time.* However, we had to keep him talking. "And?"

"I imagine they built that world you were in as a sort of relaxation area. It is a comfortable place, is it not?"

"It was until you came along," Ruby said. From the tone in her voice, she sounded ready to attack him, shock or no shock.

Norlok stared at her, and then he glanced at me. "Are all the females on your world as argumentative as she is?"

Like I knew? I didn't, and I didn't understand why he kept on with the insults. "She isn't argumentative. She's asking questions. She wants to know, and so do I."

For that, I got a harrumph. "On my world, the females know their place."

"Good thing I don't live on your world," Ruby snapped.

In my limited experience, there were the snotty women, and then there were the defiant ones. Ruby fell into the latter group, and my respect for her went up a hundred percent.

While I sided with her, getting angry wouldn't help us. Instead, I changed the conversation, steering it to something more information-based. "Do you know how the Settlers built that world? Or the others?"

Norlok's mouth opened and closed repeatedly like a fish tossed onto land. He was clearly surprised by the question. Finally, he answered. "To be honest, I do not know. Their technology is far superior to ours. We must...catch up. I believe that is the expression you Earth people use. I gleaned that information when I entered your mind and downloaded your language."

Yeah, people used it all the time. However, I had another question. "How many races are there?"

Norlok gave a very human shrug. "Countless. Your people think you are the center of this universe. You are not. I will have you know that your knowledge of your own galaxy is shockingly limited.

"As for the universe, you are even more ignorant. The universe is infinite, and we have made contact with over half a million sentient species. They think and are self-aware, as your species is, and in many cases, they have constructed great societies. In technological terms, some are behind your species, but most are vastly superior to yours. I am a member of one such superior race."

Ruby let out a harsh laugh. "You want us to be your slaves. My people used to be slaves. That isn't superior at all."

He sighed. "While you have a point, I must tell you the reason why I am here. I told you before that I was exiled for my experiments on my world. But I was also exiled due to the ignorance of the science council, who refused to believe in my theories. They sent me here. I can move between the various worlds you have undoubtedly visited. How did you do that?"

I glanced at Ruby, who nodded slightly, her signal for me to tell the truth. "We, uh, saw the pictograph, the carving at the entrance of our cave," I said. "Inside the cave, we saw the same picture. We used our hands to trace the outline of the pictures, a portal opened, and we entered. That's it. There are other caves about a mile down the trail from our first cave. I don't know about the worlds there."

All right, that was a lie. I knew about the pterodactyl-dinosaur world—sort of. But that was the limit of my knowledge. I only hoped that our jailer couldn't read minds.

However, Norlok seemed to appreciate my answer and nodded. "You entered through tactile manipulation. And the portal accepted your atomic structure. It found you compatible. Very interesting."

He pulled a small cube from his pocket. "This is how I do what you do. It operates on brainwaves. It is a portal opener my people invented. One merely thinks about where they wish to go, and the device takes them there.

"However, when I was exiled, the device the leaders gave me only allows me to move between the various worlds that can be accessed from here. I cannot return home. Still, if I can collect enough materials, I may be able to fashion a different kind of transporter that will bring me back to my world. If I can do that, perhaps they will allow me to remain among them. That is my only wish."

Ruby shot me a glance, rolling her eyes. She obviously didn't believe him for a second, and neither did I. His story sounded too pat, too simple.

"All right," I said. "If we help you, then we want something in return."

Norlok gazed at us with a bland expression. "I imagine that you wish to return to your garden world."

"Yeah, that's right."

He nodded. "Good. We have similar goals. Here is my offer. Work for me, do what I ask, and if you wish to return to your garden or another place on this world of yours, after I am satisfied, then I will send you there."

Ruby apparently wasn't satisfied with his answer. "Can we trust you? We want your promise to send us home."

His expression turned haughty—if an alien could look haughty. "I have given you my word, dark one."

Norlok's reply got my crap hot. I shouldn't have gotten angry—I'd promised myself I wouldn't—but I couldn't help it. Ruby didn't deserve to be spoken to like that—by anyone. "She has a name. It's Ruby. Not *dark one*. Go to hell with your bigotry."

Norlok's already thin lips thinned even more. "I see that you have feelings for the female. Good. They will aid you in your quest. I must prepare materials for the places to be explored. When I am ready, I will tell you what to do."

He then raised his gun, and before I could do anything, he shot me. My last vision before the table and then the floor hit my face was of Ruby toppling over. Then...darkness.

# Chapter Nine: The Quest, Part One

"*U*gh..."

I woke up in the same white cube as before. Ruby lay next to me, out cold. I struggled to my feet, my head throbbing, and paced around the room until my head cleared. My body still tingled, and sure enough, I stank. That shock gun, or whatever it was, packed a wallop. I bent over Ruby and gently shook her shoulder. "Hey, wake up."

"Leave me alone," she mumbled.

"Can't. We've got a job to do."

Ruby mumbled something else I didn't catch and then opened her eyes. "Urgh," she grunted. "My body hurts everywhere."

"Join the club."

She sat up, massaged her temples, and then asked if we were in the same place as she looked around. "Yeah, still here." She sniffed herself and grimaced. "It happened again."

"Yeah, what else is new?" I said. "You think he'll let us go?"

"No. That man lies like a rug."

With an effort, she got up, letting out a grunt of pain as she did so. "What do we have to get that he can't?"

It was a good question, one I didn't have an answer to. "I have no idea, but he doesn't look that strong. Maybe his gun is all he's got. He needs strong people to lift or carry what he needs."

We waited, but our captor didn't come. I finally got tired of standing around doing nothing and yelled, "Hey, Norlok, we're up. Let's get the show on the road."

A moment later, the door opened, and Norlok faced us, gun in hand. "By saying let us get the show on the road, I must assume that you are ready to undertake your mission?"

"Yeah, let's get to it. But, er, we still smell."

Wordlessly, he took another metal ball from his pocket. He'd probably figured we'd pee ourselves again. A toss of the ball, a puff of dust, and we were once again clean. Then he motioned for us to exit the room.

Norlok led us outside, then took the cube device from his pocket and stood a healthy distance away. "We must find three items. They are not heavy, but the places I am sending you to have an element of danger, and I do not wish to risk injury or death."

Wonderful. He didn't mind risking our lives, though. After that thought, a sense of resignation took over. "Fine. We need details. What's first on the list?"

"An eggshell."

Ruby arched her eyebrows. "Eggshell?"

Norlok explained that, unlike chicken eggs, this kind of shell wasn't made of calcium. It was metallic and would help transfer energy from one source to another.

I didn't get it at first, but then I remembered my training on my ship. We'd had to rewire circuit boards more than once. "So, it's like a wire that transfers energy from a battery to an engine. Something like that?"

Norlok nodded. "Your analogy is crude, but yes. Shall we go?"

I wondered why it was so hard to get an eggshell, but Ruby

beat me to the question. "Are we talking about an eggshell that belongs to something small?"

Norlok frowned. "No, this bird is much bigger. It has two heads and two beaks."

Uh-oh, he wanted us to enter that dinosaur land. I did not like the sound of that at all. Still, I decided to not reveal what we knew. "Does that mean we might have to kill one of those birds?"

"Perhaps."

Norlok fiddled with his cube, and a moment later, we were inside the cave where we'd encountered the prehistoric bird. Not a mark was on the wall except for the carving, as though we'd never blown it up.

Norlok gave us more instructions, using a factual tone instead of his usual arrogant one. "Now, here is what you must do. I have files on the denizens of this world. They are large and dangerous, yes, but they have one thing in common—their eyesight is quite poor, even the flying creatures you will encounter. They do, however, have a highly developed sense of smell, so you must stay downwind.

"As for your task, the eggshell I need is from a newly hatched baby from that flying species. I will only need a few small pieces. The shell is metallic, blueish-green in color. You will find it in the nest of those birds."

Now, I really didn't like the sound of this *task*. "Are you saying we'll have to climb a tree or a mountain to find these nests?"

"No. The nests are on the ground. That particular species of bird prefers to build its nests in tall grass. However, you must first pass through a forest and then enter a meadow. The nests are guarded by the parents of the eggs, so that will call for stealth and guile on your part. Once you have that piece of metal in your hands, come back through the wall. It is that simple."

Nothing was simple with this guy. However, without any choice in the matter, we agreed.

"Good," he said. "Use your hands to trace the pattern and enter. When you have what I need, return." He spoke like it would be easy.

Since we had no choice, Ruby and I did the hand thing. Within seconds, the stone wall turned to dust and revealed the portal. I took Ruby's hand and turned to Norlok. "See you soon."

\*

We emerged into a field of tall green grass that came up to my waist. The land around us looked like a primordial swamp, hot and steamy, with many insects flying around. The smallest of the bugs were thumb-sized, the largest the length of my forearm. I could only hope they didn't sting.

Sweat instantly began running down my face, and I inhaled and exhaled slowly in wonder. "This is…"

Ruby finished my thought when words failed me. "Prehistoric."

That about sized it up. I'd seen pictures of places like this when I was in school and read about them in history books, but all of it had happened millions of years ago. Dinosaurs were extinct. That's what the experts said, but apparently, we'd stepped back in time.

"Over there," I said, pointing to a collection of rocks.

Ruby held onto my hand as we quickly made our way to the wall of boulders and hid behind them. The air was thick, and I saw those pterodactyl critters flying around overhead.

Other sounds—squawks, deep-throated roars, bellows of rage, and bleats of agony—echoed around us. I couldn't see anything, but I heard everything.

Ruby gripped my hand tighter. "I saw a movie like this once, something about cavemen and women living together and fighting monsters. I thought it wasn't real. I was wrong."

"It's real, all right."

The forest lay about a hundred yards ahead, so keeping low, we moved through the grass, always on the lookout for some big or small critter that wanted to make us lunch, and we tried to stay as quiet as possible.

Lucky for us, nothing stood in our way. We reached the forest and entered another few yards to hide behind a large tree. All the while, I wondered if something was about to drop on us from the branches, but fortunately, nothing did.

After three more tree hops, we exited the forest and into a meadow, just as Norlok had described. There, we found shelter behind a large collection of rocks. We hunkered down, and I tried to catch my breath. Being inside that forest had scared me, but we'd had cover from the trees. Here, we were out in the open.

"We'll wait," I said, still gasping for air. My heart hammered, and I forced myself to take deep breaths to calm down. The humid air made it hard to breathe...not to mention the adrenalin pumping through my veins.

"Wait for what?" Ruby panted.

"Wait for the flying things to land. If they do, maybe it's near their nest."

So, we waited, and after a good thirty minutes, two of those flying monsters circled lower in the air roughly a hundred yards away, cawing madly. They landed together and fell quiet.

"Maybe that's their nest," I whispered. "Let's go."

We started out of our hiding position, only to stop when two rampaging beasts emerged on the scene. They weren't dinosaurs, not like I'd seen in the books. These creatures were well over fifteen feet tall, with five horns about a yard long atop their triangular-shaped heads. Their massive bodies were bear-shaped — only hairless — with gray skin and heavy, thick limbs like elephants.

They bayed their challenges for all to hear and then charged, their horns digging into each other's torsos. Blood — bright green and thick — spurted out, and after five more thrusts from both beasts, they fell over, twitched, and lay still. They may have been big and strong, but they weren't very bright. Or perhaps they wanted to end their battle that way. In any case, they were dead.

"Those aren't dinosaurs," Ruby whispered. "Green blood? No, they were definitely not from Earth."

"Maybe the Settlers put them here from another world." It didn't really matter who put the creatures in this world or why. We had to get the eggshell parts and get out of here as fast as possible. This area was way too dangerous to be in, at least for us.

Ruby didn't say anything. She was too busy staring at the monsters. "We got company." She pointed toward the dead creatures.

Company? That wasn't the kind of company we wanted. Scavengers, hyena-like but with larger bodies and short yellow hair, had already set upon the downed animals, tearing into them with savage grunts and snapping at their brothers and sisters.

Smaller animals the size of Earth's lizards, bluish-green, with floppy seashell-shaped ears and oversized spines on their backs, also joined the feast. Lastly, some of the flying monsters landed and stayed at the edge of the action, picking at the remains.

It was back to playing the waiting game again.

The gnashing of teeth, the tearing of flesh, the thick, heavy smell of blood…the feast continued for over forty minutes. Once the hyena creatures and the lizard things had eaten their fill, they moved off. When they did, we moved out of our hiding place to creep closer to the nest.

"We have to stay downwind," Ruby reminded me, testing the air by licking her forefinger and holding it up to check the wind. "Go right."

Downwind…right. Good thing Ruby knew what to do. It was only through dumb luck that we hadn't been detected. "This way," she whispered as she moved to her right, staying low.

Ruby led the way as we crept through the grass to where the flying creatures had landed. "There it is. Over there." She pointed at a nest around fifty feet away.

One of the double-headed monstrosities suddenly flew off, probably to find food. That meant only one critter was left to tend the eggs. I wondered if they'd hatched. If they hadn't, we'd have to take the egg back with us.

Ruby tapped my arm. "Carl, what's the plan?"

I thought fast. "All right, here's what we do. I'll get its attention while you run in and grab the pieces of eggshells. Then we go back through the forest and into the portal."

On the surface, it sounded easy enough, but Ruby started shaking her head. "That's it?"

"Well…yeah."

Now, her body started quivering. "No. I…I can't…"

I gripped her hands. It was hard for me to keep from shaking as well, but I managed—barely. "Listen, you won't be in trouble. I'll be the bait. Trust me."

"We're both bait."

That much was true. "Ruby, I can't do this without you."

She gulped and nodded. "I…okay…don't leave me."

That sounded almost romantic. "C'mere." I held her tightly and then released her, trying to put as much conviction into my next few words. "Look, we came in together. We leave together. Get ready."

I picked up two rocks. One was the size of a golf ball, while the other resembled an oversized brick. "I got my weapons."

Ruby grabbed a large, thick stick that lay nearby. "I got mine," she whispered.

We moved closer, and I hurled the smaller rock at the creature, hitting one head right between the eyes. It immediately started cawing madly, whipping its heads left and right, searching the area.

"Go," I told Ruby and took off running to my right, away from the nest, hoping the creature would follow.

It did. The damn thing flapped its wings, rose in the air a few feet, and sped in my direction. That was part of the plan.

I ran over to where a cluster of rocks stood. There, I straightened up, waving my arms. "Hey, over here, ugly!"

The giant bird came at me, and just when it was about to ram its beaks through my chest, I threw myself to the right, and it slammed into the rocks. Its beaks broke, and it fell to the ground, flopping around but still very much alive.

For good measure, I used the brick-sized rock and brained its left head. Blood spurted out, and the head stopped moving, but the right head was still snapping its broken beak. All right, batter up! Soon, it lay dead.

"Got it!" Ruby's voice rang out.

She'd done it. Good…but the mad cawing of other flying critters told me we weren't safe. I ran back to where my companion in crime was. She showed me seven shards of the bluish-gray metallic shell in her hands and then tucked them into her skirt pocket.

That was the good part.

The bad part was that three eggs had hatched, and the mini pterodactyls were pecking at Ruby's legs, making her bleed in multiple places.

"Get off me, get off me," she yelled, smashing one of the birds with her stick and sending it flying across the meadow. Surprisingly, the other two took to the air and chased us as we ran.

Mama—or Papa, I couldn't tell which—pterodactyl also flew after us. The cawing got louder, and something snapped just behind my neck. I kept running, but Ruby suddenly stopped and stood her ground.

"Hey, what are you doing?" I yelled.

"Baseball," she answered, and when the large bird flew at her, she swung for the fences and knocked it cold. The two smaller birds stopped, cawed, and flew off.

Ruby dropped her stick and swiped her hands. "I really like the Cards. Let's go."

The meadow lay ahead. We tore over the meadow and into the forest. Along the way, the lizard things nipped at our ankles as we ran past them. "Don't stop," I yelled. "Keep running!"

We reached the other edge of the forest and sped through the grass. My heart was hammering, and my breath hitched in my lungs. The wall was up ahead, and I panted, "Trace…trace the picture."

We hurriedly ran our hands over the cracks in unison. The gateway opened. I grabbed Ruby's free hand, and we dove through just as one of the lizards bit into my ankle. I kicked it off just as the gateway closed, crushing its head. Who cared? We were safe.

We lay panting on the floor of the cave, feeling the cold of the mountains quickly cooling our bodies. A moment later, we were back in the holding cell, still gasping for air, and

Norlok stood over us, weapon out and ready.

Ruby pulled the shards out of her pocket and held them up. "You wanted these?"

He plucked them from her hand with a pleased expression on his odd-looking visage. "These will do. Now, you must rest up. I have another task for you later on."

Our captor started to leave, but when he was halfway around, I told him to wait. He turned back, grimacing. "What is it, human?"

"Ruby's hurt," I pointed out. "If you want us to help you find your materials, fine, but she needs medical attention. And one of those lizard things bit my ankle." I pulled up my pant leg and pointed to where the teeth had broken my skin. Already, it was red and swollen. I just hoped the thing hadn't injected me with poison.

Norlok let out a sigh of vexation. "Very well. Wait."

He left the room and returned a moment later, holding a small tube, which he tossed to me. "Put this on your companion's cuts as well as your own. It will heal the skin and prevent infection. I will be back in three hours, so rest."

When the door slid shut behind him, I moved to where Ruby sat on the floor and started to apply the ointment to her cuts.

She frowned and put up her hand to stop me. "What are you doing?"

"Helping you out," I replied. "That's what friends do. And I couldn't have made it through without you. You saved me in there…it's the least I can do."

Her mouth moved in six different directions as if she couldn't figure out what to say or how to say it. "I suppose it's okay."

"Fine. Hang on." I gently dabbed the ointment on her cuts. The stuff smelled horrible — like wood alcohol and crap mixed together.

Ruby winced each time I dabbed her skin. "It stings. You…you playing nurse, now?"

"Someone has to," I quipped. I finished putting the medicine on Ruby's legs and then dabbed the ointment on my bite marks. It burned, but the cuts healed before my eyes. My muscles ached from all the running, and I was tired. Maybe a nap would help.

"Thanks," Ruby said, patting my shoulder. "I feel better, but I'm never going back there."

She lay down, and I joined her. We didn't say anything, but I was grateful to be alive. Exhaustion hit hard, and I soon felt the embrace of sleep closing in on me.

*

A hand shook my shoulder, waking me from a rather pleasant dream. Something about dancing with the girlfriend I'd always wanted but could never have. Of course, someone *would* have to intrude on such wonderful images. I half-opened my eyes. "Who is it?"

"It's me, Ruby. Norlok's here…it's time."

*He would have to come around.* I became fully alert and sat up. The rest had done me some good. I was still sore all over, but my ankle bite had completely healed.

Norlok stood a yard away, gun in hand, watching us with his usual bland expression. "If you are rested, then our next task is at hand."

"What are we getting this time?" Ruby asked.

Norlok ignored her, focusing his gaze on me. "It is a small device, similar to what you call a battery on your world."

He tapped something on his gun. An image leaped up. Wow, a gun and a small movie projector, too. As for the image, it sort of resembled a car battery, only it was triangular, not square or rectangular, and it was the size of a paperback.

"That's it?" I asked. "It isn't that large."

A harsh laugh rumbled from Norlok. "You are demonstrating your ignorance again. A battery does not need to be large. This particular battery carries a tremendous amount of power, something that is far beyond the biggest batteries and engines your world produces. It is the energy source I need. Its power flows through the metallic shards you have given me. This task will be harder, as mindless beasts are not involved. People are."

"People?" Ruby echoed. "Do they, uh, look like us?"

When Norlok continued to ignore her, and she pulled a face, I took a step toward our jailer. "Hey, she asked you a question. That question includes me. So, no more crap about her being inferior or that you only speak to men on your world. In case you haven't noticed, pal, you're not on your world anymore. You talk to us. Not just me—us."

Norlok's bland expression never changed, but he nodded. "You are correct. I am sorry. From now on, I shall speak to both of you."

He then tapped something on his wristband and a minor shock hit, causing me to gasp, but at least I didn't lose control of my downstairs. "That is just to show you that I do not care if you show concern for the dark one. On your world, you have a game called chess. The least important pieces are the pawns. You are both my pawns, and I shall move you and use you as I see fit."

The shock stopped, and my heart rate slowed down. "Kill...kill one of us," I managed to get out. "Kill one of us, you get nothing. Think that over."

Norlok blinked, and an apologetic tone entered his voice.

"Yes, of course, you are correct. I apologize for my conduct just now. I need you both. Now, this is what you must do."

Sadistic bastard, that's all he was. But he was still armed, and we weren't.

He explained that he'd be sending us through another portal. "This next world has patches on its stone marker outside. You will see. Then you will know."

"Patches," I repeated. "And they mean…what?"

According to him, it meant that we had to be exceedingly careful. "This world is one that is not for the weak. You must be mindful of where you step."

Where we stepped? I actually raised my hand and then felt totally ridiculous. I hadn't been in school for the past two years. "Why?"

"I take it that you have not yet entered that cave's portal." He'd finally caught on to the fact we hadn't done much exploring.

His statement deserved a sarcastic answer, but this wasn't the time. "No, not yet."

"The world is called Jerana. It means *hole* in your language."

Oh, I didn't like the sound of this.

Norlok explained that some parts of the ground of the world were porous and that we had to know where to step and where not to.

"You've been there?" Ruby asked.

"No," he replied. "But as I said before, on my planet, we have detailed files on every single world we have encountered. I remembered that fact about Jerana. Now, the people there are similar to you." He turned his gaze on Ruby and nodded. "In fact, they resemble you more than your companion."

Ruby looked confused for a moment. "You mean, they're

colored, like me."

"Yes. They have dark skin, and they are highly intelligent. But they do not take kindly to outsiders, which means you." He pointed at me.

Wonderful, they didn't like white people. "Anything else?"

Norlok chewed on his lower lip as if trying to remember the details. "Their architecture is somewhat similar to that of your ancient Egypt in that there are pyramids. As for their garb, they wear robes and are ruled by a king and queen. Although they may seem primitive, they have advanced power sources, as you will soon see. They also have advanced weaponry."

*Weapons...great. Something else to worry about.*

Norlok continued with his explanation. "Where I am sending you is the main city. It is called Pash. From where you enter, you must find a small, brown building. It is the only building of that color in that city. That is where the battery is located. It is one of two, so should they lose one of them—"

"Or someone steals one," Ruby cut in.

He glowered at her. "Yes, should someone steal one, then they have an alternate. Wait, and I shall impart the necessary information to you."

Norlok pressed something on his bracelet and then put his finger to Ruby's temple. She stiffened, wavered, and then straightened up, breathing deeply.

"Are you okay?" I asked.

"I'll make it," she said. "I know...I know what we have to do."

Norlok then did the same thing to me. My brain actually hurt from the input of knowledge, and I rubbed my temples, trying to ease the agony. It didn't help. "Why does my head hurt?"

Our jailer cut in, sounding impatient. "The knowledge I

have downloaded into your primitive skulls is taxing your minds to the limit. I appreciate the concern you have for your companion, Earthman, but I am in a hurry to get home. I am sure you wish to get home as well. Go to that world, obtain the battery, and come back as soon as possible."

It sounded easy, but then there were the patches to think about. "Uh, question," I said. "What are we not supposed to step on?"

Norlok actually smiled and lost his air of impatience. "You are learning. Good. While most of the walkways and the interiors of buildings are made of stone, the entranceway is grass, and that is where the dangerous patches are. You must step on the dark blue grass. The light blue or red patches are not safe. That is all."

Patches of danger, advanced weaponry, and probably armed guards everywhere…this sounded like a suicide mission, but what other choice did we have? Stay and die, or enter and be killed on another alien world. "Er, I don't suppose the people there speak English."

A look of disdain appeared on Norlok's face. "My patience is wearing thin again. Now, to answer your question, it is not necessary. Once you go through a portal, your brain waves become attuned to that world's language. I do not know how the Settlers managed that feat, but it is a useful feature of the portals."

He then took out his cube and pressed it. A gateway sprang up out of nowhere, and he cautioned us once more to be mindful of the dangers. "This portal will remain open. I have attuned it to your atomic structures."

"Which means what?" I asked.

"This means the portal will recognize you and only you when you approach it. You will not need to touch it and trace its pattern. Now, tarry not, and bring me my prize. Above all, be careful."

As we stepped through, I gave him a parting shot. "Mister, careful is our middle name."

# Chapter Ten: The Quest, Part Two

Jerana was hot, although it wasn't as intense as the dinosaur world we'd visited. It was a dry heat similar to our garden, which was fine with me.

Thankfully, we landed on a patch of dark blue grass in the middle of a checkerboard pattern of other squares. Most squares were dark blue, but some light blue as well as red squares dotted the area. Each was roughly a yard squared…more than enough space for us to walk on.

"Ah, we are here," I said, and we started walking hand in hand to search for our target. "Let us find this building and abscond with the battery."

Ruby suddenly stopped and let go of my hand. "Wait."

I turned to her. "What is it?"

"You heard Norlok. The people here are one color—my color. And that means the people of my color rule this world. It also means you are the inferior one here." Damned if there wasn't a tiny grin on her face.

"Are you trying to make me out as some kind of jester?" I wanted to say *Do you think I'm some kind of an idiot?*…but those words simply didn't come out.

The grin disappeared. "No, I am being truthful. Now, I must disguise myself in the garb of the people here."

All right, that made sense. We crossed the field, stepping

carefully on the dark blue squares, and hid behind a small building. As Norlok had said, all the buildings here were shaped like pyramids, but they were only two-story structures, and their color was either gold or silver.

"What do we do now?" I asked. She mentioned disguising herself, but I was also wearing my military uniform. I was pretty sure no one else here dressed like me.

Ruby gazed around the area. "Stay here," she said and started to move off. "I shall return soon with the proper regalia."

"Wait," I said, suddenly concerned. "Are you sure that you can handle this alone?"

"I received the knowledge from Norlok. I will be back soon." She gave me a reassuring smile and moved off.

Where was she going? As I crouched down, I thought something was strange, but I couldn't figure out what it was. In any case, Ruby headed toward a young dark-skinned woman wearing a spotless white robe and white sandals sitting on a U-shaped bench.

Norlok's description of the people here was right. The men were six-footers, while the women were roughly Ruby's height, dark-skinned, with curled or straight black hair, flattish noses, and flat faces. They resembled Peruvians I'd seen pictures of in a history book once. Ruby could pass, more or less, although I thought she was prettier than the native woman I'd seen. But my color clearly worked against me.

When my companion in crime approached the native woman, the woman looked up, they exchanged a few words...and a moment later, the native woman fell to the ground, courtesy of Ruby's right hook. Ruby quickly dragged the woman into the bushes and came walking over to me a couple of minutes later, wearing the other woman's robe and carrying her neatly folded uniform.

"That was an amazing feat," I said, amazed at her performance. "You are skilled at fighting, and I stand in awe of your prowess." I'd wanted to say something more casual, but that speech pattern just came out of me. Something funny was happening. Oh, wait…it was the portal. Norlok had said the portal would alter our brains, and it had.

"I was raised in an area where there was often conflict between people," she said, handing over her clothes. "Now, hold these, walk ahead of me, and let us get to that building."

I saluted her, and we started off. Along the way, we met a couple of powerfully built men with guns strapped to their sides, similar to what Norlok wielded. They also carried long and lethal-looking gold-colored spears.

"What is this?" one of them asked Ruby. "And who are you?"

"I am Nateedra," she replied. "Daughter to the high regent of the province of Lendara. I recently moved here with my family, and while walking, I caught this intruder. I am taking him to the palace for questioning."

Obviously, Ruby had been given additional knowledge to try and fool the people here. Before I could think of what to say — or not to — the second man spoke up.

"Nateedra of the province of Lendara, your province is three days journey from here. I do not know the customs of your city, but here, in the capital city of Pash, women do not capture spies like this white slug and then demand to be taken to the palace. It is simply not done. That is the job for a man. We recognize you are a stranger here, however, you must observe our customs."

Interesting. Like my and Ruby's speech, the way these guards spoke was very formal. In fact, they almost sounded like the royal kings and queens of olden times, like I'd read in books and seen in movies. Customs were one thing, but now

I was a slug, at least in their eyes. I said nothing, though.

Ruby stared imperiously at both men. They outsized her by almost a foot and probably a hundred pounds, but under her intense gaze, they seemed to wilt. "You are fools," she declared. "You are guards, are you not?"

When they mutely nodded, Ruby prodded me with her finger. "Yet you did not see this white…thing enter your city? You are incompetent and stupid. I am a new resident, and the first thing I see is this stranger. Who has trained you? Whoever they are, they are as incompetent as you are. You are derelict in your duties. I should report you to the king and queen."

The first man got a look of alarm on his face. "Please, do not. If the king or the queen learns of this incident, our lives will be forfeit."

Ruby eyed them up and down. "Very well, but I will have need of your weapons. You are not to be trusted with them."

Reluctantly, they handed them over and backed away, supplicating their hands as if begging for mercy.

Ruby prodded me with one of the guns, and once the men were out of sight and we were alone, she handed me the other weapon. "Hide this under my uniform," she murmured, then massaged her temples. "My head pains me."

My head also hurt, a dull throbbing. "It is due to the knowledge we received. We sound like they do. Those guards spoke most formally and did not know who you were."

Ruby prodded me again from behind, and it was filled with a mixture of amusement and alarm. "Understood, but we must hurry. We must find the battery and leave so Norlok can remove this knowledge from my mind. It is almost too much to bear."

Fortunately, the building we searched for lay only a hundred yards ahead. Unlike the others, it was only one story and was brown. A few people were taking their daily constitutionals, but I didn't see any guards.

However, when the citizens saw me, many screamed and ran in the opposite direction. Others walked up to me with fear and hate in their eyes and proceeded to kick me as well as spit on me before walking away.

"You are a feared presence," Ruby said.

Feared? More like hated, or what was that other word? Oh, yeah...despised. "They hate me because of the color of my skin."

A note of ire laced Ruby's next words. "This is how I was treated."

"But I did not—"

"We shall discuss this later. We must hurry."

Right, she'd said that before. We went up the steps and into the building, and sure enough, the battery sat in a glass case held by a vise. It looked like a dime store novel, triangular, and approximately six inches long at its base. It glowed a bright orange. Like a furnace, it gave off a tremendous amount of heat. I felt it even though I stood a good thirty feet away.

"Hold," a deep voice said.

We turned around to see three guards jogging toward us, their hands on their weapons, although they hadn't drawn them—yet. Maybe Ruby could talk her way out of this...but I doubted it.

"Who are you?" one of them said to her.

"I am Nateedra," she replied. "I am from the province of Lendara. I caught this intruder trying to steal the battery, and I held him here to interrogate him."

Oh, that was the dumbest lie I'd ever heard. Even the guards grew suspicious. One of them came over to eye me up and down with distaste. "Where are you from, white pig?"

White pig, white slug…how were they going to insult me next? "I am from the world of Memphis," I said, thinking fast. "I am here on a mission of peace."

I'd just topped Ruby's lie with a whopper of my own. However, that knowledge was lost on the guard, who told one of his men to fetch the king. The man took off like a shot. "Our ruler will be here shortly, white slug. He will direct us to torture you until you tell us the truth."

"That sounds delightful," I replied, giving my companion an imploring look. "I shall look forward to it."

The guard's slap was powerful, snapping my head around. "Whelp, you shall not be impudent in my presence!"

"How about in mine?" Ruby asked and fired her weapon.

It blew the guard apart, and then she turned it on the other man. He, too, went to pieces. "Now," she said, aiming her gun at the case. "We must take the battery."

Ruby pulled the trigger, but the weapon failed to fire. "It is without power," she said and tossed the gun away, imploring me to destroy the case. "Shoot now, and make sure it is a perfect shot."

I got the gun into position, but before I could fire, I was struck by a shock—similar to Norlok's—and I fell to the floor. At least I didn't lose control downstairs. When I managed to raise my head, ten armed guards had entered the room, along with a tall, strongly built man and an equally tall, slender woman. Both wore robes of red and gold, as well as golden crowns. They had to be the king and queen.

"What have we here?" the king-person asked. "You are strangers, and you are here to steal that which gives life and light to this city. Tell us your names."

Ruby answered, "I am Nateedra of Lendara. I am here on a mission—"

"To steal that which is ours," the queen-person

114

interrupted. "For that, your lives are forfeit, but before you die, we will find out who you truly are. If we must torture you, then it is because we must know the truth."

"I am Nateedra," Ruby repeated in a forceful tone. "Do you doubt my word?"

"Yes. I know of Nateedra and what her appearance is. You are not her."

Just then, the young woman Ruby had flattened rushed in, naked as a jaybird and not at all shy about showing off her body. She had bruises all over her face, and she ran to where the royal couple stood and knelt, prostrating herself in front of them. "O, King Sadim and Queen Renalla, please forgive me. I am Nateedra of Lendara. I was sent here by my parents on a mission of goodwill, and that woman beat me severely." She pointed at Ruby.

Well, I'd been right about the king and queen couple, and I took their threat seriously.

The queen clapped her hands twice and pointed at one of the guards. "Find another robe and be quick about it!"

The man ran off and returned a minute later, handing the robe to the real Nateedra. The men, including the king, turned away as the visitor dressed.

Once she was clad in her robe, the king stared down at us in what could only be called a haughty manner, the same way Norlok looked at us. "You, imposter, and you, white slug, are our prisoners. Guards! Take these two to a cell and imprison them there. I will question them later."

Wonderful, we were now the prisoners of a homicidal king and queen on a world we weren't a part of. A world that considered me a second or third-class citizen…or worse, only a thing to be hunted down and killed. I now understood the kind of garbage Ruby had to face almost daily.

The guards marched us out of the building, down an alley

to our right, and then we entered a silver building. On the ground floor, there was no furniture, only a series of circular silver cages. Some of them had people inside...but they weren't alive, only rotting corpses—and the smell was horrible.

"Do we not get a trial?" Ruby asked.

"Your trial will be by combat later on," one of the guards said. "If you do not die in the fight, then others in our service will kill you. Now, be quiet. We do not wish to speak to you any longer than we must."

Ruby got tossed into one cage, and a guard locked the door. The other nine men decided to have some fun, beating and kicking me. I fought back and managed to knock out two of them, but there were seven more contenders, and they weren't tiny guys. After they'd beaten the living daylights out of me, they threw me in a cage ten yards away from where my companion was.

While nursing my wounds, the door opened, and two guards came in, prodding two other men with the sharp ends of their spears. I recognized the two prisoners as the guards Ruby had dressed down earlier. The prisoners remained silent.

One of the guards looked at Ruby and asked, "Did you encounter these two men earlier?"

"Yes," she replied. "Incompetent idiots. They could not recognize me as a stranger, and they surrendered their weapons without objecting in the least. They are useless."

Both guards prodded the prisoners with their spears and ordered them to turn around. Once they did, the guards stabbed the hapless prisoners in their chests. One thrust was all it took. After the men fell, the guards pulled their bloody corpses out of the room, leaving us alone.

I couldn't resist asking Ruby, "Are you not shocked?"

She stared at the bloody smears on the floor, and her voice shook when she spoke. "I…I have no words right now. It is too terrible a thing to imagine."

Only we hadn't imagined it. It was all too real, and Ruby had blown away two men earlier. As I wiped the blood from my face and eyes, I realized that our perfect crime hadn't been so perfect after all. We'd become prisoners, and we could only wait to see what kind of death we'd experience from our new jailers. Fight and win, then get killed in some horrible manner, or fight and die.

Neither option thrilled me.

# Chapter Eleven: The Quest, Part Three

"How is your condition?"

Ruby's voice startled me from a semi-sleep, though not a restful one. I rarely dreamed about my childhood days, mainly because they weren't anything special. But one memory stood out. I was fourteen, near the end of junior high, and some of the kids—three in all—decided to make an example of the only Jewish kid in school.

Fights were common back then. If it wasn't a fight over someone's religion—mine—then it was a fight over which baseball team had the best players, which movie star was the neatest, or something else just as inconsequential in the long run.

Kids back then didn't think about the long run. They only thought about the immediate, the now, and what they were interested in. So fights happened. In my case, they happened because I was a fairly decent student and because of my religion. Just how it was. Welcome to Southern life.

Back to getting my butt kicked… Those three kids had pulled me around to the back of the building and threw me up against the wall. Of course, the teachers there hadn't done a thing to stop it. They never did. They were on the side of the punks who wanted to mangle me. Schools were supposed to be an impartial arena for learning. In my case, my school became an arena of abuse.

Tommy Tucker, Larry Wheeler, and Kit Harmon — their fathers were leaders in our community. Tommy's father was a Baptist preacher. Larry's father was the vice president of a bank in Memphis. And Kit's father was part owner of Dalton's, the biggest department store in Memphis.

In short, their fathers had money and power. That alone separated those three boys from the rest of us and elevated them to untouchable status. No one stood against them. No one could. Other kids had tried, but after getting their faces kicked in a few times, they'd stayed on the sidelines. Just how it was back then.

From the time I'd entered junior high, I'd listened to their insults, been pushed around by them, and put up with being abused on an almost daily basis. At first, I ran home. I still got beaten up the next day. I ran home the day after that. Once more, I got my butt kicked from here to breakfast.

My mother worried, what with me coming home three or four days a week all banged up.

On the other hand, my father said that if I wanted to win, I had to stand up for myself. "These kids are nothing but *momsers*. They know only one way, and that's violence. You got to fight back."

*Momsers* was a Yiddish word for punks, or gangsters.

His advice given, my father returned to his store while I did some soul-searching. Being smacked around and my father's words had taught me one lesson — running was for losers. Additionally, all those punches had taught me to duck. I still couldn't punch my way out of a paper bag, but I'd learned how not to get hit—mostly.

After thinking long and hard, something stirred inside me. I recognized it as resolve, and I realized I didn't feel like running from the bullies. Not anymore.

When the terrible trio approached me again, I squared off and said, "Okay, if you guys want to fight, let's do it one at a time. That way, you get to beat on me some more."

Tommy, the leader of the mini gang, said, "You got it."

"Who's first?"

Kit stepped forward with a grin. "Me." He was short, thickset, and had a mean face, like an ugly pug dog. He charged, and like a matador, I stepped aside at the last second, and he rammed headfirst into the wall. His head hit with a crack, and he slid to the ground, unconscious, blood coming from a cut on his forehead. A massive bruise was also starting to form in the center of the sliced-up skin.

Larry was tall for his age and skinny like me, but he had fast hands. He tagged me with a shot to the side of my head that made me see stars. When he leaned forward to grin at me, he got two fingers in his eyes, and he screamed in pain. A shot to his throat left him gasping for air and writhing around on the ground.

"Just you and me now, preacher boy," I said, turning to Tommy. "You want to call this off, or do you want to go to the dentist?"

"Fight," he snarled.

We tore into each other like wild animals. Tommy was stronger, but only his right hand did any damage. His left hand was weak. I was also weak, but I'd learned how to hit with both hands, which gave me an edge.

One minute and forty seconds later, Tommy lay on the ground, bleeding from his mouth and nose. His two front teeth lay next to him. I had a bloody nose, too, and when I went home, the mirror showed that I had a magnificent shiner.

I didn't care. I'd won, but the next day, three different kids decided to challenge me, and it was fight night at Bryer Hill Junior High all over again...

\*

Shift. Two years later. Leaving home.

Sixteen now, and after the argument with my father, I'd packed a small bag and taken off, determined to see the world. I was tall — six-one — but skinny, and while I looked older than I was, I doubted the army or marines would take me.

But I'd heard about the Merchant Marines, so I'd gone to someone in Memphis to get forged papers. Cost — four hundred bucks. Luckily, I had a gold watch I'd gotten as a bar mitzvah present when I was thirteen. I hocked it and a few other things which gave me enough money to pay for everything, including some photos the forger needed.

The forger was a man named Nick — he didn't give me his last name. Short and barrel-shaped with spotty skin and of indeterminate age, he reminded me of a toad. I half expected him to have a croaking voice. Sure enough, he did.

Nick worked out of a small, dirty office located above a pawnshop. It smelled of smoke and stale wine. He sat behind a cracked and broken desk with an aged typewriter in front of him, asked me for the photos and the money, and then told me to take a seat.

"This'll take some time," he'd said as he lit a cigarette.

"Do I need all this?" I asked as I sat on a rickety chair.

"Yeah, you do. Private companies run the Merchant Marine. You want to get a berth on a ship, you need to be a graduate of the Merchant Marine Academy. That's how it works now."

I didn't know a damn thing about sailing, so Nick clued me in. "They'll give you a rule book when you board your ship. Read it, memorize it, keep your mouth shut, and you'll be fine. Now, be quiet and let me work."

His fingers, cracked and blackened from ink, worked deftly as he typed things up, cut and pasted the pictures, and made everything look normal. From time to time, he took a drag on his smoke.

Finally, he was done. He stubbed out his cigarette in an overflowing ashtray and waved me over. "These'll get you on a good ship," he'd said as he handed over the papers. "These are good enough to pass muster with anyone. Great picture, great work, if I do say so myself. Carl Allen Goodman, graduate of the United States Merchant Marine Academy in King's Point, New York."

"New York?"

"That's where you gotta go, kid." He got up to walk over to a closet. "You'll need a uniform. You're going in at the lowest rank."

He picked out the uniform for me, I tried it on, and it fit fairly well. He seemed pleased and instructed me on what to do next. "When you get to the office, wear your uniform. The other guys'll be wearing theirs. Speak to a guy named Dave Martinson. Tall, skinny guy, like you. Red hair. He'll help you out. Good luck."

Yeah, good luck. I had just enough money left to buy a one-way ticket to New York. Since the office in New York was fairly new, and the Merchant Marines were chronically short of men, they took just about everyone. Lots of veteran fishermen and itinerant sailors signed up and went through the academy, which took them about a year and a half. My *schooling* was completed in about thirty minutes.

At the recruiting office, I stood behind a yellow line with others waiting to hand in my papers. A skinny man in his early thirties with a shock of red hair sat at the desk, reading and stamping the documents. I tried not to fidget and glanced at the clock. It was two-thirty p.m.

After another twenty minutes, my turn came. The man scanned my papers, looked up, and murmured, "Nick send you?"

I figured this had to be Martinson, and he knew my papers were forged. One word from him to the authorities and I'd end up in jail, but it was too late to back out now. "Yes, sir," I whispered.

"Congratulations, sailor," he replied in a hearty voice as he stamped my documents. "Report to the ship docked in the first berth at the Brooklyn Shipyards. You ship out in six hours."

"Thank you, sir," I said, saluted, turned sharply on my heel, and left the office walking on air. Martinson probably got a kickback from Nick, but I didn't care. On January seventh, nineteen-forty-three, I had my ticket to sail.

Onboard my ship, I worked hard, learned quickly, and had few fights, but life was good. Then my ship was sunk, and my life changed forever...

\*

Shift. The present.

My consciousness slowly returned with lots of images replaying in my mind like a bad B-movie. I'd arrived on a hot world where everyone hated me because I was white...I'd been beaten up by a mob and couldn't fight back...and...

"Carl, rise!"

That got me up and more alert, only to experience a vicious headache that pounded like drums. My body felt like a giant hematoma, and my nose was caked with blood. Still, they hadn't tied me up, so that was something. When I looked at Ruby, she was wearing her uniform. "You are wearing your old garb."

"While you were unconscious, a female of this world gave me my old clothes. I am now dressed like you."

"I comprehend," I replied, wishing I could speak casually and knowing I couldn't while we were on this world.

"Good. We must leave this place."

Yes, true. "If you have a plan, I shall listen." It was hard to keep from sounding sarcastic, but I managed. I then wiped the dried blood from my nostrils in order to breathe. "Do you?"

"No."

Silence fell. Finally, Ruby said with a tone of sadness, "I took the life of two guards yesterday. I feel a great measure of guilt over it."

She shouldn't have. "They wished to deprive us of our lives. I believe that we were only acting in self-defense."

Ruby considered my words and then bobbed her head. "I agree with what you say, but I have another more pertinent question."

"What is that?" Once again, I wished that I could speak normally, but it just wasn't going to happen.

She bit her bottom lip. "Do you feel badly knowing that you are considered a lesser race here?"

A number of thoughts ran through my head at light speed, chiefly the one about being a lesser race. I'd never thought of myself as being better than anyone else because I was white. Yet, here, I was considered less than nothing. "Yes."

"Then that is enough."

"I have a question for you."

Ruby looked at me. "Yes?"

"Do you feel the same way as they do?"

Her answer came instantly. "No. What I feel for you is…affection. I felt that way for you in the garden during our evening together. Even before that, to be honest. You are kind and good, but I…my history…I should not have vented my wrath on you before, or now. I care for you…if I may be so bold."

Well, at least she cared for me. That was a good thing, but I could tell she still carried that chip on her shoulder. I couldn't blame her. Back on our world, the deck would always be stacked against her, which was just wrong. Here, the deck was stacked against me, and that was equally wrong, but in a different way.

When I served on my ship, some of the men had brought books to help pass the time. One man, a chief engineer named O'Halloran, had been a university graduate of history. He'd wanted to become a professor, but for some reason, he'd been denied a professorship, and then the war interfered.

Still, he recognized that I wanted to learn, so he lent me some of his books, mainly about Irish history. "These'll open your mind," he'd said.

I'd read about indentured servants and heard from him about how badly the Irish were treated when they first arrived in America centuries ago. Their problems were terrible, but could I really compare them to what colored people had to go through? I asked O'Halloran about it. It was late February. We were on deck and off-duty at the time. Although it was frigid outside, it was better than being below in the foul air. He was smoking a cigarette, staring out at the water.

"Comparisons," he said, looking surprised, but then his mood turned reflective. "I suppose you could say that my ancestors had it tough," he finally said. "But I'm not sure you could compare the two."

He drew on his cigarette and then flipped it overboard. "It's true that many of the Irish in the sixteen-hundreds and early seventeen-hundreds were indentured, but that wasn't for life. They had some rights. The negroes had none. So, you can't compare the two."

It was a revelation for me to hear someone tell me differently than what most history books said.

He left me then to go below, but I'd never forgotten his words. My mind came back to the present, and I finally understood the cause of Ruby's anger at racial inequalities.

Yet, Ruby had just said that she cared for me. I hadn't expected that, but it meant we were more than friends…and that was special. "It is all right, Ruby. I have similar feelings for you, too…"

We were interrupted by the sound of the doors opening. The king and queen entered, flanked by six guards who wore those pulse guns at their sides and held their golden spears. The king also carried a gold spear, but his was longer than the others and studded with jewels along the shaft.

"I see that the prisoners are awake," he said, grinning at our plight. "I wish to know your real names and where you are from. If your answers please me, I shall make your deaths painless. If you displease me, then I shall torture you slowly. Think wisely upon my offer."

His offer was no offer at all. "I am from the world of Memphis," I repeated. "And I demand that you let me out of this cage."

The king laughed. "White slug, you are in no position to make demands. But perhaps you would like to fight for your freedom?"

It had crossed my mind. "I shall be happy to do so."

He clapped his hands twice, and one of his guards came over to unlock the cage. Once I stepped out, the other five men piled into me, kicking and punching and using the butt ends of their spears to whack me all over, chanting, "White pig. White pig. White pig."

Trying to fight back didn't help. While I managed to smack a few of them around and inflict some damage, in the end, it proved to be too much. The last thing I heard before passing out were the words *White pig* and Ruby screaming…

# Chapter Twelve: The Quest, Part Four

$\mathcal{I}$ woke up to more pain. Every muscle hurt and every nerve screamed for mercy. It went without saying that my head hurt. I couldn't take much more of the abuse, but I'd have to. I was still in my cage, and when I tried to move to pat myself and check for broken bones, my body let me know it didn't like the movement.

Ruby sat beside me and whispered, "Are you going to live?"

Her soft voice interrupted my self-examination. "Yes, but I shall not enjoy it."

Fortunately, nothing was broken. Ruby then told me I'd been out for most of the day. She'd been given some kind of meat dish, but I'd had nothing. At that moment, the thought of eating made me ill.

"It is afternoon now," Ruby said. "The king will return soon. He wishes to know more about our world, but I did not tell him anything."

"Did he torture you?" The mere idea made me angry and frightened for her. My only thought was that if the king had tortured her, then nothing would save him from my wrath.

Wrath was an old term, but it fit.

"No. He said it was because I resemble his people." A look of agony crossed her face. "My head pains me severely."

Wonderful. So did mine, and speaking of *wonderful*... The door opened and the king, the queen, and six guards walked in. The guards were armed, but the king and queen weren't.

The king strode over to my cage. "White pig, tell me the truth about your world, and your death will be quick."

What to tell him? No matter what I said, he wouldn't believe me, so I replied, "In your society, do you believe in hell?"

He nodded. "Yes."

"Then go there and kiss the ruler's buttocks."

His face flushed an angry purple, and he stepped closer to the cage's bars. "You have shown insolence to me and my queen for the last time. However, I shall still give you one more chance to earn an honorable death. It is much more preferable than the dishonorable execution of those two worthless guards of mine. You will face my finest warrior."

He motioned one of his men forward, a man a couple of inches shorter than me but much thicker all around. He held two spears, and their ends looked wickedly sharp.

"I accept," I replied. "If that is your best, then I do not have to worry."

Ruby started to protest, but I cut her off with a cheery grin and commented, "I shall triumph. I already know my opponent's weaknesses. Do not worry." Of course, that was a lie, but I didn't want her to worry more than necessary.

My reply earned me a laugh from the other guards, but they shut up when the king snapped his fingers for quiet and then directed another man to open our cages.

I stepped out, shook my arms and legs to get the blood flowing, and stood ready. My opponent tossed me one of the spears. I caught it, spun it, noting its perfect balance, and nodded. "Let us do this."

"You sound overconfident," the king said. "That is admirable, but it will not matter. You are to fight…and then to die."

"And if I should triumph?"

A mean smile crossed his face. "You will fight again until you are dead."

That was no comfort, but I couldn't think about it as the king yelled, "Begin!"

My foe stepped forward, spear at midriff level, and he wore the grin of someone who enjoyed killing. He was right-handed, I noticed, so to throw him off a bit, I switched to a left-handed grip on my spear and moved to the left. We circled each other, he jabbed, and I backed out of range.

While sizing him up, a memory floated back to me, a memory of a beating and a feeling for revenge…

\*

Onboard my ship.

During my first week, one of the crewmen, a man named Blair, continuously went after me. Taller than me by an inch and much heavier, with a bald dome and a pug face. He bullied the other new guys, too, but for some reason, he took a special dislike to me. As I was the new kid, he probably felt like he could do what he wanted and not get into trouble.

One night, he and a few other men trapped me and dragged me to a room. They had a lookout, shoved me inside, and at first, I thought they were going to rape me. It happened on ships and in prisons…everywhere, in fact…unfortunately.

Fortunately, no rape occurred. Blair, though, had two of his friends hold my arms while he proceeded to beat the living hell out of me. Only after I couldn't stand up did they let me go. It was supposedly an initiation rite of sorts on a ship, and the captain overlooked it.

The next day, it happened again. Same man, same accomplices. A day after that, another sailor noted the bruises on my face while I was swabbing the deck. "Blair get you?"

"Yeah." I stared at the floor.

"He gets all the new guys. They ganged up on you, right?"

"Yeah." I still couldn't look at him.

"I can teach you to take on four men at a time and win. You want to do that?"

It sounded too good to be true, but if this worked...I picked my head up. "Yeah."

"You're gonna start with the basics, kid. Get ready for an education." His name was Walter Gomez, a veteran sailor who'd been all over the world. In his mid-thirties, short and thickset, he knew how to box and taught me the basic moves of blocking and slipping punches, as well as throwing combinations. My old fighting style was crude and consisted of weak kicks and roundhouse punches. I needed to upgrade.

Gomez became my teacher in some martial arts moves in addition to his boxing skills. Mainly striking in rapid combos from multiple angles, kicking straight ahead high and low, and using various kinds of elbow and wrist locks to disable my opponents or break their bones, if necessary.

After my first sparring lesson, battered and bruised, I asked him where he'd learned it all.

"Been on the sea since I was eighteen," he said. "Been everywhere and learned how to take care of myself. I lived in China for three years before joining up with the service— tough crowds there. Got my face beat in a lot, so I learned from a couple of the locals what to do. What I'm teaching you is called *Gong-Fu,* learning a skill through hard work."

Call me a willing student, and after our shifts were over, Gomez took me to a storage room where he beat the hell out of me until I got the idea. Then I hit back. That went on for almost two months. During that time, I put up with Blair smacking me around. I hated it, but I took it because I wasn't ready.

One afternoon, though, after my session with Gomez, he announced I was ready. "Remember," he counseled. "Keep your guard up and fight to disable him. Not to kill him."

"What if he tries to kill me?"

Gomez offered a grim smile. "Then do what you have to."

Good advice.

At the evening meal in the mess hall, Blair slapped a tray full of food out of my hands. He had a grin on his face, as if he expected me to run. Not this time. "Up top, Blair. Let's go."

A grin painted his face. "Oh, this is going to be fun."

Blair was big and strong, but like many big men, he relied on his strength and size to win, usually with his buddies to help administer his beatings. This time, it was just him and me.

We fought it out on deck by the light of a full moon. All the off-duty crewmen formed a circle, watched, and rooted — most of them placing bets on Blair to win.

Even though I was scared when Blair lunged at me, my training didn't fail me. I blocked, parried, kicked him high and low, and then let loose with a right cross that snapped his head around. He fell on his face and got up unsteadily after a few seconds, blood dripping from his mouth.

"Using that judo shit," he snarled and spat out a river of red. "Let's see how you do against a blade." He pulled a switchblade and flicked it open.

One of the junior officers, a man named Edwards, yelled,

"Hey, toss that pigsticker away!"

My opponent didn't listen and lunged at me again. I spun to my left and chopped at his neck. He went down like a sack of potatoes, much to the surprise of the crewmen watching. A few started cheering for me, but I ignored them and concentrated on winning.

Blair turned over, swinging his knife at me, but I kicked the blade from his hands. "Chickenshit maneuver," I growled. "Pure chickenshit." Without hesitation, I straddled his chest and beat his face without mercy.

Gomez ran over and caught my fist before I went for a throat punch. "You want to kill him, kid?"

At that moment, my thirst for revenge left, and I got off the sack of shit under me. "No."

Silence fell as Edwards walked to our combat zone. "All finished, Goodman?"

"Yes, sir."

He stared at Blair. "Get up."

Blair couldn't rise and ended up in the infirmary with a broken nose and a broken orbital bone around his right eye, and I'd cracked his jaw as well. I got reprimanded due to Blair being a higher rank than me, but the captain didn't throw me in the brig. Best of all, after that, no one bothered me again…

\*

The present.

"Watch out!"

Ruby's yell yanked my attention back to reality just in time to see the guard lunge at me, just like Blair with his knife. And just like that fight, my training kicked in. I spun around with my spear ready and plunged it into the back of the guard's head. He gasped, fell to his knees, then fell onto his face — dead.

Gorge rose in my throat. I'd never killed anyone before, and the thought made me sick, but I couldn't dwell on it as another scream rang out. Ruby had snatched a spear from a guard and held it menacingly, shifting it between the queen and the guards. One guard raised his spear, but I thrust mine into his side, downing him.

That gave Ruby all the time she needed to run behind the queen, loop the spear over her head, and put her in a chokehold. "If you try to slay me, she will die first," she growled. "Choose wisely."

The king started to move, but Ruby squeezed the spear tighter against the queen's throat. The queen grabbed the spear at her throat and gurgled, "Stop."

Ruby didn't move and repeated, "Choose wisely."

While the king and his men appeared indecisive, I dropped my spear, grabbed a gun from one of the guards, and fired at each of them. Within five seconds, the guards were ashes, leaving only the king and queen. Once again, I felt sick at having to kill people, but if it was a choice between them or me, then I chose me — and Ruby.

Ruby released the queen and quickly stepped back.

Her royal lowness turned around, sneering, "You have soiled me with your touch."

Without a word, Ruby dropped the spear, leaped forward, and knocked the queen cold with a single straight shot to her jaw. The queen collapsed without a word.

As for the king, he stared at his downed wife, then turned to me. "What will you do now?" He was at a disadvantage, yet he retained his aura of command.

"You are going to let us go," I said. "That is easy enough to comprehend, is it not?"

The king smiled grimly. "You cannot leave my kingdom unless I give the command. No ship will take you from here to Lendara, or wherever your companion says she is from. Not without my order. You are trapped."

I tossed the gun away, picked up the spear, and walked over to him. His expression of haughty superiority changed when I rammed the butt end of the spear into his gut. He fell to his knees, puking. I stared at him, wanting to do worse but refrained from doing so. "Let us worry about that."

Ruby rubbed her temples and then told me to disrobe the king.

"Why?" I asked.

"We must bind their limbs and silence their mouths," she replied. "I will do the same for the queen."

Well, well, my companion in crime was one step ahead. We stripped the royal couple, bound and gagged them.

I snatched two guns, handing one to Ruby, then went to the door to check if someone stood guard outside. The coast was clear. "Let us leave."

We ran out of the prison and over to the building where the battery was. Surprisingly, I saw no guards despite our break-in the day before.

We entered, and Ruby pointed straight ahead. "It is there. We must get it now."

*Tell me something I don't know.* I aimed the gun at the corner of the case and fired. A burst of yellow energy shot out of the muzzle and shattered the case. The battery fell from its holder to the floor, losing its orange glow.

Hesitantly, I touched it…it was cool, so I grabbed it. "Let us leave now."

The small device wasn't very heavy, perhaps two pounds, so I tucked it under my arm, and we ran through the door and past the startled citizens.

Six men were guarding the city entrance, but we managed to sneak around them and took off across the checkerboard grass.

"Dark blue areas," Ruby reminded me.

"I remember. Hurry."

We jumped and ran on the dark blue patches. Behind us, the cries of the guards indicated that at least one of them had stepped on the wrong square. I stopped once, turning around and seeing a man step on a red patch of grass and disappear into the ground. Good Lord, this planet ate people.

That spurred me to start running again. "Keep going," I cried.

Ruby hadn't stopped, and she was fast on her feet. I closed the gap, and we joined hands. My breath came in short, sharp gasps, and the pain in my head was growing worse. We were running out of energy and time.

Moreover, shots of energy started whizzing over our heads. The king's soldiers were finding their range.

"There," Ruby gasped and pointed at the wall where we'd come in. "Over there."

As if sensing our presence, the portal began to glow. Just a few more feet…a few more…we stepped on a dark blue patch, and the portal opened wide. We jumped through, tumbling to the floor of the white room.

Norlok stood over us, waiting, his expression impassive. "You have been gone a long time. What happened?"

After my breathing calmed, I gave him a quick rundown about what we'd gone through.

He seemed surprised and impressed. "You have done well."

Whoopee, a compliment, and I held up the battery. With a glint of greed in his eyes, Norlok plucked it from my hand.

"Listen," Ruby said. "Take whatever you put into my head

out. Now. It's going to explode."

Wordlessly, he touched something on his bracelet, then put his finger to her forehead. She stiffened and then lay still, eyes closed. A second later, she started to snore gently.

"She will be all right," Norlok assured me. "The implantation of knowledge is sometimes painful to the recipient. Her mind, though, is quite adaptive. I was in error before. She is very much your equal."

He then did the same for me, my mind cleared, and I replied, "Nice to know. What's next?"

Norlok meditated on my question for a time after tucking the battery under his arm. "For now, you and your companion must rest. You are both drained from your ordeal. Sleep, and tomorrow, we shall resume the quest. I will be joining you."

"Why? Just tell us what to get and —"

"What I seek is something that was hidden away by an ancient race, and it is in a very hostile area. Therefore, I must go with you. Now, rest. I shall return tomorrow morning."

Norlok left the containment cell, the door closed, and sleep soon pulled me under.

# Chapter Thirteen: Escape

"*T*his will be the hardest task of all," Norlok told us the next morning after saying that we'd been sleeping for about seven hours.

We sat at a table, eating the square egg-type sandwiches, and our jailer ate with us. He'd strapped the battery to his side, saying it had to be within easy reach. "There are no words I can say to express how serious a matter this is."

"I think you just did," I grumbled, relieved to be speaking normal English again. Speaking formally, combined with the embedded knowledge of that last world, made me wonder whether I'd gotten brain damage or not. For now, I felt okay. "So, where are Ruby and I going?"

Norlok glared at me, looking displeased. He really didn't like being talked back to. "This matter concerns me as well as both of you. We must obtain a scepter. It is in a rather inaccessible place, but between the three of us, it will be possible to obtain it."

"A scepter?" I queried. "What kind of scepter?"

Norlok's look of displeasure deepened, but then he changed his tune and explained what the deal was about. We were going to a world called Gamga. A primordial world of land that was still forming, identical to how Earth had formed billions of years ago. It had no life forms and was considered dangerous beyond belief. As for the scepter...

"The scepter is the final key to our search. I have the battery and the metal shards. When we retrieve the scepter, I will link them all to the transporter cube I carry. It will have sufficient power, I feel, to take me home as well as send you home, as I have promised."

I wondered why someone would hide a scepter on a world like he'd described.

Our captor must've been a mind-reader, as he asked, "Do you not know the story of Velarus of Tiannon?"

Ruby's expression was blank, and I responded, "I'm not as well-traveled as you are."

Norlok laughed. He seemed genuinely amused at my reply. "That is a fair reply, and no, it was foolish of me to expect that you would know. Velarus was a former soldier of Tiannon, a planet in the galaxy I am from. He ruled over five hundred of your years ago, and his exploits were legendary as a soldier and later as a statesman.

"He eventually became a king, but we were alike in one way—we were and are great inventors. The scepter he invented was made of a rare metal that reputedly carried enormous power."

"And?"

As it turned out, this Velarus guy was a cruel and unjust ruler who got rid of the opposition by bumping them off through his court of assassins. The story was fascinating, and Norlok spared no details.

In the end, with a sense of wonder, Ruby asked, "That really goes on out there?"

Norlok let out a harsh chuckle. "Assassinations and machinations within governments happen in every culture and in every corner of the universe. If there is something to be gained, then unscrupulous men and women will do whatever is needed to gain the item they crave. I am sure that in your culture, there have been some people who were and are the same way."

He happened to be right about that. I wasn't much of a historian, but I'd read about gaming the system and assassinations in various governments that had happened since time began. It was nothing new. "I guess greed is everywhere," I said.

Norlok bobbed his head in agreement. "It is. And I stand before you as one accused of the same thing Velarus was accused of."

"So, what happened to him?"

Norlok shrugged and waved his hand. "From what our files tell us, the very people who had supported him for many years, the same people who had helped him achieve his status as king and undisputed ruler of his world, overthrew him and sent him to a penal colony, where he died after many years. Such is the fate of foolish tyrants."

Norlok wasn't much better, but I didn't tell him that. "So, what happened to the scepter?"

He steepled his hands under his chin and spoke like the words were memorized by rote. "Those who overthrew him hid it on many worlds in our galaxy and others. This was done in order to prevent any unscrupulous people from obtaining it." His gaze locked with mine. "Your race is on the verge of discovering the stars, but where I am from, we have great ships that easily traverse the universe. Plus, we have transporter cubes, as you have seen."

Norlok then leaned back in a more relaxed manner. "At any rate, the scepter passed from world to world over the centuries and finally landed on Gamga, the world I spoke of earlier. Our files indicate it is perched atop a high mountain in the middle of a lava pit."

"A lava pit?" I echoed. "They chose a good place to hide it."

He laughed at my reply. "Yes. Not many people will risk going to such an inhospitable place. Now, I will be able to transport us to the base of the mountain. And to answer your unspoken question of why we cannot go directly to the top, it is because of the scepter. Its power is such that it prevents direct transmission of people or things. However, we can get close to it."

He paused with a heavy sigh. "I agree that it is most inconvenient for all of us, but we must help each other if I am to reclaim what I consider my prize...and if you wish to return home."

I definitely didn't like the sound of this next task, and from the look of fear on Ruby's face, she didn't like the idea either, but what choice did we have? None. "Okay, let's do this."

Ruby nodded. "Yeah, it should be a piece of cake." She acted bravely, but the tremor in her voice indicated otherwise.

Norlok took his transporter cube out. "Then let us go, and may good fortune favor the bravest of us all."

What he said sounded good, and I hoped his prediction would come true.

\*

We landed at the base of a mountain in an incredibly hot area. As Norlok had said, the world was one of lava flows, with small islands of rock and smaller mountains dotting a sea that was on fire. I'd read books on astronomy that showed what Earth was like when it was forming millions of years ago...but this was something else.

Right away, sweat popped out from every pore. It was hard to breathe, much more so than in dinosaur land. While trying to inhale and exhale naturally, Ruby grabbed my hand, not so much out of affection but for reassurance.

"This is like hell," she whispered. "My mama used to tell me that if I wasn't good, then I'd wind up here. Maybe I haven't been so good after all."

"Good has nothing to do with it," Norlok said with a touch of harshness. "It is what this world is like and nothing more. I do not know of this hell you speak of, but this is science, not some imaginary belief."

He was right, but it was a hellish landscape, all the same. "What now?" I asked, looking at the mountain. "I don't see any handholds. We need tools to climb."

"Correct," Norlok said, reaching into his pocket and pulling out twelve pinky-sized metal rods. Six were silver in color, while the other six were dark green. He handed us two green and two silver rods each, pointing out the tiny buttons on their ends. "Press the buttons you see and watch what happens."

I wiped the sweat from my eyes and pressed the buttons as he instructed. Instantly, the two silver rods formed into pitons, and the two green ones transformed into climbing boots with spikes on the toes. That was…pretty different.

"Put the boots on," Norlok said. "They will aid in your climb. Use the pitons to stab the rock and pull yourself up."

I stepped into the boots, surprised when they reformed to fit my feet. Once I was ready, I stole a glance at Ruby. She looked terrified, but she followed Norlok's instructions. I admitted I wasn't feeling so brave myself.

Once we were all geared up, Norlok pointed to the top of the mountain. "Now, we ascend."

I'd climbed trees in the past and had recently climbed into the treehouse in our garden world, but this was different. I had to hug the rock, which took a lot more strength than I expected.

Not only that, but the heat of the place also made it hard to breathe and sapped my strength, making it more difficult to climb. Add in the explosions from the lava. Softball-sized lumps of magma shot past us, scaring the hell out of me. One of them seared my right ear, and the pain almost made me let go of the piton.

But the worst part was the atmosphere. The thick and heavy air seemed to settle in my lungs and weigh me down. Ruby and Norlok didn't appear to be doing any better. We had to stop every half-minute or so to catch our breaths.

While there were ledges along the way, they were few and far between, small, barely able to hold two people. They provided occasional places to rest but didn't provide shelter, and the magma balls seemed to like landing in those exact spots.

So, we climbed. As for the mountain...it was moving. Could mountains move? Ruby asked our jailer-guide about it.

Norlok yelled back, "I neglected to tell you. The mountains here are part of this world. They are very primitive forms of life, but they exist."

Lie number one...Norlok had told us there was no life here. What else wasn't he telling us?

A second later, I took back that thought. It didn't matter. What mattered was that we were here, and the only important thing was to climb or die.

Ruby maneuvered her way over to me, cautiously inserting her pitons and boots into the rock and then just as carefully extracting them. "This is garbage," she murmured, just loud enough for me to hear. The explosions from the magma, not to mention our heavy breathing, made it difficult to catch anything.

"Just keep climbing and be careful. I briefly let go of one

piton to pat her shoulder.

Norlok chose that moment to bellow, "Climb, you two. Let go of a piton, and you might perish. Climb!"

We climbed. The mountain shook, rumbling deep within its belly, and rocks jutted out here and there at random, almost as if the mountain was trying to knock us off.

"Be careful," I yelled to Ruby.

"I am," she called back, her voice filled with terror. "I am!"

Our ascent seemed to go on forever. Eventually, though, we reached the top. It was flat, and the three of us lay on our backs, gasping for air. My throat burned, and I wanted water in the worst way, but we had nothing to drink and no time. I let go of one piton, sticking the other in my pocket. I had no strength to take off my boots.

Norlok recovered faster, got up, dropped his pitons, and took off his boots. He walked over to a small scepter, about the size of my forearm, that sat in a small crevice, untouched by the lava blasts flying over our heads. It appeared to be made of a golden metal with a small star at the top. While it didn't look overly impressive, it began to glow a bright blue when Norlok touched it, so it must have had some kind of special power.

"This is it," Norlok exulted. "I finally have it!"

He pulled the battery off his belt, then took the shards of metal from his pocket. Suddenly, I knew what his plan had been all along. He was going to transport himself directly to his world and strand us here. *You are slime!*

Still, maybe we could talk to him. He had no reason to leave us to die here. I struggled to my feet, pulling Ruby up with me. "All right, Norlok. You got your prize. Now, send us home."

In answer, he uttered a harsh laugh. "I will send you to your deaths." His eyes shone with madness. "A fiery death in the hell you two so richly deserve."

Norlok reached for his gun, but before he could take it out, Ruby uttered a war cry. Together, we charged him, using our forearms like battering rams and slamming into him. He gasped in surprise, dropped the shards and the battery, and staggered backward.

Norlok managed to latch onto my shoulder, and we went over the edge together, landing on one of the small ledges below. The impact knocked the breath out of me. A second later, the scepter landed next to my right leg. It had lost its brightness, so maybe its magic was limited.

But when I got my breath back and picked it up, my foe kicked me in the gut. The scepter fell from my hand, and when I got to my feet, Norlok kicked me again, this time in the ribs. Pain or not, I summoned up enough strength to slug him on the side of his misshapen head when he came close enough.

He staggered but recovered quickly and cried, "You think that you can best me? Me?"

Agony, accompanied by anger, surged through me. "Yeah, you."

Norlok reached behind his back and brought out a metal rod. "It is time to feel agony, Earthman." He pressed a button on the end, and the rod immediately elongated, becoming a flexible whip. He proceeded to whip my shoulders and my back until I fell to my knees.

I'd been in fights before but had never been hit so hard— or whipped. Through the pain, I grunted, "Not man enough to take me on hand to hand? You're nothing but a dirty rat."

He gave a sadistic grin. "You call me vermin, but you are not a man. You are a putrid slug, a useless piece of effluvia."

He continued whipping me, but he made one mistake. He came too close. I caught his whip, pulled him in, and head-butted him. The whip went flying, as did he, right to the edge.

Norlok was stronger than he looked as he regained his balance and moved toward me, his hand reaching behind his back again. He brought his gun around...too slowly...allowing me to use a move that Gomez had taught me — I grabbed Norlok's wrist and twisted his arm around his back sharply. A loud snap sounded.

Norlok bellowed in pain and fired into the air. "You..."

"Yeah, me."

I slammed his hand against the rock, and his gun went flying into the magma. With a growl, he twisted around and clamped his free hand on my face. Although he had a powerful grip, that wasn't going to help him, not this time. I still had one piton left, I took it out of my pocket and stabbed him in his side.

He screamed in agony, his hand dropping from my face to grab his side. "You have wounded me!"

"Is that all you have to say?" I bent down, snatched the scepter from the ground, and got ready. "Go ahead. I'm listening."

With another scream, he pulled out the piton and lunged at me. "If I must die, then you are coming with me."

As I twisted out of the way, I said, "Think again," and drove the scepter into his throat.

Norlok gaped at me as gray blood dribbled from his mouth, and then his eyes began to roll up in his head. I pulled out the scepter, and a gush of blood erupted from the wound.

Norlok still managed to gasp out, "You..."

"Me...what?" I couldn't resist. He'd tortured us — me more so than Ruby — he'd threatened to kill us, and now, when his life was about to end, he wanted me to suffer with him? Not gonna happen.

He didn't answer, only made horrid gurgling noises as

more blood ran from both sides of his mouth. It was time to end this. I used my left hand to secure my hold on the ledge and latched onto his uniform with my right. "This is where *you* fall to your death," I said and pushed him away.

Norlok fell backward and plummeted into the lava flow. It was a long way down. His body flamed briefly, and then he was gone. I looked up and found Ruby peering over the edge.

"Are you okay?" she called out.

"I'll make it. You?"

"Still here."

Good news.

I panted unsteadily, but I'd come too far to fail now. "Throw me your pitons so I can climb back up."

She tossed them down. I shook the excess blood off the scepter, tucked it into my pants, and managed to clamber up to her position. Once there, I took off the boots and surveyed our surroundings. This was an awful place, and I couldn't wait to leave.

But how—that was the question. "Uh, do you have any idea of how we'll get home?"

Ruby gave me a tired smile and held up our former captor's transporter cube. "He told us this would take us back to our cave. I grabbed it from his pocket just before we pushed him over the edge." Smart, she was beyond smart.

"Then let's go home."

She pressed the button on the cube...and nothing happened. "It must be damaged."

Maybe it was, but then I had an idea. "Let's link the cube and the other items together. That might work." Whacky idea or not, we had to try something. The heat was too much.

Ruby put the cube on the battery, grabbed all the shards she could find, and laid them on top of the cube. Then she touched the point of the scepter to the shards with one hand

and reached out to me with the other. "Take my hand." When I did, she added, "Let's say the magic word."

We both said *Memphis* at the same time, but nothing happened. Had Norlok lied to us? Or maybe the cube wasn't geared to take us back to Tennessee.

"Maybe we should use another word. Let's try *garden*," I suggested. "Get a picture in your mind."

"All right."

She gripped my hand tighter, I concentrated, and we both said, "Garden."

Within seconds, the scepter began to glow, as did the shards and the transporter cube. In another second, a portal opened. We stepped through it, finding ourselves near the treehouse under the rays of the glorious sun.

Behind us, the gateway shut with a snap, leaving the cube and the shards behind, but we didn't need them. We still had the scepter, even though it had lost its glow. Whether we could use it again didn't matter.

Ruby leaned against me and whispered, "That wasn't much fun. But it's finally over."

"Yeah." Nothing else came to mind as I wiped the sweat from my face.

Ruby had other ideas, though, and proceeded to mimic the actress from the Oz movie. "There's no place like home."

No, there wasn't. We were now home, and this was where we were going to stay.

# Chapter Fourteen: Recovery

Exhaustion hit me hard, my body folded in on itself, and the ground came up to meet me. While lying there, I touched my shoulders…ow. Then I felt my back and my ear…painful, too. In fact, everything felt like it was on fire. "Ouch," I managed to get out.

Ruby turned to face me, and her expression became one of concern. "Carl, you're hurt."

"Thanks for telling me," I grunted. "You, too."

"I just got barbecued a little. What can I do?"

"A little medical attention would be nice."

She didn't answer, just got to her feet slowly and went to the treehouse, returning a few seconds later with the med kit. "Take off your shirt," she ordered. "I'll see what I can do."

I sat up and slowly removed my shirt, wincing at every movement. Norlok and his damn whip. I winced again as Ruby patted my back, shoulders, and chest with something that stung like crazy. She got my ear, too.

"It's iodine," she said, dabbing here and there. "It'll kill any infection, if there is any. I'm going to put sulfa powder on your cuts, too, just in case. It's going to sting a little."

"Okay," I mumbled and then yelled as the yellow compound hit my wounds and scoured my nerves with fire. Sting a little? No, a lot. "Ow!"

"What are you, a baby?"

"No."

"Then don't act like one," she replied. "You'll live."

It still hurt. "I probably won't enjoy it."

We both laughed at that. I carefully put my shirt back on, although I didn't button it. My mother used to say it was best to air out a wound, not cover it up. Suddenly, fatigue washed over me, and I crawled over to the shade of a nearby tree.

Ruby followed me over, folding her hands across her chest. "You going to take a nap?"

"Unless you have something better to do." I was drowsy, and I needed to rest.

"Not really." She went to put away the med kit, and when she returned, she added, "Think I'll pass out, too."

I waved my hand in a lazy gesture. "Plenty of space."

Ruby took her place beside me. "This here's a good space."

Well, I couldn't object to that. I lay down and closed my eyes, but before I fell asleep, I felt Ruby snuggle close to me and place her arm over my chest.

\*

Some minutes or hours later.

I woke with a start. My back still hurt, but it felt much better. Stiff muscles or not, I got up to gently stretch out. Ruby was still asleep, curled up on the grass. I let her sleep and walked over to the stream, feeling my muscles cramp up at first and then loosen some with each step. I drank some water, felt infinitely better, and the skin on my back started to loosen, feeling almost normal again.

Once more, I wondered if time spans were the same everywhere in the universe. I'd lost track of how long we'd been here. In the outside world, we'd spent three…maybe four days in the cave before discovering this place. Since then, I had no idea how time worked. It was like we were outside time, although if I told anyone else that, they'd think me a nutcase. I could hardly believe it myself.

But facts were facts. We'd come here, and even if I couldn't explain it, Ruby and I existed in a different world.

I returned to Ruby's side, noting the even rise and fall of her chest and the prettiness of her features. I couldn't forget how much she'd helped me fight off Norlok or how she'd almost sacrificed herself. Was it because she really liked me, or was I just imagining things?

Maybe it was because it was just us with no one else around to talk to or be friends with. That could be it. Confused by my feelings, I sat and tried to put things into…I searched for the word…oh, yeah, perspective.

Growing up, I'd never had any contact with colored people other than seeing them on the street every now and then. My parents weren't exactly against them, but they weren't for them either. Their attitude was that everyone should stay with their own kind.

"It's easier that way," my father once said. "White with white, colored with colored, Chinese with Chinese, and so on. Same thing with religions. Mixing just doesn't work."

From his perspective, he thought it natural, but it didn't sit well with me. If we were all people, and we were all God's children, then why stay separated? That had never made much sense to me. My parents, though, were products of their upbringing. Same with the parents of the other kids I knew. And those kids said the same thing as their parents. Like father, like son, and all that… But they hadn't entered an alien world. And they weren't Ruby…

"Hi." Ruby's voice snapped me out of my reverie. She sat

up and scooted beside me. "You take a walk?"

"Yeah, just to stretch out. I'm feeling better, so…yeah." There it was…my lack of ability to say anything interesting.

Ruby, though, didn't seem to mind. "Glad you're feeling better. I was dreaming about us…being caught by Norlok, I mean."

"And?"

"He was evil, but he…I don't know… Did he deserve what happened?" That was Ruby. Always looking on the sunny side of the street.

"Well, just to help you out, he kidnapped us, tortured us, and almost killed me, but you think he didn't deserve what happened?" For my question, I got a pout. It looked cute, but if I said so, she probably wouldn't appreciate it.

"Carl, you're not wrong, but…but we're supposed to be better than that."

"We are better," I rejoined. "Look, I didn't like doing that to Norlok. I just wanted to get home, but you saw. You know. He wanted to kill us, plain and simple. You were there, and… Never mind."

It wasn't worth arguing over, so I got up and started walking, stopping at the lake. Ruby was a nice girl, but she was wrong on this. Our little world seemed to agree with me, as the sun seemed a little brighter, the air sweeter, and the atmosphere…better. I couldn't say why, but a feeling of positivity came over me.

A hand tapped me gently on my shoulder, and I turned around to see Ruby wearing a look of contrition.

"You're right," she said. "I try to be nice. My mama raised me to be nice and to forgive, even if someone did me wrong. But…Norlok wasn't into forgiveness, and you… You were so brave. It was…I mean, your fight with him…I never saw anything like it." She turned away, perhaps embarrassed by her admission.

Well, I'd take what she said as a compliment. To change the topic, I asked her if she wanted to go for a swim. "It's a bath, really, but after that, a swim."

Ruby turned back to me, her eyes bright. "Sure thing."

I turned away to give Ruby privacy when we got to the lake. I heard the rustle of her clothes being discarded, followed by the sounds of splashing.

Seconds later, Ruby called out, "I'm ready."

Cue me. I slipped out of my clothes and joined her in the lake. The water stung the wounds on my back and shoulders, but for some reason, my body felt more normal. I laughed internally. Must be magic water.

I swam over near Ruby. "Um…are you up for a race to the other end?"

"You're on."

We started swimming. She matched me stroke for stroke, and I barely managed to beat her to the finish line. Once there, I sat on the soft sand, keeping everything below the waist underwater and hoping nothing would crawl up my nether regions.

Ruby obviously didn't feel any embarrassment because she hauled herself out of the water, naked as the day she was born. However, she sat next to me and hugged her knees so everything was hidden. I'd caught a glimpse, though, surprised by the beauty of her body. I stared at the center of the lake, trying to stop thinking of my reaction to her, but for the life of me, I couldn't.

I finally found my voice. "Some race."

"You're good," she said with a note of admiration. "We tied last time, but no one's ever beaten me in a race before."

Words failed me, and after a few seconds, Ruby said, "Carl, look at me."

Trying to be noble and not succeeding, I turned my head and saw her as she was—a beautiful woman.

"I've been wanting to say this for a long time," she whispered.

"What?"

"What I said to you on Jerana, that's how I really feel. I care about you. I wanted to tell you before, but I couldn't, not the whole thing, and now…"

"Now, what?"

"Please kiss me."

Up until that point, I'd never kissed anyone. "Are you sure? Not that I don't want to, but…uh, well, I mean—"

She looked at me with limpid brown eyes. "I know. You told me already. I haven't been with anyone, either. But all this time, it's been just us, and after everything we've been through, the trouble…the pain, I don't want to be alone anymore. I don't want to die without…"

Ruby didn't have to finish her sentence. I knew, and I felt the same way. "Is it because there's no one else here?"

She reached over to grip my hand. "Even if there was, I'd want to be with you and only you."

There were times when feelings couldn't be denied. This was one of those times. Slowly, I pulled her toward me, and the warmth and strength of her came through. And even more slowly, I bent down to kiss her, our lips locked together, our tongues entwined, and after that… Nothing—*nothing*—could ever top the feeling of kissing Ruby. If I'd died that same day, then my life would've been complete.

# Chapter Fifteen: Rescued

"What are we going to do today?" Ruby called out to me as she waded out of the lake to let the sun dry her.

Her clothes were in the treehouse, as were mine. It wasn't as if we needed to wear them, anyway. They were sort of ragged, and the weather was always perfect.

Come to think of it, it was too perfect if such a thing was possible. It never rained or snowed or turned cold. While I wasn't sure, I guessed the temperature hovered around seventy-six degrees during the day and around seventy at night. It had been that way since we'd arrived here.

So not wearing clothes wasn't a big deal. After all, it was just the two of us in this idyllic world. Initially, I'd felt a sense of shame in being naked. Now, none. My girlfriend—I smiled thinking of Ruby that way—told me she felt the same way. Therefore, since no one else could see what was going on...

"Carl, you got an idea?"

Her question broke into my reverie. "I thought we'd explore the outer caves again," I said as I sat up. "There might be another doorway out of here."

Ruby sat beside me with a serious expression. "Do you really want to leave here?"

"No!" My answer came out too quickly. "No, just that…you saw what happened with the first cave we went to. Then we went to Jerana and the lava world."

"I remember."

I rubbed my hands together. "I'm just curious, is all. I mean, the doors we've entered only went back to our cave. Maybe there's a portal that leads back to some part of our world. I'm just not sure what'll happen if we go into a world, and for some reason, the doorway won't let us come back."

"Maybe we should try," she said, although she didn't sound very confident.

"We can, but like I said, one door might lead us back to our home or even a better place than where we are now." I leaned over and took her hand in mine. "I love living here with you, but aren't you a little tired of the same ol', same ol' every day?"

Ruby leaned against me, and I felt her warmth and strength, so much of the latter coming from her small form. It amazed and excited me at the same time, not so much sexually — although I had to admit being with her that way was a wonderful part of our relationship — but because I was able to share my life with her. My hopes and dreams were now hers, and her hopes and dreams were mine. It was as simple as that.

"Yes," she admitted after a pregnant pause. "I mean, you and me, we're good together, and I love you. You know that."

It was the first time she'd ever told me, and something I couldn't define surged through me. I realized I felt the same way. "I do. And I love you, too."

She giggled. "You sound so serious. Like we were taking our vows and standing in front of a preacher."

"I'm not exactly the stand-in-front-of-the-preacher type."

That got another laugh out of her. "I don't think religion

has much of a place here. I haven't thought about going to church for the longest time. But you know, we're together, and that's all that matters."

It was, and what she'd said made me think about things. Here, there was no civilization, no religion, no law. We were the only inhabitants, and we made the law. It was as simple as that.

Ruby remained silent, but her expression indicated that she must've been thinking the same thing. If we ever got back, we had no idea where we'd end up or how much time had passed.

Moreover, no one would believe our story. It was all too fantastic. If the authorities found us, then they'd call us liars. Or they'd dismiss us as lunatics. And it was a sure bet that no one would understand our relationship.

That was my biggest concern. The laws in the US prohibited interracial marriages. Interreligious ones happened, but they were sort of rare. Still, after all we'd been through, I would not—could not—ever be without her again.

Ruby's voice interrupted my self-examination. "I don't think it'll hurt if we check out the other caves. We don't have to stay long." She twisted a lock of her hair in a shy yet winning manner. "Then, we could come back here, take a swim, and...you know..." She didn't finish the sentence, but then again, she didn't have to.

Sex was an unspoken thing, something people in love just felt and wanted to do. Perhaps all newly married couples felt the same way. Marriage or not, Ruby and I had been fooling around every night—and often in the daytime—for the past three months, by my reckoning. Who needed a court of law to tell us what to do, anyway?

However, we weren't the law when it came to all things biological.

Ruby and I were in our treehouse bed, and things took a more serious turn when she asked about nature possibly taking its course. "What if I get pregnant?"

*Oh.* I hadn't thought of that, but now I had to. "Are you?"

She brushed her damp hair away from her eyes. "No, I don't think so. I haven't had my, er…that…since we got here. I can't remember when."

Call me unaware, but I'd never thought much about it, which was shortsighted on my part. Not that I knew much about women's cycles, but I figured that Ruby would go off on her own and take care of such things. Still, searching my memory, no, she hadn't. And that made me think again about time. Some of the days seemed shorter, while others seemed longer. I'd guessed we'd been here for at least three months, but who really knew?

I'd read in a book that time was a construct, a way of giving order to our lives. Telling time had been around since sundials and then watches, and time zones had been standardized in the late eighteen-hundreds. But here, without a clock, it had no meaning.

My thoughts came back to Earth when Ruby touched my hand. Her skin, warm and soft, always sent an electric thrill through me.

"I'm not worried," she added. "If I do have a baby…"

"We'll raise him — or her — the best we can." That was what responsible people did. "In the meantime —"

"In the meantime, we can go exploring," she murmured as she rubbed my chest. "After that, yeah, we can come back here and…"

Her hand went lower, traversing a zig-zag path down to my stomach and lower still. My hands also explored her body, eliciting a purr of pleasure from her.

"Mmm… Are you sure you want to check things out

now?" Ruby whispered as she proceeded to kiss me on the lips and then trailed lower to kiss my chest.

Fire now scoured every part of my body. "Later." Exploring could wait as I gave myself over to her.

\*

Two hours later.

We'd constructed two torches from the crate slats, and I packed some matches to light them when necessary. We also dressed in our old uniforms and included the bomber jackets. After passing through the gateway to our old cave, we ventured out into the cold, carefully climbed to the top of the stairs, and walked along the trail toward the other caves.

"Light me," Ruby said at the mouth of cave number five, which she picked randomly, avoiding the dinosaur cave.

Right. Match out, torches lit, we went inside and found a pictograph that hinted at a world of eternal twilight. The carving had moons on either side of what looked like grass, and when we opened the portal by tracing the full moons, we entered a dark world.

All was still for a few seconds, and then the sounds of large animals roaming around reached our ears, followed by growls and inhuman screams. When heavy hoof stomps and cries of pain and agony got closer and louder, Ruby looked at me and said, "This place isn't for us."

We backed out. I took a small stone and etched an X into the wall beside the pictogram.

We ignored cave one—the dinosaur cave, which remained sealed after our last visit—and continued choosing at random. The world in cave two was one of too much heat, cave six led to an icy cold world, and cave nine was another lava world.

Thankfully, we encountered no flying monsters and met no more aliens from other places in the universe, but I marked each with an X.

When we entered cave three, we found a pictogram of a tree only, with no other carvings surrounding it. In pretty much every culture, tree symbols meant life, which meant it was safe. And it had turned out to be a world much like our garden of paradise, only not as fertile, and I sensed there might be some danger there. Perhaps whoever had built it had neglected the place over time. How long was anyone's guess.

As for cave number four, the carving at the entrance showed a swirling image, which indicated either water or sand — or maybe wind. It also had the usual two-hand opening symbols, but between them were stick figures. Multiple entrants, maybe? I wasn't sure.

At any rate, when we went inside and to the rear wall, the cracks spidering along the rock seemed familiar — but not. Under Ruby's gentle touch and my more ham-handed approach, the wall split open to reveal another glowing doorway.

"Should we enter?" I asked.

"Let's try it."

Hand in hand, we went in, but after two steps, I yelled, "Stop."

"Why?"

We'd entered a desert radiating heat of maybe a hundred degrees Fahrenheit, if not more. A hot wind swirled around at a high speed, blowing sand in our faces. When I shielded my eyes and focused, I discovered we'd arrived in a place dominated by sand and scrub brush, burned-out cars and trucks, and an unpleasant smell in the air — one of war and waste and death.

"What happened here?" Ruby asked, plainly confused. "Maybe these people had a war."

"Maybe. I don't know." That was my initial answer since my confusion matched hers. The area looked like pictures I'd seen of deserts on Earth, but the shapes of the cars and trucks didn't look as though they came from our time. Some were large, square vehicles, and some were smaller, sleeker designs. Maybe they were from our future… They definitely weren't nineteen-forties style.

Ruby took my hand, and we moved closer to one of the wrecked cars. The rust-covered chassis and two skeletons in the front seat brought to mind a horrifying thought. One of the guys I'd served with on my ship, Millard Anderson, had told me about a super-bomb. Intrigued, I'd asked him what he meant by a super-bomb.

He'd replied that his cousin worked at Los Alamos. "He's assisting the guy who's in charge of the program. I don't even know what it's called, but it's top-secret stuff, I tell you…top-secret."

That was all he'd said about it, and a week later, he went to the bottom of the sea with all the other sailors on board when our ship was sunk by the Japanese. Now, the possibility of a super-bomb made me wonder if that was what happened in this place.

I pointed at the car. "This…these cars, they might be from a future Earth."

"Our Earth, or another one?"

Ruby's question caught me off-guard. I hadn't thought about another Earth. I'd thought there was only one, but Norlok's words came back to me. If what he'd said was true, if there were other universes, other dimensions, then there had to be other Earths.

However, if this Earth was our future, then how far in the

future was it, and what had happened? Anderson's words came back to me. It would be a terrible thing if this war, or conflict, or plague, or whatever it was, came to pass.

Finally, I confessed that I didn't know which Earth this was but hoped it wasn't ours. While I was thinking, a noise from up ahead caught my attention, a groan combined with a horrid moan that made the hairs on the back of my neck stand up. Figures in the distance were coming toward us, but they didn't walk normally, not exactly. They seemed to shamble.

Ruby squinted, trying to see through the swirling dirt. "What's wrong with them?"

The figures drew closer, and the smell of their rotting flesh tipped me off. That, along with their growls of hunger, told me that we'd entered a place that no rational person should try to enter. "A lot. Let's leave, and I do mean now."

We quickly retraced the pattern on the wall. With all the dust flying around, it was hard to see, but we managed to open the portal and dove into our world. The gateway closed just as those people-not-people lunged at us.

For a change, entering a cold climate was welcome. I took a deep breath and shook off the images. I'd read about the undead in some horror books I got from someone, but those were more about vampires. I'd also seen a couple of horror movies, but that was my first time seeing the real thing. I hoped it would be my last.

Ruby leaned against me, murmuring, "I think this place is a write-off, too."

Cave number seven had no pictogram on the entrance. "I guess this place doesn't have a doorway." I shrugged, but we decided to check inside the cave anyway.

As we'd suspected, there was no gateway. I felt disappointed and wondered why the Settlers, who'd made all those different worlds, had decided not to create a garden or river or strange creature-land like they'd done with all the other caves. I etched another X into the wall, just in case.

As we left, I figured the Settlers had gotten tired of building. Norlok had said they were a very secretive people. Maybe they'd simply gotten bored, gone home, and decided to never return to visit what they'd built. Maybe not.

Further down the line, cave number eight led to a water world that consisted of a beach that stretched in either direction to infinity, an ocean of red water, and nothing more. The sky was a reddish-pink, and the vague light of three moons shined through. The temperature was comfortable but a little hotter than our garden, maybe eighty degrees.

"Interesting place," Ruby said as she reached down to grab a handful of sand, slowly sifting it through her fingers. "Seems like regular sand. Maybe we could have a picnic here one day."

At least it didn't move, and nothing popped out to terrify or maybe eat us. We took baby steps to the ocean. The sand was...sand. I took off my shoes and dipped my toe into the water. It was cold, but not excessively so.

Ruby took off her shoes and did the same. "I've never seen the ocean, only the rivers in Tennessee. And they were kind of dirty."

I scanned the horizon and the water in front of us. "This place seems fine." I still wondered if it was safe, but since no monsters had risen from the sand or surf to attack us... "Yeah, we'll come back." We'd also check it out at night. Maybe things changed then.

We exited, and I stole a look at the other caves. There were twelve in total. Later...we'd do it later. The rocks were slippery, but my girlfriend proved to be part billy goat, and her footing was sure. I clambered to the top with her, and we returned to our garden, our home away from home.

Once there, I felt a sense of renewal. My body felt more in tune with the surroundings, as though the place liked us. It was a silly thought, really, but it was there all the same. With the warmth, the fullness of nature, and the calmness of the water in the lake, it felt like paradise.

"Back home again," I said before asking Ruby what she wanted to do.

Ruby was already in the process of shedding her clothes. "Take a dip, have lunch, and have fun," she said with a smile and gestured at the water. "Are you coming?"

I undid the button on my pants, let them drop, and then slipped the rest of my clothes off. "I'll be right there."

*

Keep busy. That's what Ruby always said. So we spent time shoring up our treehouse with more staves and constructed a crude pipeline to pull water from our lake through a pipe into an overhead shower. Swimming was fine, but showering after a hard day's hike…call that luxury.

Plus, we built a table and two chairs. Even though I enjoyed eating while sitting on the ground, Ruby pushed for a little more civilization. I had to admit it was nice to sit at the table and look across at my girlfriend.

We still managed enough free time to explore the remaining caves. Cave number ten was a forest world, while numbers eleven and twelve were ones of stone, minerals, and gold nuggets covering the ground, along with various gems.

Alien worlds or future Earths…I wasn't sure. They were habitable, though.

Once again, the question of the Settlers came to mind. They'd built these different worlds, but why? Norlok had given us part of the answer but not the entire answer.

Ruby and I discussed the matter over dinner one night. I brought up the idea that maybe these places were sanctuaries for different races, not just places to relax.

"So, if these Settlers built the doorways, then why aren't they here? And why aren't other alien races here?" Ruby posed the question while we feasted on our orange bread-and-butter fruit.

She'd asked me the same question before, and I gave her the same answer. "I don't know." I paused to take a bite of my meal. "Maybe…maybe the Settlers went to another world, or they went home. And maybe the other races haven't come yet. No one knows."

"Except us," Ruby said with a grin. "We found a miracle. Maybe it's the biggest miracle of all…but no one will believe us."

And therein lay the problem. We knew that alien life existed, but since there was no way to prove it to anyone, we decided it didn't matter.

"Oh, wait, we've got some proof," I said. "We could show people those carvings or tell them about them. I mean, we haven't been able to figure them out except for a couple of the symbols, but still, that's our proof."

"Li'l green men? Ruby giggled, and then she abruptly sobered. "When I was small, my folks talked about things like that, but I figured it was just stories. It's all true, isn't it?"

It seemed to be, so I nodded. Just as we got up and decided to take another swim, a faint voice echoed over to our position. "Sir, we found something. It's an engraved picture of…just come and look at it, sir."

*What in the hell?* I looked in the direction of the voice. It came from behind the main wall. "C'mon," I said and grabbed Ruby's hand.

We retrieved our clothes, got dressed, then ran to the wall.

The sounds from the other side were louder. I looked at Ruby. "Should we go out there?"

My girlfriend bit her lip, her indecision easy to read in her eyes. "If you go, I'll go with you."

It was a foregone conclusion we had to go through together. So, after we did the hand-tracing thing and the portal appeared, we went through the gateway hand in hand, emerging on the other side in the cave we'd abandoned so long ago. A man wearing a solid yellow jumpsuit knelt on the ground with his back to us, placing something in a box. Another person, wearing the same color suit and holding what looked like a radio, froze in place and gaped at us like we were ghosts.

The cave surprised me. Far from being cold, the interior was warm. Small, square machines that radiated heat sat around the area. Other boxes held metallic objects — probably instruments of some kind — and two boxes held explosives, marked clearly on the side.

The man who'd been kneeling on the ground looked at his colleague, who pointed at us. He turned around and viewed us with alarm. "Who...where'd you come from?"

I jerked my thumb at the barrier. "From behind there. Who are you?"

The man straightened up and brushed off his uniform, his eyes radiating surprise. However, a measure of self-confidence surfaced when he spoke. "I'm Jonas Arthur, with the American Paranormal Research Institute Laboratory — APRIL, for short."

"Research for what?"

"I just told you. For unexplained phenomena. Paranormal stuff...and this is it." Arthur pointed at the barrier which had closed behind us. "What's behind there?"

"Another world," Ruby said. "Uh, you're American, aren't

you?"

"Yes."

She had another far more relevant question. "Is the war over?"

The man — Arthur — looked confused. "Which one?"

Which one? "Uh, World War Two," I said.

Arthur shook his head. "It's been over for a long time."

The question was, how long? Ruby beat me to the ultimate question. "What year is this?"

"It's two thousand twenty-eight, October eleventh."

I started to repeat the date, then stopped. This man had no reason to lie, but the impact hit me hard. We'd been away for eighty-five years. "That's...that's impossible," I managed to get out. I glanced at Ruby, her mouth hung open like she, too, had trouble processing the date.

Arthur, though, simply shrugged. "You have a story. I want to hear it."

*

An hour later.

Ruby and I sat on the hard ground, having shared what details we could remember since we'd crashed on the plateau. Arthur gave our names to one of his assistants and told him to check with the State Department and the military branches.

Arthur sat back and looked at us with a stunned expression. "That's an amazing story. I...I have no idea what's behind that barrier. But I'm looking at your clothes, and they seem authentic enough."

Our clothes could wait. I had to know. "How'd you find us?"

"A hiking party came across the wreckage of an old plane.

They notified the Nepalese authorities, and their government contacted our State Department. Both countries agreed to cooperate in the interests of international amity. We found this location with the help of the hikers and satellite imaging. This mountain range has hundreds of caves that haven't been explored due to the height and danger. We're at roughly the thirteen-thousand-foot level. The air's thin but breathable. It took us a while to acclimate before we could start our investigation."

I remembered the difficulty we'd had when we first crashed here. We were lucky. Being young and stupid helped. As I mused over the intangibles of luck, one of Arthur's assistants came over with a piece of paper, handing it to him and whispering something in his ear. The assistant then left after giving us a curious glance.

"What is it?" I asked.

Arthur read the paper, then took a deep breath and whooshed it out. "We had the State Department and then the Air Force check their records from World War Two. Most of them were destroyed, but some of the descendants of the fliers in Tsu-yang airbase had heard your name from their grandfathers. They reported you were around twenty back then. That right, Carl?"

"I was eighteen. I, uh, lied about my age when I enlisted in the Merchant Marine." Enlisted wasn't the right word, but getting in with forged papers…well, I wasn't willing to admit that out loud.

However, if Arthur knew, he had the decency not to say anything. All he did was look at the paper again. "All right, so, just to get the facts straight, your full name is Carl Allen Goodman."

"Yes."

"And your, uh—"

"Carl's girlfriend," Ruby supplied.

Arthur nodded again and looked at her. "Your full name is Ruby Laverne Matthews."

"Yes," she answered.

I looked at her. "Laverne?"

She shrugged. "It's a name."

Right. I turned my attention to Arthur. "So, where do you come in?"

Arthur sat a little straighter and proudly stated that he'd been in charge of the research institute for the past ten years. "We research various paranormal activities. When we got the information about strange pictograms, the institute dispatched us here with the blessing of the Indian and Nepalese governments. We didn't find anything at first except for the remains of the C-46 you two were on, along with three skeletons." He looked at the paper again. "The plane was officially listed as lost in action. The same notation was made for you two and the pilots."

Silence fell as I digested the news, and then I nodded. "The pilots were Johnson, Morton, Etheridge...they died in the crash."

Then I thought about how much time had passed. "Eighty-five years. I know my parents are gone, but I'd like to know...when...where...that kind of thing."

Arthur reached into his pocket, pulled out a small object, and tapped its face. "Do you know what a smartphone is?"

It looked like something Norlok had used, but his was a weapon. This device didn't give me the same impression. In any case, I said no, and Ruby shook her head.

"It's like a portable telephone," Arthur explained. "I can reach anywhere in the world with this. It also has access to a database for research."

"Database?" I echoed. "Data...like a library?"

"Something like that," Arthur agreed as he continued tapping the device…the smartphone. A troubled expression came over his face. "Carl, the war ended in nineteen forty-five. Your parents died five years later. Ruby, we know that your parents passed away before you were listed as, uh, missing."

Ruby received the news calmly enough, although a few tears slipped from her eyes. She leaned against me, and I hugged her, whispering that time was a thief. She whispered back, "I'm sorry for you, too."

Arthur cut in to gently say that he didn't mind leaving us alone for a time to collect ourselves.

Ruby wiped her eyes and said, "No, I'll be fine. Uh, what happens now?"

"That's up to you," he replied, getting to his feet. "If it's acceptable, we'd like to take you back to the US. Our main office is in Washington, DC, and if you agree, we'd like to run some tests on you."

Initially, I'd dreamed of the day we'd be rescued, but now, a sense of uncertainty gripped me. This was a huge step, one I never figured I'd have to make. "If we go back with you, how long will it all take?"

"It's about a seventeen-hour flight back to the States, then perhaps a week or so at our facility."

Ruby whispered that she'd go. I got up, pulling her up with me.

"All right," I said. "We'll give you ten days. That's all. Let's go."

# Chapter Sixteen: Tests And More Tests

*W*e descended from the plateau in a helicopter. I'd seen pictures of helicopters during my stay at Tsu-yang, but they were primitive compared to this model. We got inside by using what Arthur called zip lines. It was something new for Ruby and me, and we jumped when someone on the helicopter shot a line into the rock above the cave with harnesses attached. After a brief explanation, I went first, then Ruby, and then Arthur. The other techs stayed behind.

We flew slowly to a lower level to help us acclimate to the drop in elevation and stayed overnight at a campsite. While there, a doctor looked us over. He took blood samples from us and declared that we carried no diseases. In fact, he claimed we were beyond healthy. That was nice to hear.

The next day, we did the helicopter thing again and flew directly to the airport in Kathmandu, Nepal, where I saw my first jet. I'd heard about them but had never seen one. When I noticed all the other airplanes there, I couldn't believe it. They were so different from what I remembered. Arthur shepherded us through the terminal, bypassing all the customs checks as we didn't have passports. Before we got on the plane, I saw our ride through the window in the terminal.

"Is that safe?" I asked. After the disaster with the C-46, I'd sworn never to get on a plane again.

"It is," he replied. "It's safe, fast, and you'll love it."

"A real jet," I breathed.

A grin painted Arthur's face. "Private, too. Room for fifteen, and it's all bought and paid for."

"Who's footing the bill?" Ruby asked.

A guarded look crossed Arthur's face. All he said was something about private investors. Fine, it wasn't worth digging for details…for now.

Once we got onboard, I expected a bare-bones setup, but no. The seats were comfortable, and we even had food on the plane. Steak for both of us with all the trimmings. It was the first time I'd had steak in almost ninety years. It tasted all right, but my jaw muscles cramped repeatedly. All in all, it wasn't worth the effort.

Ruby expressed the same thing. "It's okay," she said between bites. "I haven't had meat for…for—"

"A long time," I finished for her.

She laughed. "Yeah, that long."

After a refueling stopover in Singapore—where we saw lots of neon lights at the airport and heard a double-dozen languages as our minders shepherded us around for a quick tour—we flew on to Washington, DC. Once we got there, Arthur led us to a limousine waiting for us. We sat in soft seats, Arthur gave us bottled water from a cooler built into the seat, and we cruised around the city.

Call this luxury with a capital L. When I lived in Memphis and went to the movie theater, I saw pictures of Hollywood stars being driven around in limos. Now, we were in one. I relaxed, thinking about how far we'd come.

After our sightseeing tour, Arthur said, "Almost there… That building up ahead is our destination."

The limo slowed and then stopped in front of a tall building on the outskirts of the city. Oddly enough, no other buildings were nearby, only empty lots. I wondered why. Washington had always been a big city, but it had gotten larger since we'd been gone with high skyscrapers and department stores that seemed like small countries.

Yet, this building was all by its lonesome and had no name or number to identify it. Maybe it was for privacy. That was all I could think of.

Then Arthur opened the limo door. "This is it. Let's go inside."

We piled outside and stopped at a small glass-encased device next to the entrance to the building. "Retinal eye scan," Arthur said as a light played up and down his face, and then the door to the building opened automatically. That was…different.

Inside, we saw a sign that floated in the air. There were no wires, and it had no depth. "What is that?" I asked while walking around it. It looked like something straight out of the science fiction novels I'd read long ago, but this wasn't fiction…it was fact.

"Hologram," Arthur replied. "Like a projector, but different."

Yeah…different. Times sure had changed. Anyway, the hologram sign said that this facility had seven levels. An elevator took us to the fifth floor, and from there, we strolled along seemingly endless passageways and doors that held all kinds of secrets behind them, or so I figured.

As Arthur guided us along the corridors, we passed by some rooms with windows. Inside, I saw people sitting at tables, tapping what looked like keys on fold-out metal cases.

I asked if they were modern typewriters.

Arthur chuckled. "Those are laptops. They're like typewriters, but they do a whole lot more."

Ruby also seemed impressed by this truly amazing modern age. "I guess we got a lot of catching up to do."

Arthur smiled. "I imagine you do."

The facility was surprisingly sparse, without any fancy doodads that usually marked a laboratory. I expected lots of beakers and vials filled with liquids, bulky machines, rheostats, and other things that involved electricity.

However, the large room Arthur brought us to consisted of desks, laptops, masses of papers, and photos of phenomena from around the world posted on the walls. Arthur signaled a tech—one of twenty hovering around the room—to come over.

A smiling young man in his late twenties with slicked-back black hair trotted over. "Sir?"

"Show these two how to work the internet."

"Yes, sir."

The tech took us to a table and gave us a crash course in operating the laptops and navigating the internet.

Ruby was astounded. "Y'mean, like a library, all in this, um, computer?"

"That's right." He showed us what to do and then left us alone.

While I sat at my laptop station, tentatively tapping the buttons, I marveled at how fast technology had developed since the war. We'd gone from piston-engine fighters to jets that flew faster than sound. The cars were smaller and sleeker, and we were told that some even ran on electricity.

And now, I'd just started using what Arthur called a laptop—an actual computer. When I was around fourteen, I'd read some science fiction stories about machine-like computers that developed the ability to think for themselves and wanted to control humanity.

Just make-believe, I'd thought, the dreams and figments of a writer's imagination more than anything else. Plus, as described in the books, they were massive machines, larger than a building.

However, these small, sleek machines could do practically anything. Information seemed just a few hunt-and-peck movements away. Ruby seemed to take to the laptop and internet search faster than I did, and her fingers danced over the keyboard.

Curious, I asked, "What are you looking for?"

Ruby stopped typing and gave me a brief smile. While her expression remained impassive, her eyes radiated uncertainty, a sure sign that my girlfriend didn't want to disclose anything. "For reports of what we went through. Li'l green men, aliens…the strange things we saw."

That sounded interesting. I got up and went to her side, leaning down to peer at the screen. As I did so, I felt a mild pull in my lower back and grunted, "Nnngh… What've you got?"

Ruby pointed at the screen. "These are all the results for what we saw. There are over a million sites, but there's nothing about the caves in our old place. I typed in Himalayas and then Nepal, and…" She stopped and furrowed her brow, looking as if she was unsure. "Oh, yeah, I cross-referenced that with caves and aliens, and I got nothing."

Disappointment rang in her voice, but then she leaned closer to me and whispered, "I also checked on this place. It isn't listed."

I glanced around, but no one seemed to be watching us. Still, I also lowered my voice. "You mean, top secret stuff?"

"Yes," someone said behind us. "Top secret stuff."

We turned around and found an older man wearing a general's uniform facing us. Around sixty, he still possessed a powerful build, and even with his craggy features and grayish-white hair, he projected an aura of strength and command.

The man introduced himself. "My name's General Parley Bayliss. This institute is off the books, and we're the only ones who know about your existence."

Arthur had said something about private investors, so maybe having a general involved was why this place wasn't known to anyone.

"So no one else knows?" I said. "Top secret, classified stuff, right?"

Bayliss pulled over a chair and sat facing us. "Yes. That, as well as where our funds come from and how those, shall we say, donors shelter their money. It's all very complicated."

Complicated? Not really. I may have been born a century ago, but when the general mentioned sheltering money, it seemed like he was hiding something illegal. "And what about the techs here? Are they getting paid well?"

The general didn't appreciate my reply, as his face reddened. Ruby chuckled, though. He responded in a huffy manner. "I'll have you know, Goodman, that I take care of my people."

*Uh-huh.* "Like keeping this place secret?"

"Yes."

*Uh-huh...again.* "Can you trust everyone?"

Bayliss cracked his knuckles and leaned forward. "There are only twenty technicians working here. Four doctors. Fifteen security personnel. One second-in-command — Jonas Arthur. The circle here is small, very small, and they've all signed NDAs."

"A what?"

"Non-disclosure agreements," he explained. "If they talk, they end up in jail for the next fifty years. That's called keeping a secret. Long story short, to the world, we don't exist, and neither do you.

"In fact, officially, neither of you has existed since nineteen-forty-four. Your airplane went down a year before that, but you weren't officially declared missing in action until about a year later."

He cleared his throat and got up. "Now, I'm going to assume that you had a good rest. For now, all we need to do is to take some samples from you."

"Samples," Ruby echoed. "As in blood samples?"

"Yes."

Her lips thinned, and her eyes sparked with anger. "We already gave when we were at your base camp on the way down from the mountain we were on." She pointed at the bandage on her right elbow. "And we're not lab rats."

Bayliss put up his hands in a gesture meant to placate us. "No, you're not. And we heard from the other doctor at the base camp that you're not carrying any harmful pathogens."

Pathogens? I wasn't sure what the word meant, but Ruby obviously did. "You're talking about viruses. We've been where we were for nearly ninety years. We never got sick. And you just told us that the doctor didn't find anything wrong with us. In fact, I recall him saying we were beyond healthy."

Bayliss nodded again. "Yes, but we need to know why you are, er, like you are. All we're asking is that you give us blood and urine samples, along with a small skin sample. That's it. We'll examine them to see why you haven't aged. I must say, you're the best-looking century-old people I've ever seen."

He turned to leave, but I stopped him, wondering about something, and asked, "Uh, aren't you surprised by us?"

The general turned back, gazing at us with a confused expression. "What do you mean?"

Ruby glanced around the room, but when no one bothered looking in our direction, she whispered, "He means us, me and him." She gestured to me. "I'm colored, he's white. Aren't you bothered by that?"

Bayliss' mouth opened in a perfect O before he chuckled. "Not at all. I understand why you must have reservations, but things have changed a lot since your time. We did away with the laws that segregated people long ago. Interracial relationships are pretty common these days."

He brushed off some nonexistent lint from his neatly pressed suit. "By the way, we don't say colored anymore. I had POCs in my units when I commanded in the field, and we all got along just fine."

"POCs?" I had to ask because acronyms had always confused me.

"People of color," he explained. "And from what I hear, the proper term is either black or Afro-American. Your choice, Ms. Matthews, of course. Or should I call you Lieutenant Matthews?"

"Ruby is fine," she replied. A look of relief flashed across her face. Acceptance was always welcome.

As for Bayliss, he offered a reassuring smile and turned to leave, tossing over his shoulder, "Sit tight. We'll take the samples, and then we'll go over your story again."

\*

Forty minutes later, we'd given our samples to a technician while sitting in a private room. Another tech came and took our measurements.

"For clothes," the guy explained. "You need new ones.

We'll get them ready for you."

"Yellow for me, please," Ruby said. "It's my favorite color."

The tech then asked me if I had a preference.

"Dark blue or gray is fine."

He jotted down the information on a pad. The first tech then led us to the main room, where we rehashed the details of our adventure once more with Arthur, another tech—a small, slender, dark-haired man in his thirties who didn't give his name—and Bayliss.

The three men sat in a row across a table from us, with Bayliss in the middle, and asked us numerous questions as if trying to trip us up. I figured they thought we were lying. But with a story like ours? Not likely.

In the end, though, Bayliss glanced at Arthur and then spoke with great seriousness combined with a hint of wonder. "This is amazing. If what you say is true, then we've found the secret of entering other dimensions. Or other universes. Or perhaps both. From your descriptions, I'm not sure."

The tech beside Bayliss murmured something about national security.

Arthur got an alarmed look on his face and turned to Bayliss. "Sir, I'm prepared to believe their stories. After all, I observed them emerge from the portal they described. But, uh, shouldn't we discuss this further?"

"I'll take any suggestions under advisement," Bayliss replied. "In private." He got up from the table and dismissed Arthur, then turned to the unnamed tech and directed him to take us to our rooms.

I was definitely feeling tired. Arthur had said I was suffering from what he called jetlag. In any case, I thought of little else save getting into bed. And since I'd tweaked my lower back, perhaps a good night's rest would help.

Mr. No Name led us through the door, down the corridor, and stopped outside a room with the number three-B painted on it. "Here we are," he said with an air of forced cheerfulness. "It isn't the Ritz Hotel, but I think you'll both be comfortable." After handing us key cards to the room and showing us how to work them, he wished us a good night and left.

I paused in the doorway, glanced around the room, and then up at the ceiling. Even though Arthur said this was a research facility, it smelled like military, and Bayliss's presence confirmed it. No cameras that I could see, but that didn't mean they weren't there.

Ruby leaned in and whispered, "What are you looking at?"

"Just checking something," I said and shrugged.

We walked in, our feet treading on the soft carpet. The door closed and locked automatically behind us. The room was plain white all around, a double bed stood against one wall with two bathrobes on it, a large box with a slightly smaller rectangular screen sat on a low dresser, and a full-length mirror hung on the wall next to it. A refrigerator plus two chairs completed the main room. No windows, though.

"Hey, we got us a shower," Ruby said as she checked out another door. "Oh, and a separate toilet. This is so...modern."

She sounded more enthusiastic than I felt. I sat on the bed, noting its softness, quite a change from the hard-as-rock mattresses I'd lain on in my Merchant Marine days. It was way softer than the grass I'd slept on in our garden world or the floorboards of our treehouse. "I guess it is. What's that big box?"

Ruby studied it, cocking her head to the side. "Not sure." She finally picked up a small rectangular object next to the box and poked the red button. "This says power..."

The screen lit up. Despite my fatigue, I jumped to my feet.

"It's a...it's a picture box. Wait, no..." A memory came back to me, something I'd seen in a newspaper long ago. "It's a television."

Ruby came over and sat beside me, her eyes widening with surprise. "I never saw anything like that before."

"Me, either, but I remember this...wait, I saw an ad in a paper I read showing this thing off. It was a big box with a tiny screen, though. Things sure have changed."

"They certainly have," Ruby agreed and peered at me closely as if checking for signs of illness. "You look tired."

My exhaustion hit me hard, and I lay back on the mattress. "I am. Must've been the flight out. Think I'm...think I'm going to lie down."

Ruby fluffed up the pillows and chuckled. A moment later, she took her place beside me. "You're already lying down, silly. It was a long flight."

"Yeah..."

She pressed the power button to turn off the television, snuggled up to me, and smiled drowsily. "I'm feeling tired, too. Nap time." She then passed out.

Darkness washed over me, and I fell into its embrace.

*

When I woke up, I felt stiff and sore all over. I'd never felt this way—ever. Ruby lay beside me, still sleeping, her chest moving up and down rhythmically. She looked fine, but my back still bothered me. Perhaps I'd tweaked it on the flight, sleeping in the wrong position. Yeah, that had to be it.

Slowly, I got off the bed and sauntered over to the washroom. After going, I washed up and examined myself in the mirror. Same as always. Fine...I'll be fine, I thought. I exited the bathroom and dropped to the floor to do some push-ups, sit-ups, and bodyweight squats.

After five rounds, I was breathing heavily and sweating, so I took a shower and felt the tightness in my muscles slowly relax. I left the washroom and put on my bathrobe. As I swung my arms around, Ruby woke up.

When she saw me, a smile — the smile I loved so well — lit up her face. "Hey, boyfriend, how are you feeling?"

"Much better," I lied. "Just fine. You, uh…you want to do something, like go for a walk or get something to eat?"

She reached for me, and a second later, I was lying facing her. "Later," she whispered as her lips met mine.

Fine, I could do later.

\*

The next day, a technician delivered three pairs of slacks, three short-sleeved shirts, two long-sleeved shirts for me, and boots for both of us, made to measure. Ruby got her yellow pantsuits plus skirts and blouses in the same color, and she seemed happy with her new duds. We also got jackets to cut the wind. Washington was sort of chilly at night this time of year.

Once we donned our new clothes, we toured the complex with Arthur. He mentioned that his team was still analyzing the data from the samples we'd given.

"We should be done soon," he said as we walked along the corridors. "General Bayliss has put a priority on getting the results."

"Can you tell us anything?" I asked.

Arthur didn't speak for a moment, and when he did, his voice was guarded. "I only saw the results of your blood tests. They were perfectly normal. No abnormalities. We're still going over your DNA tests."

Ruby arched her eyebrows. "Meaning what?"

Arthur stopped walking and bobbed his head with an apologetic smile. "I'm sorry, I forgot you're still not up to speed on modern technology. We can look into your cells now and see how they work. Medical science has advanced a lot in a century."

"I see."

As our walk continued, Arthur said they'd discovered two things so far. One, we weren't carrying any harmful diseases, which we already knew, but the second results were more important. Our telomeres were extremely long. He explained that telomeres indicated how long a person would live, and in our case, our telomere strands were ten times longer than usual. "But we're still examining the data."

\*

Over the next forty-eight hours, Ruby and I were subjected to more tests. We were given a reprieve between with a brief outing where Arthur and another man in plain clothes—probably a soldier or security officer—came with us. We went shopping downtown, toured a department store, had pizza and ice cream, and even took in a movie. Its special effects made my eyes pop, and Ruby was equally enthralled.

At first, the noise of the city was overwhelming. I'd grown up with the sounds of cars honking and insects buzzing, along with the chatter of people. When I'd visited Memphis with my parents, I'd had a ball checking out the bookstores, the movie theaters, and the bowling alleys.

But in Washington, all the sounds seemed to hit me at once. Higher voices, faster speech, more languages than I could count, a riot of colors and busyness that made me uneasy. It was hard to adapt, and as much as I'd railed against the quiet of the garden at times, I now missed it.

Still, Ruby was with me, which helped, and we discussed our future over dinner. Arthur and the other man sat at a table nearby, keeping tabs on us, I figured. Ruby ordered a fried fish dish, and I had a steak.

For most people, steak would've been a treat, but I'd eaten that on the airplane back from Nepal. I hadn't enjoyed it that much, and now, I didn't care for this dish either. It tasted strange and almost...alien.

The sounds of music playing from all around us also distorted things. "It's called pop music," Ruby said while forking a piece of fish into her mouth. "Dig that rhythm. I still love Lena Horne, but this is nice to listen to."

Well, if she said so...

"I'm a little old-fashioned, so give me Benny Goodman or Artie Shaw anytime." Ruby chuckled. "Get with the times, boyfriend."

She put down her fork and leaned forward to kiss me. She tasted of goodness and hope and more.

"Does that mean you love me?" I asked in a low voice.

"You know I do," she murmured.

We continued to talk in low voices when a woman's voice with a pronounced drawl interrupted us. "'Scuse me, miss, may I speak with you?"

We looked up to see a woman in her mid-twenties with bleached blonde hair, slightly overweight, plain but pleasant features, and startling green eyes. She slung a large bag over her shoulder and apologized for interrupting our dinner.

Ruby blinked and asked, "Yes, what is it?"

"I know this sounds silly, but were you once a nurse?"

"Yes, but that was a long time ago."

"Really? You look around twenty-five. I mean, it's just that my grandmother...she served as a nurse during World War

Two, and she used to talk about her time in China."

This was weird and getting weirder.

The woman tapped the side of her head as if trying to draw out the details. "My grandmother said that she knew a black nurse, someone...um...Ruby Matthews...a lieutenant. She described you in detail...but you can't be her. You look too young. Wait, I have a photo."

She dug into her bag, pulled out a faded photo, and handed it to Ruby. I saw an attractive brunette standing next to a woman with lighter hair. In the background was my girlfriend, wearing her old brown uniform. No mistake. It was her, all right.

Ruby's features shifted, though a very subtle shift. Considering what she'd told me about serving with a white woman's nursing corps, this was bound to trigger some bad memories. "What was your grandmother's name?"

"Mary Bettache."

Ruby's lips tightened, but her eyes betrayed nothing, and then she handed the picture back. "I'm sorry. Your grandmother was very pretty, but I don't know her. And my name's not Ruby. It's Frieda Carlson."

She'd lied about her name, but why? No matter—I'd ask her later on. Out of the corner of my eye, I noticed our minders tense, but I quickly made a signal of waving them off. We didn't need to make a scene.

As for the young woman, she stowed the picture away in her bag. "I'm really sorry. The way my grandmother talked of this nurse..." She shook her head and turned to leave. "Anyway, sorry."

However, Ruby called her back. When she spoke, her voice sounded colder than a winter's day, and her body stiffened with what I recognized as barely suppressed rage. "What did your grandmother say about this, uh, Ruby person?"

The woman bit her lip, and a look of pain flashed in her eyes. "To be honest, nothing nice. My grandmother came from Louisiana. Deep south…I mean, really deep. And…she was a bigot. Her parents were also bigots, and so are my parents."

She rubbed her eyes as if to take away her inner turmoil, but from the way she spoke, I doubted that would ever happen. "I broke ties with my family a couple of years ago, moved from Louisiana up to New York, met different people…made new friends. Still got my drawl, though."

She huffed a soft, self-deprecatory laugh. "You can take the girl out of the country, but you can't take the country out of the girl. When my grandmother died, my mother gave me that picture. She said that I had to honor my grandmother's memory."

A single tear traced its way down her right cheek. "I kept the picture, but I couldn't judge people like my parents or grandmother did. It hurt to leave, and… Well, I haven't spoken to my folks since I moved away. I don't think I ever will. Now, I'm here with my husband, sightseeing. He's from New York. Then I saw you and thought you might be related to that person in the photo. Sorry to have interrupted your dinner." She pivoted around and walked quickly away while wiping her eyes.

We watched her go, and I saw the tension gradually ease from my girlfriend's body. I touched her shoulder. "Ruby, are you okay?"

A few of the other patrons gave us curious looks, but then they turned back to their meals.

"Ruby," I said. "What is it?"

Her voice shook. "I remembered that woman, Mary Bettache. I used to call her Mary Bitch. So did the other white girls. Mary was the one who gave the order to leave me behind after we landed in Tsu-yang. I never forgave her for that. None of the other girls disagreed. They didn't like Mary, but they hated me even more, and they were all like, *leave the colored girl here*. They all agreed with Mary, and now…they're gone."

She inhaled and exhaled forcefully. "That's why I used a fake name. I don't need anyone digging up my past. I can't hate on Mary's granddaughter for that…but I sure hated Mary and the rest of them. I shouldn't be bitter…but I am."

"Ancient history," I said. I got up, went to her side, and wrapped my arms around her.

"Ancient history," she echoed, wiping her eyes. "My history was pretty bad. Her family history has to be worse."

# Chapter Seventeen: A Turn of Events

Eight days later. The facility. Our room.

Ruby and I hadn't left the facility since that dinner. That meeting with the granddaughter of the woman my girlfriend had known—and despised—had almost gone south, but Ruby had kept her cool.

Still, it had been a close call, and we didn't need any more people dredging up our pasts.

Bayliss wasn't overly happy when he heard the news but dismissed it as purely coincidental. "The chances of you running into someone you knew…and you didn't know her, only her grandmother…astronomical. Pure coincidence, and I'm sorry you had to go through that."

He sounded sincere enough. At the same time, though, he said incidents like that had to be avoided at all costs. "That's why you two are staying here."

Staying at the facility and boredom went hand-in-hand. Our lives consisted of having breakfast, lunch, and dinner at selected times. Going to briefing sessions with Bayliss and that unnamed tech who'd shown us to our rooms on our first night here also became part of our routine.

I suspected the unnamed tech was one of the investors or connected to the government in some way. No one we asked seemed to know anything about the guy, or so they said.

Moreover, when I asked Arthur or the other techs about returning us to our cave—Ruby and I claimed homesickness and that we'd fulfilled our end of the bargain—they claimed no official word had come from Bayliss, who apparently ran the whole show.

One afternoon, while Ruby was taking a nap, I left our room and wandered around the facility. It was immense and quiet, with only the hum of electricity and the hiss of air through the vents to break the silence.

On the first floor, a lounge offered free coffee, so I figured I'd get a cup, but when I entered, I spotted Bayliss sitting on a couch facing a man in his early seventies. They were the only two people in the room. The visitor was tall and thin, partially bald, and wore an elegantly tailored gray suit that nevertheless hung on his narrow shoulders.

But it wasn't the man's skinny physique that made me look more closely. It was his grayish-yellow skin color. He was clearly sick with something, and he swallowed continuously. Neither man noticed me, so I ducked behind a cabinet and cautiously peeked around the corner.

The older man spoke in a querulous voice, "You know what you have to do, General Bayliss."

"Sir, yes, sir, I do," Bayliss replied. "But these tests, while promising, take time, and—"

"Time is a luxury that I don't have much of," the man interrupted and chopped the air as if to excise the general's statement from existence. "You know what kind of treatments I'm taking."

*Treatments? Maybe he has cancer or something equally rotten.*

The visitor continued talking, his tone urgent. "My specialists give me about a year, so I'm not asking you, Bayliss, I'm telling you. Get. The. Job. Done. I've invested a lot in this project, and by God, I expect to get value for my money."

Bayliss wasn't the type to back down or crumble, but he did in the face of this man's anger. "Of course, Senator Mulholland. I'll tell the lab boys to double their efforts…"

I had to know more, so I entered the main room and asked a technician if I could use a laptop. "Information search," I told him. "Trying to get up to speed."

The tech set me up on a laptop and left me alone. I searched for any information on Senator Mulholland. Lo and behold, I found a few files on the guy, and they all said the same thing.

*Senator James Xavier Mulholland, son of billionaire Francis Richard Mulholland…age sixty-one…born in West Virginia…still serving in Congress despite fatal cancer prognosis…*

I shut off the computer. I now knew all I needed to know. Bayliss had said that the tests were promising. He meant the blood and DNA tests on me and Ruby. I didn't know much about science and even less about medicine, but it didn't take a genius to figure out that Mulholland thought something in my DNA could cure him.

"Is there anything I can do for you, sir?" A tech's voice interrupted my thoughts.

I came back to reality with a start. "Uh, no. I'm fine. Thanks. Think I'll, uh, head on back to my room."

With that, I got up and returned to my room. I decided not to tell Ruby about what I'd heard. No sense in upsetting her, and when I opened the door, I found her waiting.

"Go for a walk?" she asked as she got up to hug me.

"Yeah, I, uh, I couldn't sleep, so I figured I'd get some exercise in." It was a rotten lie, and my lower back started stiffening up something awful, but Ruby looked worried. "Something wrong?"

Ruby spoke quietly with a troubled expression. "I have to

tell you, Carl. I got this bad feeling that they're not going to let us go. We have to get out of here."

I'd already figured that out even before seeing Bayliss kowtow to Mulholland. "How are we going to do that? They know everything about us. Even if we manage to escape, we don't have money or passports, we don't have connections, and we don't exist, remember?"

Her eyes held concern. "I know. That's the hard part. Let me ask you something," she whispered as her arms went around my neck. "Do you want to go back?"

"Yes."

"Me, too."

Since there was nothing else to do, we relaxed on our bed, watched some mindless television program, and then I felt the pull of sleep. I didn't want to, but it came up to catch me, anyway.

\*

Four days later. Two weeks-plus at the facility.

We'd endured more tests, mainly physical ones. They tested our reflexes, gripping power, coordination, and strength. Ruby and I had lost a lot in all departments. And after the tests, it took us longer to recover.

Then there were the mental tests — memory tests, as one of the doctors explained. He told us he was a gerontologist.

"What does that mean?" I asked.

"Er, we study the aging process and elderly patients," he replied.

The man was middle-aged with a flabby, jowly face. He was bald, wore glasses, and had a soft-spoken, officious manner. I took an instant dislike to him.

So, according to him, we were now considered elderly. "Fine, we'll take your tests."

We aced the tests, but to my surprise, I occasionally forgot things. When the doctor asked me where I'd been born, for a moment, I couldn't remember. Finally, it came back to me. "Uh, Bryer Hill, near Memphis."

He tapped something on his laptop. "That can't be. There's no such place. You must be forgetting things."

I instantly got angry. "It might not be there now, but I was born in...in..." I searched my memory and got a little frustrated for not remembering right away. "I was born in April, nineteen twenty-five. Bryer Hill existed back then. I know it."

Ruby got the same response when she said she'd been born in a small town near Memphis that apparently no longer existed. "Nellis Point. It was a small town back then. Check the records. You must have them."

The doctor thought she was also lying. Finally, when he mentioned we might be suffering from the early stages of dementia—and I knew what that word meant—I slugged him in his flabby face, knocking him to the floor and bloodying his nose.

Old, was I? I still had a good right hook. "Get out," I said, breathing hard and aware that my heart was beating too fast for its own good. "We're old to you now? We were young a couple of weeks ago."

All right, that sounded crazy, but it was the truth. Mr. Old Age Doctor picked himself up and practically crawled out of the room.

A few minutes later, Arthur came by to ask us what had happened. He wasn't happy about me beating up an employee, but after we described the doctor's rotten bedside manner, he told us to forget about it. "We won't be sending him your way again."

I was incredibly grateful for that.

I wasn't grateful, though, when we sat in on our daily briefing with Bayliss. As the overall leader, his words carried the most weight. What he said went without question. And he was dismissive of our concerns.

"Trust me, Goodman," he said. "I have your best interests at heart."

After the meeting I'd witnessed with Mr. Rich and Powerful Senator, the short answer was no, he didn't. When Arthur came by, we told him about Bayliss's response and asked him again about the tests. And once again, he told us that the techs were still checking things out.

Right. *Evasive* was his new middle name. I now knew that this research institute was simply using us as guinea pigs. Escaping became our top priority, but armed guards stood at the exit points — all three of them — effectively blocking any chance of us getting out of there.

Ruby had also figured things out. Back in our room, she picked up the pad of paper Arthur had given her. She waved me to her side and scribbled her thoughts on the paper. *I don't trust them. Bayliss is a liar.*

She'd said that before. I grabbed a pen and responded. *I know that, but what can we do?*

My girlfriend shrugged as I handed the pen back and wrote, *Wait. That's all we can do.*

Once we finished messaging, she tore the paper into tiny bits and flushed the scraps. After that, we made small talk simply to throw off anyone who might have been listening, and then we took a nap.

Our frequent napping bothered me, especially now that I knew it wasn't just jetlag. It was something else.

More than the sleep issue, I had aches and pains I'd never

experienced before. A sore lower back and stiff shoulders, and for the first time in a long time, I had trouble going to the bathroom. I mentioned it to a technician.

"Stopped up?" he asked.

"Yeah." It was embarrassing, but it was the truth.

He offered a sympathetic smile. "My grandfather has the same problem. I'll handle it. Don't worry."

Later on, someone came by with what they called magnesium pills. "Take one at night, before bed," he told me. "That should help."

It did, but the constant napping still plagued me. I'd nodded off and subsequently woken up to find two hours had elapsed. I wandered into the bathroom, feeling my back act up again. The pain was there, but it was bearable.

However, what shocked me was my appearance. The mirror didn't lie. I'd aged. Gray hair, a few crow's feet at the sides of my eyes, and my muscle tone wasn't as good. Overall, it seemed that I'd aged forty years. I realized then that we didn't have long to live if we stayed.

Someone knocked at the door, and I went to answer it, knowing I'd probably get angry with whoever was there. "Who is it?"

"Jonas."

I opened the door, asking, "What's next? More tests? More talks? Someone else wants to look at the zoo specimens?"

The APRIL leader shook his head with a pensive expression, but once he focused on my face, his eyes widened. "I came to tell you about the test results. I wasn't sure at first, but now I know. Our tests showed…showed…"

"We're aging?"

He nodded. "Yes. I'm sorry. I honestly didn't know."

With a grunt, I folded my arms across my chest. I didn't know what else I could do, but this visit called for a gesture of defiance, however small. "You didn't know. You yanked us out of our home, didn't bother asking us how we felt about it, and you're probably going to chalk it up to science, aren't you?"

Arthur bobbed his head again. "Like I said, we didn't know then. We know now."

"So, what are you going to do about it?"

"Tell Bayliss. That's all I can do."

# Chapter Eighteen: The Return, Part One

*F*our days had passed since Arthur's declaration. We'd been at the facility for almost three weeks. Bayliss hadn't shown his face, and the word came down that he was occupied with administrative matters. Various intermediaries—they called themselves intermediaries, while I called them lackeys—told us that Bayliss was tied up in meetings with his investors.

Right, he was probably kissing Mulholland's butt, along with the other rich and powerful members of Congress or the business world. Pointing out his behavior wouldn't help Ruby or me, so we kept our mouths shut.

Keeping our mouths shut meant we spent most of our waking time watching television. Everyone thought it was a great invention, but I only saw images of disasters, sickness, and death.

India, a country I'd been supposed to fly to before my life with Ruby began, had experienced a major earthquake across the nation that exceeded anything the Richter scale had ever recorded. Nepal had also suffered major damage. The devastation was terrible.

I'd searched the internet for stories about World War Two, trying to catch up on my history, and the statistics for the dead and injured were staggering and horrifying, particularly the death camps in Germany and Poland. Six million lives were snuffed out for being a different religion—my religion. Another million-plus for being homosexual or gypsy—the modern term was Roma or Romani, so the internet said—or mentally defective, according to the Nazis back then. All of them had been slaughtered over roughly three years.

India's earthquake had wiped out over five million people in the space of seven minutes. The news reports said twice that many victims were buried under rubble. Survivors said it was like a million giant hands had erupted from the ground all over the country and toppled everything like a child pushing over building blocks. It was the worst crisis ever in modern history, and the US and other allies were flying in supplies and medical help twenty-four hours a day.

Nepal's situation was even more dire. They had a smaller population and a weaker infrastructure. Their airports were also destroyed. All those people were gone, wiped out in a matter of a few seconds. Had those people thought about their mortality? I couldn't answer that.

However, during that ninety-six-hour period, I had no choice but to contemplate my own mortality. I'd aged even more. Of course, the process had begun earlier, but now it seemed to move faster. The mirror showed a hint of white that poked out from the gray in my hair, my muscle tone had gone down at least fifty percent, and it became harder and harder to haul my butt out of bed in the morning.

Ruby also showed signs of aging, though she still looked much better than I did. "Got a stiff back this morning," she said after we'd gotten up at five a.m. to use the bathroom, another sign of old age. Leaky bladders sucked. "Stiff shoulders, too…stiff everything. I could go for a massage."

"Yeah, me, too," I replied, thinking about the times she'd used her small but strong hands to knead the muscles in my back when everything tightened up. "You first, then me?"

"You're on."

She slipped off her pajama top and lay on her stomach. I gently pushed my thumbs into the spots she told me to massage, and she grunted with pleasure. After ten minutes, she said, "Enough. Your turn."

I pulled off my top, lay on my stomach, and she performed her magic on me. Once she finished, I turned over, and seeing her pretty face made me think of all the times we'd spent together.

She leaned down and kissed me, then reached for her pajama top and put it on. "For the first time since we got together, I don't feel like having fun," she admitted with distinct notes of sadness. "Everything hurts, and I'm sagging in all the wrong places. Is that what getting old means?"

I sat up and wrapped my arms around her. "We'll get through this."

Ruby leaned her head against my shoulder. "Yes, we will."

But deep in my heart, I had the feeling we wouldn't. I'd watched a movie where the main character said something about time slipping away…and they were right. Our time was rapidly running out.

One decent thing our overseers did was to comply with our wish to visit Memphis. I wanted to see my parents' graves, and Ruby also asked to see her parents' graves. Arthur contacted General Bayliss, who gave his assent. We took a private plane with Arthur, two security officers, and a doctor on board…just in case.

In Memphis, our minders had rented a van, and they drove us from the airport to the cemetery where my parents had been interred. It was chilly, with a cold wind that rattled my bones. Ruby and I walked hand in hand and followed an official who led us to where my parents' plots were.

My parents were buried next to each other in simple graves in Beth Israel Cemetery, the main Jewish cemetery in the city. Well-kept with Dusty Millers surrounding each plot, I noted the neatly cut grass and the quiet, somber atmosphere. Judith and Albert Goodman, their birth dates, and their death dates were the only things on their headstones besides the Star of David that symbolized my religion.

Our minders stood a healthy distance away, watching the scene for any kind of trouble. So far, there hadn't been any.

I stood at the foot of the graves, saying goodbye to my parents. We hadn't had the best relationship, but they'd been my parents and tried to raise me the right way. I didn't agree with it, and that's why I left, but I now realized why they'd done what they'd done. In the end, that was all any of us could do.

After I finished saying goodbye, Ruby took my hand, and we walked around the area. In the far-left corner, I saw a small grave. I stooped down to grab a quick look. *Carl Allen Goodman, born April 5th, 1925.* There was no date of death. That figured. Well, I doubted anyone bothered looking there, and I wasn't dead…yet.

Ruby and I turned away and started walking. A few other people were there, some with children, and they glanced at us as we passed by. One short and portly man in his late thirties with prematurely gray hair murmured something about why a black person was there.

Idiot. I confronted him, saying, "Mister, she's my girlfriend. Got that? Say what you said again. She's just dying to hear it. So am I."

Yeah, we were dying…in more ways than one. As rotten as

199

I felt, I didn't have to take that crap from anyone, and neither did Ruby. Even though I was chronologically thirty-something years older than the guy, nothing could've stopped me from beating his face in.

"Girlfriend?" The guy laughed. "Mister, you're older than I am."

That's when I lost it and smacked him. Not with my full strength because I didn't have it any longer. However, it was enough to put him on his ass.

His wife, short and chubby like him, pulled him up, apologizing for her husband's insensitivity. "I guess you're grieving, too," she said.

As if she meant that, but whatever. That was a common saying for me these days—*whatever*. Life was too short to get angry over stupid people. Arthur and the security detail led us to our van, and off we went.

At Dane Creek Baptist Church, Ruby's parents' graves were even simpler and not as well cared for. Time and neglect had allowed the weeds to multiply. We stooped to pull a few of the offending plants out, and my back rebelled.

"This is hard for me," Ruby said with a catch in her voice. "I'm going to need some time."

I left her alone, and luckily, a preacher showed up. While I sat and massaged my lower back, he kindly said a prayer for her parents, assuring her that their souls were with the Lord. Ruby wiped her eyes, and I listened to the prayers and bowed my head.

After the preacher was done, Ruby wandered off and stopped at a small, weed-covered area. I went over to her as fast as my stiff legs could carry me.

"That's me," she said in a deceptively quiet voice, pointing at a small marker with her name on it and a small cross in the center. "Born January seventeenth, nineteen twenty-four, no date of death. Isn't that something...I don't exist."

"Neither do I," I answered.

When she turned to me and spoke again, it was with a sense of urgency. "Carl, I want to leave here. I...I'm done with my life in Memphis."

Our brief stay was over. We stopped for a simple lunch of burgers and fries at a local eatery. Arthur, the doctor, and the officers left us alone, and no one bothered us. Ruby and I didn't talk, we only focused on our food, which still tasted bland and couldn't compare to what we'd eaten in our garden.

Back at the facility, the doctor who'd accompanied us examined Ruby and me, and took more samples. After waiting an hour for the lab technicians to go over our umpteenth blood test, the doctor finally got a call from the lab with the verdict.

We sat in the main room with Arthur off to the side. The doctor seemed reluctant to speak, and an uncomfortable silence fell over the room while he read the report.

I wasn't expecting good news and didn't believe in miracles, but my patience was wearing thin, so I decided to break the ice. "Okay, doctor, we know we're getting old. What else did they find out?"

"As you said, both of you are showing signs of accelerated aging," the doctor replied in a quiet voice. "You've aged about forty-five years in the time that you've been here. I'd guess that both of you are in your early to mid-sixties. Maybe even older. Carl, you have signs of arthritis in your knees, hands, and lower back, and your liver is showing signs of damage, as are your kidneys.

"Ruby, you have the same symptoms of rapid aging. Your blood profile is also showing high cholesterol and heart disease. Your, uh, womb..."

"What about it?"

"It seems that it isn't there. There are no signs you ever had one."

That's why she'd never gotten pregnant. All this time...

Ruby's lips thinned, but she remained calm. "All right...but can you tell us why we're getting old?"

His hesitation infuriated me, although I should have expected it. "I can't explain why it's happening, but..." He shrugged and then stated the obvious. "It is what it is."

All of which didn't please us one bit. In fact, I got downright angry and turned to Arthur. "Didn't you think this would happen if you took us out of there?"

He gave me his classic I-don't-know evasive gesture, but his expression signified he regretted something. It was a gesture meant to appease, but it didn't help the situation at all.

I slammed my hand against the table. It hurt, but I ignored the pain and sputtered, "You're...you guys are scientists. You're supposed to know!"

Arthur had the decency to wince. "I'm sorry. This is unprecedented. And you agreed to come along."

With an effort, I stifled a four-letter, extremely nasty response. The man would have to toss the you-agreed-to-come-with-us argument at me. But facts were facts. We *had* agreed, and getting angry wouldn't change things. "Isn't there anything you can do?"

Arthur appeared sympathetic, if not necessarily helpful. "This is a first for us. But I can see that things aren't going right."

Ruby quickly interjected, "Yeah, they're not. We gave you everything we had. We told you where we were and how we got there. We gave you the details. We gave you samples. What more do you want, to see us turn into mummies and die in front of you?"

Arthur's mouth moved in a dozen directions before he managed to get a word out. "I don't have the pull to get you out. If I could, I'd send you back today. But General Bayliss is the man in charge. He's got the contacts, not only within our government, but also with the Indian, the Nepalese, and the Chinese governments, and that takes a lot of smooth talking and some concessions."

What the hell was this all about, I wondered. "What kind of concessions?"

"Trade deals, lifting of embargos, weapons...that kind of thing. High stakes, really."

"And we're not high stakes or important?"

I'd had enough when Arthur gave the I-don't-know gesture again, followed by another apology. I grabbed the younger man by his collar, pulled him across the table, and started choking him. "I don't give a damn what you're going to do with our blood and skin. I can guess, but that doesn't matter. I'm not asking you this time. I'm telling you. Get Bayliss in here, let me talk to him, and if I can't make him see the light, then I'll beat his goddamn head in."

By the time I finished my rant, I was breathing hard and sweating. Ruby pulled on my arm, asking me in a quiet but firm voice to let Arthur go. I did — reluctantly.

A security officer walked over, hand on his holster, although he didn't take his weapon out. "Trouble, sir?" he asked.

Security officers, I thought savagely. We're prisoners. "Yeah, there's trouble."

Arthur, though, put up his hands. "No trouble, officer. Just a minor disagreement. Has General Bayliss returned?"

The security officer, young, strongly built, and with a mean scowl, touched something in his ear and then spoke into a microphone attached to his collar. "Sir, this is Officer Jenkins on the bottom level. I'm in the room where the subjects are being held."

"Subjects," Ruby growled, suddenly as angry as I was. "Lab animals, you mean."

From the look on the officer's face, he really wanted to use his weapon, and we were the targets, so I hushed her. Jenkins stared at us while listening intently to the instructions he had to be getting. Finally, he clicked off his com-link and spoke to us. "General Bayliss is en route to this base. He'll be here within an hour."

"Then we want to speak with him," Arthur said.

"I'll give him the message." Jenkins saluted and left.

With that, Arthur relaxed, rubbed his throat, and asked me if we wanted to rest up while we waited.

"We will," I replied. "But when Bayliss gets here, we want to talk to him. Right away. Got it?"

Arthur nodded. "Understood." He turned and disappeared down the corridor.

Ruby pulled me to our room, hugging me tightly. "What if they say no?"

Something suddenly occurred to me. It should've happened earlier, but better late than never. I leaned down to whisper in my girlfriend's ear, "I have something to trade."

\*

Seventy-three minutes later.

A security officer came to get us, saying that General Bayliss had returned and wanted to speak to us on the double. We'd been watching the news, and I wondered how the world had survived the past few decades. People hadn't changed much. There was still racism, anti-Semitism, anti-black hate, and much more. Too much division. Too much strife. I wanted out in the worst way.

Bayliss had to offer that way out. In fact, he was the only one who could.

We entered the main lab, where Bayliss sat at a table with a mug of coffee in front of him like a potentate in charge of his kingdom. He arched his eyebrows in surprise when he saw us but recovered quickly and offered to get us a beverage. We declined.

He sipped his coffee and remarked, "Well, what a difference four days make."

*Stick the knife in a little deeper.* "Yeah, soon, we'll be able to apply for a pension."

"Considering you don't exist, good luck with the application. But you're serving your country, I'll have you know, just by being here."

I'd already served my country, and he was a heartless bastard. "How?"

Bayliss put his mug down. "Advancement of science, of course. New discoveries in medicine, science, and yes, weaponry. You two may not realize it, but you're the key to a whole new age."

"How's that again?" My body hurt, and my backache had gone from dull throbbing to a full-blown stabbing at the base of my spine. But I didn't show him that I was in pain. Show no weakness—that was the rule.

A grin painted the general's craggy features. "Your blood samples, Goodman, and yours, Ruby, have properties in them that can slow down the aging process in our population. The original samples, I mean, and what we can do with the first samples, well, the possibilities are limitless."

At least he was admitting it. "Is that what you told Senator Mulholland?"

His eyes widened. "How did you know?"

"I was going to get a cup of coffee and overheard your conversation in the lounge. I can guess you made a deal with the senator, right?"

Ruby glanced at me but then stared daggers at Bayliss. She slapped his mug, knocking it right into his lap and spilling the coffee all over his neatly pressed and starched uniform. "You bastard."

He sputtered something incoherent while she yelled, "Does that mean killing us? I don't know who this senator is, but from where I'm standing, you got what you wanted. You don't need us, so let us go back."

Bayliss grunted angrily, got up, and brushed the excess liquid from his uniform. When he spoke, his voice had an edge to it. "Let me lay a little reality on you. It isn't that simple. We had to get permission from the Nepalese government to access those caves the first time. That took time, but since we're on friendly terms, they allowed us in. The concessions we made to them were modest.

"However, India and Nepal recently had a major earthquake across their respective countries. Two days ago, in fact."

"I saw it," I replied. "It was tough to watch."

Bayliss grunted. "It's tougher for their people. The damage...India has practically reverted to the stone age. Nepal is already there. Every single one of their airports is wrecked, they're worried about the spread of cholera and other diseases, not to mention half their populace freezing or starving to death or dying from injuries, and we're doing what we can to help them out."

He inhaled and blew out a deep breath. "You have no idea about the logistics this kind of endeavor involves. It means flying in food, medical supplies, rescue crews, dog teams to sniff out the survivors...the works. And we're working twenty-four-seven to do it. Fifty other countries are doing the same thing, and many more have promised to help out. Our government has put top priority on saving what's left of India and Nepal."

My hopes sank. "So, what now?"

Bayliss offered me a mollified look. "Oh, now you want to be nice? Your girlfriend should learn better manners."

"When we're being messed over, why bother," Ruby interjected. "You want to play with your lab rats? Do it without me." She turned on her heels as if to leave.

Bayliss's words made her halt. "Wait. Before you start throwing things at me or throw another tantrum, we have an alternate route."

Ruby turned and glared at him, hands on her hips. "Where?"

"Through China. We've already contacted the Chinese government, and they'll allow us a stopover in their country. It wasn't easy convincing them, but we managed."

Ruby's glare intensified. "And how did you do that?"

The general shrugged. "It's all about concessions."

"Meaning?"

He sighed. "Meaning that we share what we find."

Bayliss then turned his gaze on me. "Now, what are you prepared to share with us. And I mean, only us?"

That figured. Bayliss was in it for the advancement and the money — if there was any to be made — but I'd already come prepared. "When we get to the caves, there's a barrier. I don't know if you can enter. Jonas and his team couldn't, so chances are you won't be able to either. But Ruby and I can."

Bayliss chuckled, but there was no humor in it. "That doesn't solve my problem."

Oh, he was a tough nut. "I'm not finished. Above the cave

where you found us is a pathway. It leads to other caves. We can reach them, but we'll have to take the overland route."

A glint of curiosity and greed sparked in the general's eyes. "We know about the trail. Our team there has already walked it and found the caves. The question is, what's inside them that'll be of use to us?"

I glanced at Ruby, who wore a tiny smile, clearly understanding what I was getting at. "Like the place we were in, they're doorways to other worlds. Those worlds have riches in them. Deposits of gold, diamonds, and other gems and metals I got no idea about. Plant life, animal life…it's all there. Maybe oil, too. Who knows for sure? We'll help you. If you can't enter, we can at least bring pipelines in, equipment for testing, or bring out samples. That's worth a trip back, isn't it?"

Bayliss nodded slowly as if weighing the odds, and yes, the look in his eyes meant he saw a huge payday, both financially and scientifically. "If what you say is true, then it's something we can all benefit from." He turned to his techs. "All of you are staying here. I'll go with our new best friends here."

I'd read a line in a book long ago that greed could be a powerful inducement. It clearly was in this case, so I forced myself to smile, one that said I'd caved to the general's wishes. I gave no hint that I had no intention of following his wishes or orders or anything else, not when I knew who and what he was. "Do we have a deal, sir?"

Bayliss extended his hand for the obligatory handshake. "We most certainly do, Goodman."

"Call me Carl. I'm glad we're friends." Lord, that was false as hell, but he bought it.

The general beamed. "We do, indeed. We most certainly do."

I got up. "When can we leave?"

Bayliss rose and straightened his tie. One thing about him...he always made sure his uniform was impeccably cleaned and pressed, though the coffee stains would be harder to wash out. "Give me some time. I have to contact their government officials, but I'm sure I can work things out."

With that, we went back to our room. Once there, Ruby faced me. "Carl, I love you, but don't you think about hiding anything from me. We've always been upfront with each other. Keep it that way."

"Sorry." Guilt swept over me, knowing she was right. "I, uh, didn't want you to worry."

"Too late for that."

She parked herself on the bed and lowered her head. "I just hope Bayliss can do this for us." Her sigh sounded devoid of hope.

I sat beside her and threw my arm around her shoulders. "Me, too."

So, we waited. Nothing happened the next day or the day after that, but on the third day, a knock sounded at our door at seven in the evening.

Ruby opened the door and said, "I hope you have good news."

Bayliss stood a couple of feet away, flashing a mile-wide smile. "It is beyond good news, beyond anything that I figured would happen. The Chinese government agreed to work with us. We still have to make a few concessions, but if what you told me is on the level, then giving up a few things will be worth it."

Business...it was all about business. I wasn't concerned about making money. I never had been. But I had to pretend that I was. "Well, if it's a good deal for you, then I'm all for it. When do we get out of here?"

My heart skipped a few beats when he replied. "Tomorrow. Pack your things."

# Chapter Nineteen: The Return, Part Two

*A*rthur and Bayliss had contacted our federal government, and they quickly replied with a blunt, short answer — no — end of story, no question asked, but I'd sort of expected it. After all, we were dealing with bureaucracy, and even in my day, cutting through red tape was a major hassle.

Bayliss actually chortled when he read the message. "Get a load of this crap. He turned his laptop around to show us the message.

I'd never imagined anyone could send an electronic message through a computer. In my day, it was done with telegrams, but this was a modern age with modern equipment. As Ruby once said, we needed to upgrade.

Even though my body hurt, I had to laugh when I read the message on the laptop. *No!* It was such a simple yet dramatic answer.

Bayliss decided to ignore the message and hustled Ruby and me, along with Arthur and seven members of the research team, onto a private jet. We took off, he contacted no one, and no one sent him any messages.

"Aren't you afraid the Army will bust you?" I asked.

He laughed. "Let them charge me. What we discover and bring back will get them to change their minds. Believe me, it'll cement my reputation for all time. This is going to be the game-changer of the century."

I had no handy response to that without giving my plan away, so I said nothing. Ruby and I settled back and tried to sleep. It didn't come, and we hadn't slept much the night before, either.

Ruby had been upset at finding out that she couldn't have children. I didn't want to say anything about it, but it was her choice to discuss the matter.

In the privacy of our room, she lay beside me after I'd crawled painfully into bed. "Carl?"

I twisted over to face her, ignoring the twinges and tweaks in my lower back. Wonderful, now I had trembling muscles. "Yeah?"

"Are you upset about me... I mean, that I can't have a baby?"

"No." I wasn't. All I wanted was good health for my girlfriend and nothing more. "I didn't know, and neither did you. It doesn't change how I feel about you."

A few tears slipped from her eyes. "When I was still in Memphis, I figured I'd find someone, get married, and then have a baby. It's what a lot of women want, and that's what I wanted. Now...we're old, and even if we weren't, we'd never be parents."

I wrapped my arms around her. "Ruby, it doesn't matter. I love you, no matter what. I've spent, uh, ninety-something years with you, and for us, it's just like a marriage. And they always say that marriage is for better or worse."

Her voice came like a whisper on the wind. "This is about as worse as it can get."

She cried a little more, then slipped into an uneasy sleep, twisting and turning all night. I felt bad for her, but I knew she was wrong. Things could always get worse.

And now, we were on a jet back to where it all started. I tried to get a nap in but failed. Instead, Ruby and I watched a movie and ate the first-class food they served, which didn't thrill me. During the meal, I shifted around from time to time to relieve the pain in my lower back. Getting old was for the birds. What did younger people say? Oh, yeah, it sucked.

\*

We reached Beijing Airport sixteen hours later, and after a discussion with the authorities, we transferred to another plane with Chinese markings that took us through the mountain range. Clouds above and below us provided a cushion, and the weather was unusually cooperative as there was very little turbulence.

For the first five hours, I thought about what would happen when we arrived at our destination. After that, age and tiredness caught up to me, and when I noticed that my girlfriend was finally sleeping beside me, I followed her into slumber.

Strangely, I experienced no dreams, and when I woke— Ruby still sleeping beside me—I felt older, the aches and pains in my knees and lower back worse than before. My accelerated aging reminded me of something I'd seen in a Ronald Coleman movie long ago. Only that was a movie. This was real, and my pain intensified with each passing hour.

One of the techs gave me a small hand mirror that showed a deeply lined face, white hair, and rheumy eyes. The doctor had said I'd reached my late sixties. Now, it appeared as though I was way over seventy. I sort of resembled my father, although he'd died way too young. I already had thirty years on him. A closer look at Ruby showed the same signs of aging. She also had gray hair, liver spots on her hands and face, and a hunch in her back. We were cutting it way too close.

Bayliss didn't seem to notice our conditions, or if he did, he didn't care. He was too upbeat. He asked me a lot of questions about the new worlds, if they could be colonized, or if they were too inhospitable.

"Uh, they're all different," I replied, building on lie after lie. "I don't know why. I don't even know who built them. But they exist, and they have a lot to offer."

Bayliss nodded, rubbing his hands together with an expression that looked like a child expecting a huge toy on Christmas day. He even took out a flask from his hip pocket and twisted off the cap. "This calls for a celebration." He held up his flask. "To you and Ruby."

The sharp smell of alcohol wafted through the air. I remembered the smell. It was cognac. I'd had the stuff only once during my stay at Tsu-yang, and I'd thrown up. "Congratulations to all of us," I forced myself to say.

When Bayliss went to the bathroom, Arthur moved closer to us. "We'll be staying at the ten-thousand-foot level for the night. We need to acclimate. Has General Bayliss already told you about our deal with the Chinese?"

I nodded. "Yeah, he did."

While the general's demeanor was friendly, Arthur's expression appeared pensive, as if he was unsure about telling us too much. "All right, since you know, no sense in repeating it. I was told they've already dispatched two representatives from their government."

Bayliss came back. He must've been listening in because he muttered that they had to make deals with the devil all the time. From what I'd picked up from the internet, I knew the

Chinese weren't into sharing. During the war, they'd been our allies. Now, they were rivals and perhaps enemies.

Immediately, my suspicions peaked, and I asked, "And what are you going to share with them?"

The general barked out a laugh as he sat. "Nothing. As far as I'm concerned, we haven't found anything, and that's just what we'll tell them."

Arthur turned to him. "But, sir —"

"Stop." Bayliss held up his hand and glared at Arthur. "Listen carefully. Say nothing, Jonas. The funding for the lab comes through me. I'm the link with all the private investors. They want a return on their investment, and I'm the only one who can make it happen. Remember that."

Arthur's face reddened as he mumbled something about obeying orders, returned to his seat, and said nothing the rest of the trip.

Once the plane glided to a stop along a rough airfield, two of the research team who'd originally stayed behind met us as we disembarked. Two Chinese men of medium height and stoic expressions stood ten yards away. They wore khaki green uniforms with pistols strapped to their sides. I had a feeling this encounter wouldn't be brief or cordial.

"All set up, sir," one of the American techs said, jerking his thumb at the Chinese soldiers. "Our, uh, contacts are waiting. Are you ready?"

The question was ostensibly meant for us, so I replied, "Yes, we're ready."

"We are," Ruby echoed. "Let's go."

We grabbed our bags with our new clothes in them and slung them over our shoulders. As we trekked along the uneven ground, I reflected that it had been a long journey, and it wasn't over yet. The only question was whether the barrier still existed, and if so, would it recognize us?

Five minutes later, we reached a small helipad. A helicopter sat there, its rotor whirling around slowly. "This is how we'll get you up there," Arthur said. "Climbing takes too long, and it's too hard. No sense in risking anyone's life."

Arthur helped us onboard, and the pilot took off, slowly rising through the mist until we reached the first base camp at ten thousand feet. The air seemed thinner than I remembered but still breathable, and we stayed overnight, with the doctor in attendance keeping an eye on everyone to ensure we were all okay. Altitude sickness could hit anyone at any age or level of fitness, and Ruby and I were apparently at a greater risk.

Still, we managed.

\*

The next morning, since we showed no symptoms, we headed up again. The Chinese soldiers eyed Ruby and me curiously, clearly trying to figure out who we were, but they said nothing. I hated being stared at, but that was how things went. I just hung onto the safety strap and watched the ground disappear below us.

At the escarpment, the pilot hovered as close to the edge as possible while one of the Chinese soldiers shot out a zipline dart that embedded itself in the rock above our cave. He attached several harnesses to the line, then turned and said, "We are ready."

"Okay, let's go," Arthur yelled above the roar of the engine. "Who's first?"

Ruby raised a shaky hand. "I'll go, but I don't like this."

"No other way. Sorry." He helped her into the harness, making sure it was secure.

Ruby held her bag close to her chest, and then Arthur

shoved her across the zipline. As she sped along the line, she let out a scream, but four researchers were by the cave to catch her on the other end. I went next, feeling my adrenalin spike. Arthur followed me across, then Bayliss and the American techs. The two Chinese soldiers went last.

Once everyone was across, one of the Chinese soldiers detached the cables, and the helicopter co-pilot reeled them in as they disappeared below the mist. A cold wind whipped around me, but I was grateful there wasn't much snow.

"Find anything of value here?" Arthur asked his men.

Collectively, they shook their heads, and one of them said, "Nothing, sir. We checked out the wall, ran radiation tests, checking for any signs of contamination...it's clean. We couldn't find a thing except smashed tin cans from a century ago."

The Chinese soldier who'd shot out the zipline spoke up in clear, unaccented English. "Are you sure we are in the right place?"

Bayliss stared at the other man with a glare so intense I was surprised the soldier didn't flinch. "Yes, this is the place. We found Carl and Ruby here, and this is where we're going to search."

The Chinese soldiers consulted each other in their language, and then the first man faced the general. "Our government has made it clear that any findings are to be shared, no matter how meager they are. Shall we inform them you are...reneging on the deal?"

*Man, that is arrogant.* Back in the day, I'd spent some time with Chinese soldiers. They were stubborn, but I figured it was due to the war. Now, these men were being stubborn for an entirely different reason.

Still, Ruby and I had to get out of this mess, and the only way to do it was to make sure Bayliss and his Chinese counterparts trusted us.

The general protested. "Son, no one is reneging on anything. My research team simply said they didn't find anything in this cave. That's all. But there might be something else inside that we haven't seen yet."

"Our prior research shows nothing but rock and the aforementioned tins, which can be fakes, inside this cave. Please do not insult the intelligence of our government or our goodwill."

"Listen, men, I promised to share our findings, and that's what I intend to do." To his credit, Bayliss sounded sincere, even though I knew he was lying. The man didn't have a sincere bone in his body.

From the looks of it, the Chinese soldiers apparently didn't believe him either.

When an argument started, I intervened, putting down my bag first. "Uh, guys, don't flip your wigs. If you want answers, then we have to go to the other caves up top."

The soldier who'd done all the talking stared at me. "Who exactly are you?"

"I'm Carl, and this is my girlfriend, Ruby. We're the keys to all this. Trust me. You won't find anything inside here, but the caves I told General Bayliss about are the ones that everyone can benefit from. They're about a mile away on that overhead trail."

Arthur cut in, suggesting we wait another day. "Altitude sickness is often delayed. It's better to wait."

I didn't know if Ruby and I had another day, but we agreed. Tents had already been set up, along with oxygen tanks and medicine, just in case. Ruby and I spent the night in our tent holding onto each other, and fortunately, outside of a little shortness of breath and overall weakness, we easily found sleep.

\*

The next morning, I felt well enough and anxious to get the show on the road. We shared a simple breakfast of bread and coffee with the general and the two Chinese soldiers.

After we finished eating, Bayliss suggested we go check out the caves. "Since this is a joint venture, Carl assured me there's enough for everyone," he said in a hearty tone.

I whispered into Ruby's ear, "Feel up to a walk? Or are you too tired?"

She leaned against my chest. "You know you can't go anywhere without me. Let's go."

One of the techs gave us heavier coats, and the Chinese soldiers quickly climbed to the top of the steps. Despite his age, Bayliss went next and did the climb easily. Then the three of them turned and helped pull Ruby and me up the last few steps. On the trail, a strong, cold, and biting wind swirled around us. The frigidity of the air crept through my coat and seeped into my bones. Getting old stank in more ways than one.

"Which way do we go?" one of the soldiers asked, gazing around the area and shivering. "This trail leads in two opposite directions."

I motioned to our left. "North. We have to go that way. Ruby and I will go first and show you."

One of the soldiers had brought a length of rope with him, and we all tied the rope around our waists. Call that paranoid, but it was just as much for safety as for keeping tabs on us. Ruby was behind me, followed by Bayliss, and the soldiers brought up the rear. The wind buffeted us from side to side, and I struggled to keep my balance. My body screamed for a breather, but we kept going.

However, it all got to be too much, so for the last five hundred yards, Ruby and I slung our arms around each other's waist, and we counted together, "One, two, one, two..."

Finally, we reached the stairs leading down to the caves, and I managed to get Ruby and me sitting on the top steps. At the bottom, the first cave stood out, just as I remembered it. "We're here," I yelled above the sound of the wind. "This is it, but Ruby and I need a break."

When my breathing returned to normal, I managed to get to my feet, helped Ruby stand, and we slowly descended the stairs. Everyone else followed me down, and Ruby leaned against me, breathing hard. "Are you going to make it?" I asked.

"For better or worse," she muttered. "I'll live."

We bypassed cave number one, although the other members stopped briefly to ask me to translate the symbols on the outside of the cave. Despite the frigid weather, Bayliss beamed and whipped out his smartphone to take a few pictures.

"This is amazing," he enthused. "It's the find of the century." He turned to the Chinese soldiers. "What do you think?"

"It is all very interesting," the first man said in a voice devoid of emotion. "But we have seen nothing of importance yet."

Bayliss looked at me. "Well, Carl?"

Ruby nudged me with her elbow. "Start talking," she whispered.

It was time for the acting role of my life, so I put on my best tour guide demeanor as we all removed the ropes from our waists. "Number one's a write-off, at least, for tourists. Prehistoric monsters rule inside there. The place, though, has a lot of precious metals, but you'd have to bring an army to claim it."

"Oh, I think we can do that." Bayliss grinned. "What's next?"

"Number two is empty." Yes, it was a lie, but they didn't have to know. "Number three is like our garden, but it's not as well kept. And numbers five and six are also bad. One of them's eternally dark, and we think there are monsters inside. We were there for about two minutes. Again, if you go in there, then you're going to need an army. Another cave leads to a lava land. It's got nothing but magma and small islands and high heat. Forget about it."

The second Chinese soldier said, "Tell us about number four."

Ruby started to say something but cut herself short and covered it by emitting a wracking cough. I took that moment to rub her back and said that four had to be the lucky number, so we walked over to the cave, entered, and the soldiers took out small penlights to light the way. Sure enough, at the back, we saw the symbols.

"This is it?" Bayliss asked as the soldiers played their lights up and down the rock.

"It is," I said. "Now, if you want to take a look, we can open it."

The general nodded. "Sounds good, but maybe we'll do it later."

"You will do it now." Chinese soldier number one had his pistol out and aimed at Bayliss. His comrade pointed his at Ruby. At such close range, they couldn't miss.

"Boys, we had an agreement," Bayliss said in an aggrieved tone, though he didn't make a move. "Damn it, we had a deal!"

"Deals change," the second soldier said and turned to me. "Our government has sent aid and personnel to Nepal and

India. It is our goodwill gesture, and we have done it willingly.

"Our government has also charged the two of us with obtaining any and all pertinent information regarding these caves. Those symbols outside are interesting, but how do we know they aren't fakes? Anyone can carve symbols into rock."

We were dealing with paranoiacs, so I confronted Mr. Stubbornly Stupid. "Did you ever wonder why two senior citizens are with you? You were staring at us in the helicopter. I told you before that my girlfriend and I were the keys to this. Okay, here's another truth. We were in our late teens when we were found about a month ago. Now, we're old enough to be your grandparents."

Both soldiers glanced at each other and then at me, and soldier number one said, "We thought it strange that two elderly people were with us. But we imagined you two were part of the corporation that funded this venture for your country. Now, we must know who you are."

"I just told you. We used to be young, and we used to live inside one of those caves. We're telling the truth here."

Finally, a tiny smile emerged on the first soldier's face. "I doubt your word, but if you want to continue being a part of this expedition, then you will have to show us."

With a gasp, Ruby fell to one knee, her breathing ragged.

Concerned, I knelt beside her, feeling my back protest. "What's wrong?"

"It's my heart," she whispered. "Same as my mama."

*Oh, God.* "Can you do this?"

She looked up at me with a fierce gaze. "Help...help me up."

I gently pulled her to her feet, and my back protested even more.

Ruby glared at the soldiers. "We're going to open things

up, but we have to do it together."

The lead soldier nodded. "Go ahead."

Ruby and I joined hands and nodded. I put my hand on the wall first, then Ruby did. We quickly retraced the shape of the sand dunes. Within a second, the wall's composition turned to finely sifted sand, and the kaleidoscopic gateway appeared.

I barely held back a whoop of joy to see the magic or science or whatever it was still held. "This is it." I waved at the portal. "Whatever you want is behind there."

"Inside," the first Chinese soldier said. "You lead. We will follow."

Boy, they were pigheaded to the nth degree, but as the old saying went, there were none so blind as those who would not see. "You can't. Only Ruby and I can get in there."

Soldier number two aimed his pistol at my stomach. "I doubt that. If you can enter, then so can we."

If I was right, we could all go in, but this had to be executed perfectly. I slowly raised my hands in surrender. "Okay, I wasn't being entirely honest before. If we form a line, Ruby on one end and me on the other, then we might get in. We have to join hands…that'll connect us." I glanced at my girlfriend, and she offered a faint nod. Her face was pale, but her spirit was strong. We'd finish this together.

A smirk appeared on the soldier's face, clearly thinking he'd won. "A wise decision."

This was going to be close. With no choice in the matter, Ruby and I formed a bracket, with Bayliss and the two Chinese soldiers between us. We joined hands and had just enough room to squeeze through. "All right," I said. "Everyone, step inside…now." I breathed a sigh of relief when the door accepted us.

"We're in," Bayliss exulted as he let go of my hand. "We're

in!"

His joy got cut short when the wind and sand immediately blasted us, but Ruby and I knew what to expect and shielded our eyes. I squinted and just barely made out the shapes of those shambling creatures we'd seen before. Apparently, they had no problem seeing through the storm.

Bayliss and the soldiers were temporarily blinded, and the portal was still open, but it wouldn't be for long. Without hesitation, I grabbed my girlfriend's hand, and we jumped back to the Earth side of the gateway.

The portal closed and the wall began to reform. As it did, I heard the screams of the three trapped men, winced as the sound of shots being fired came through, and listened to the growls and grunts of hunger from the starving undead. A moment later, the shots stopped, and shortly after, so did the screams.

With a rumbling sound, the wall rebuilt itself. Silence fell. They were gone.

It was over.

# Chapter Twenty: Home Free

*S*ilence surrounded us, as did the cold of the cave. Ruby remained silent, and so did I. We'd just lured three men to their deaths. It made me sick to my stomach, and as if on cue, I vomited, and my girlfriend followed suit.

Once I finished retching, regret filled me. Killing was wrong. Yes, I'd killed before—icing the guards on Jerana and pushing Norlok into the lava. Both times had been in self-defense to save Ruby and me. And now, this...

I wanted nothing more to do with death.

When I'd joined the Merchant Marines, it was as much out of a spirit of adventure as of patriotism. Most of the sailors and soldiers I'd met had joined to defeat the enemy and make them pay for what they'd done to our troops. I'd served honorably, even though I hadn't seen combat...not until the day the Japanese sunk my ship.

But I'd never killed anyone. Sure, I'd been in fistfights, and yes. I'd hurt others.

Then I'd crashed here with Ruby, we'd discovered a new universe, been in battles on alien worlds, and I'd killed to save our lives. Now...

No. I shook my head, striving for a little clarity. While killing was wrong, a little logic shined through. Those soldiers had been intent on robbing us of our lives. Of that, I was sure.

I was equally sure Bayliss wouldn't have let us go, either. His greed wouldn't have allowed it. In the end, though, it came down to self-defense once again.

I wondered if I should say something about the situation but decided to say nothing. I merely cleared my throat and muttered something about being incredibly tired.

Ruby finally broke the silence. "I didn't want to do that."

If she was going to give me another Norlok speech, she could save it...but she didn't, simply adding that while she hadn't wanted to do it, she was glad we did. "We didn't have a choice," she said after regaining her breath. "I'm not going to cry over them."

My Ruby always surprised me. "You're right, but I'm done with it, and our ride isn't over."

"No, it isn't over," she echoed with a tired smile. She then spat out some junk. "Are you feeling okay?"

That was all the encouragement I needed. "Yeah. Let's go back, sweetheart." Call that a lie. I was truly tired now. I'd probably aged a decade in a matter of minutes.

We left the cave, grabbed some snow, and washed out our mouths. It wasn't perfect, but it would have to do. Once we climbed to the overhead trail and started walking, Ruby, who was in the lead, stopped and turned around.

"What is it?" I asked.

A strange smile painted her face. "You called me sweetheart. You never called me that before."

"Give me time, and I'll use it again."

She leaned into me and stood on her tiptoes to kiss me on the cheek. "If we have time. C'mon."

Right...if we had time.

Slowly and carefully, we moved along the trail and

retraced our steps back to our old cave. The sharp, biting wind was still blowing, but we'd come this far, and getting back to the first cave remained our priority. We couldn't quit now.

It took a long time for us to reach our destination. My muscles and joints ached beyond belief, and Ruby had to stop often to catch her breath. My heart was pounding, and I worried my girlfriend would have a heart attack. Or I would. Or both of us. It seemed like nature or the cosmos was playing a cruel trick on us. So close, and yet so far.

"Stop," she called out halfway down the steps to our cave.

We sat for a few minutes, with me holding her. Once her breathing returned to normal, we finished our hike.

Fortunately, our hearts didn't let us down during the arduous journey back to our cave. By the time we reached the entrance, we were nearly frostbitten and shivering, not to mention exhausted.

"Hey, we were worried," Arthur said when he saw us and ordered his men to bring blankets. He sat across from us, craning his neck to look outside the cave as his men slung the blankets over our shoulders and offered us hot drinks.

While we sipped from steaming cups of coffee, Arthur asked the obvious question. "Uh, where are Bayliss and our two Chinese friends?"

"They took a trip," Ruby said without a trace of irony. "One-way."

Arthur appeared to take Ruby's comment in stride. Even though his eyebrows arched, his expression remained impassive, and he remained silent. I gazed at the array of equipment surrounding us, most of which I couldn't make head or tail of.

Ruby seemed to have gotten her second wind, her color returning to normal as she said, "Carl, we have to check things out." She immediately handed Arthur her cup, tossed off the blanket, and walked to the back of the cave.

I gave him my cup as well and followed closely behind her. Along the way, I noticed the lights had been strung overhead that illuminated the area. A few steps further, I found my girlfriend running her hands over the pattern on the wall. "That's the way in," I murmured. "Are you going to ask for my help?"

Ruby offered a toothy smile. "Well, I need you, but I'd like to think it needs a woman's touch first. Now, which lines did we touch before…"

She spidered her slender fingers over the rock. "Work with me, Carl," she whispered, breathing on the stony surface as though it was her baby.

We ran our fingers in unison over the lines and cracks of the pictogram. Once we finished, we watched as the familiar dark blue cracks appeared, the rock sloughed off and turned to dust, and the kaleidoscopic barrier appeared. Just like it was the first time.

Arthur had come over to witness our actions, accompanied by the rest of the researchers, who crowded around for a better look. "Holy geez," he said in awe. "You did it. You really did it."

Ruby turned around with a triumphant grin and grabbed my hand. "Yes, we did. Carl, let's go." And we slipped through the portal before anyone could stop us.

*

Inside the garden, it was as if we'd never been away and that the place had known of our arrival or had recognized us and allowed us to enter.

"It looks the same as it always did," Ruby said, beaming with excitement. "Carl?"

I nodded. It did look the same. I breathed in deeply, feeling my lungs expand and my aches and pains slowly disappear. A sense of well-being filled me, but that got cut short when a sharp stab of pain hit my lower back and traveled up to my head, and then it migrated to my entire body. It was so intense that Norlok's shocks were mild in comparison.

"C-Carl," Ruby called, looking as though she was filled with the same agony. "What...what's happening?"

"Some...some...something good," I managed to get out. "Maybe. Hang on."

Fire painted my nerve endings and every muscle in my body. It felt like everything inside me had turned into liquid and was being poured into a different, more youthful mold. I fell to one knee, then flopped onto my back, writhing around in exquisite agony. I heard nothing, felt only the pain, but out of the corner of my eye, I saw Ruby going through the same process. I could only hope she'd make it through.

"Sweetheart, hang on," I said through gritted teeth, reaching out to touch her.

It felt as though an eternity had passed when, in reality, perhaps forty seconds had elapsed. Finally, the pain faded. I sat up and then stood with no pain and no difficulty. My heart rate and breathing returned to normal.

I glanced at Ruby. My girlfriend lay still and hadn't grown younger. Worse, she wasn't breathing. *No, no, no!* I dropped to her side, gently holding her shoulders and shaking her. No response. "Don't leave me, Ruby. Please don't leave me. I love you...we were so close...don't leave me!"

Still no response.

*Oh, God, what did I do to deserve this?* I wrapped her in my arms, rocking back and forth, calling out her name. Still no response...but then her chest heaved. She took in a deep breath, let it out slowly, then inhaled and exhaled again. Oh, yes! As I watched, wiping tears of gratitude from my face, her features started to change back to those of a young woman.

Finally, her eyes opened, and she whispered, "You're looking good, Carl. Just like old times."

"You, too." The renewal process completed itself, and I beheld the same woman I'd met and fallen for those many years ago. Our garden had given her back her youth and her beauty…and more. "You know, you're still as pretty as ever…sweetheart."

"You are such a flatterer." She blushed, but she sat up and slapped my arm playfully. "But thank you. How do you feel?"

What else could I say? "Younger."

"Same here."

We leaned against each other for a kiss, and it was just as sweet as I remembered it. Then we headed for the portal. "Do we surprise them or what?" I asked.

Leave it to my girlfriend to give the most practical answer. "They're going to ask about us sooner or later." She grabbed my hand and pulled until we were halfway through the portal. Once we could see the research team, she announced, "Guys, I think we're going to stay."

Arthur's eyes practically popped from their sockets. "Carl, you're…you're young again. You too, Ruby."

I couldn't help but smile. "Yeah, it's pretty neat, isn't it?" Did people still say neat? No matter. I'd said it. "What's the problem?"

Arthur recovered from his surprise and shook his head in short, angry jerks that signaled his frustration. "We can't enter."

Of course, he was angry. He was going to miss out on the find of the millennia. While the conga line thing might have worked again, I didn't want anyone spoiling our home with gadgets, bottles, or any possible contamination. And even though I liked Arthur—a little—I still didn't entirely trust him. Sometimes, it was better to keep a few things secret. This was one of those times. However… "Well, uh, I think we can help out," I said.

His face brightened. "Could you—"

"Do your experiments for you? Sure. Show me what buttons to press."

One of the techs showed us how to work each machine. We wore gloves, used sterilized pincers and cutters, and had a hundred different kinds of plastic and glass bottles.

As for the machines, we had one for air samples, one for radiation, and one for toxic elements. I did as they asked, and Ruby took various soil, plant, grass, and water samples, along with samples of every fruit available, even the green berries. When we went outside to hand over our first round of samples, someone gave me a camera and asked us to take a few pictures.

Why not? After a few hours, we were done, and we went through the barrier to deposit the remainder of the samples and the machines we'd used in front of Arthur and his crew.

"All done, Jonas," Ruby said. "Maybe it's not as thorough as you want, but that would take years, and we don't have time for that."

Actually, we did, but I got Ruby's point.

As for Arthur, he sighed as if disappointed, which didn't make sense since he now had evidence of what he'd been searching for all this time. "This is fine. We can analyze all this at our lab. For what it's worth, if you come back with us, we'll try to help you. It's the least that we can do."

"We're not going back," Ruby stated in a no-nonsense tone. "You know we can't. This is our home now."

She had my vote, and I slung my arm around her

shoulders. "I'm no scientist, but something tells me that if we leave again, we'll age just like before. We're back to what we were. Maybe it's the water here, or the air, or the food, or all of them together, or none of them. But we're, uh, linked to this place. If we go back with you, we'll start aging again."

"Wait—"

"No, you wait." I held up my hand to silence him.

Arthur had a lot of brass trying to convince me to do what I didn't want to. The rest of the research team stood as still as statues and said nothing, but I realized they were all armed. The question was, would Arthur double-cross us?

I cocked my head, barely maintaining my calm. "Are you going to use those guns on us, Jonas?"

After a moment when I was sure he'd say yes, he turned to face his men. "Take the equipment and the samples. Leave the explosives."

Arthur, Ruby, and I watched in silence as his crew took everything out. After thirty minutes, they were done, and we three were alone in the cave. Arthur heaved a sigh. "You got anything else to say?"

I did. "Listen, Ruby and I are happy here. I don't know why the people who built this place allowed us to stay, and I don't know why things here work like they do. But this is our home. We got lucky, and you want to take that luck away? Sorry, no deal."

Although my mini-speech sounded good, Ruby did better by stepping in front of me and holding out her arm with a tiny scar where they'd taken the skin sample. "I used to be a nurse. I saw what they did with lab animals. We gave you the samples you wanted. We told you the truth about our stay here. We even helped you with your experiments, so why do you want to take us back and keep us prisoners? We're not guinea pigs. We're people. This ain't the nineteen-forties anymore. You're supposed to be modern. Act it."

Arthur didn't say anything for a moment, and then, in a slow, steady move, he took out his pistol and three clips of ammo from his pocket. Slowly, he handed them to me. "You might need this…when you go back."

I felt a smile begin to stretch out the corners of my mouth. "Thanks. I probably won't need to use it, but it's nice to have, just in case."

"You're welcome."

He turned to leave, but I called him back. "Uh, Jonas, I have a request."

"And that is?"

I grabbed Ruby's hand. "Could you contact someone to marry us? I mean, her…me…marriage."

Ruby spun around to face me with a smile. "You're asking me to marry you…now?"

"Well, we've been living together for a long time, so, yeah. I want to make an honest woman out of you." Sure, that statement was probably way outdated, but being modern wasn't always the best thing.

Ruby smiled. "And I should make an honest man out of you, too."

Arthur uttered a brittle laugh. "You've been there over ninety years, and you want to get married?"

It seemed like the right thing to do. Ruby held my hand, and we replied together, "Yes."

Arthur rubbed his jaw as if wondering how to approach this situation. "I suppose I could contact a minister or a rabbi or a priest. It would have to be done online, but it would be valid…even though you technically don't exist."

He called out to one of his men, who came running over. He explained what was needed and then spun around to face us. "Please wait. My guy will get everything set up."

Ruby offered him a tiny smile of gratitude. "If you got a justice of the peace, that'll be enough."

It would have to be since they apparently couldn't contact a minister or a rabbi in time. However, Arthur spoke to one of the techs, and his subordinate managed to get through to the American consulate in China by internet to explain the situation. The officials said they'd try to link up with someone.

After an hour, the tech announced he'd gotten through to someone and handed over a laptop to Arthur. Before he opened it, he admitted that they'd had to tell a little white lie.

"Which was what?" I asked.

"Your birth dates. He wouldn't have believed me if I'd told him you were both born a century ago. Don't worry. I'll figure out something."

Well, if he said so.

He unfolded the laptop and said, "Now, look at the screen."

Ruby stared at the screen. "What is this? Is this real?"

"As real as it gets," the man onscreen said.

His name was Fayden. He was a justice of the peace, currently on vacation in China with his wife. In his sixties, he had a fleshy face that was red from too much booze, but he had a ready smile and a glint of mischief in his eye. "I'll have you know that you interrupted my tour. The officials brought me to the American consulate in Beijing."

"It's a special occasion," I said. Yeah...a wedding eighty-five years in the making.

He laughed. "This is a first for me. My first trip to China and my first wedding ceremony performed here, too."

"As long as it isn't your last," Ruby quipped.

"Wait and see," he said with another laugh. "All right, let's do this before we lose the reception."

He then went through the service after we'd given him our

names. Once we said our vows, he said, "By the power vested in me, I now pronounce you man and wife. Carl, you may kiss your wife. Ruby, you may kiss your husband, and good luck to you both."

As Ruby and I kissed, Arthur signaled the tech to shut off the video feed. "Signal the helicopter to take everything down to the base camp below us. You and the others go first, then send the copter up for me. Do it now."

His assistant hesitated, looking confused. "Sir, are you going to be all right here? I mean, with them?"

A pained expression crossed Arthur's face. "Don't worry. Get going."

The man took off, and soon, the helicopter could be heard outside the cave. Once everything was aboard, the helicopter took off, leaving Arthur alone with Ruby and me.

Arthur went over to the box of explosives, took out two bricks, slapped them above the archway of the cave entrance, and affixed timers to them. We waited around twenty minutes, and then the sound of the helicopter approaching spurred Arthur to action. He switched on the timers.

"All right, you two. You'd better get in there. I've set the timers for ten minutes. See you."

My heart took flight. "What are you going to tell the authorities? You got a lot of backers. They'll have questions. This could cost you a lot of money."

"It'll probably cost me my job," Arthur replied with a hint of a grin. "As for what we're going to tell our donors, we're going to say that this cave had already been destroyed, and we found no evidence. After you go inside, the explosive will blow up the entrance to the cave. Once I get back to the US, I plan to destroy all the evidence at APRIL. The world doesn't have to know. Not this time."

"What about Bayliss and the two Chinese soldiers? How

are you going to explain that?"

He pursed his lips and then blew out a puff of air. "We're a long way up," he finally said. "Bayliss was a loose cannon. He disobeyed orders, tried to find the caves without permission, and lost his balance on the trail up top. So did the Chinese soldiers. Treacherous footing. They slipped…bye-bye. Since I was the second-in-command, I'm now the official leader.

"And Senator Mulholland?"

Arthur's eyes grew round. "You know?"

"Yeah. I know he's sick, but our blood may not work on him."

"I guess he'll have to find his fountain of youth elsewhere." He inclined his head at the portal. "Get moving."

I wondered if Mulholland would really let things go. A politician as powerful as he was would probably cause trouble, but Arthur's excuse sounded plausible. And we wouldn't be there, so the government could go and stuff itself.

I had one more question, though. "What about the techs? They know."

His eyes twinkled. "They signed a nondisclosure agreement with our division. Even if they say anything, they'll have zero proof. I wouldn't worry about it."

I'd have to trust him. I was done with bureaucratic red tape. It was nothing more than a huge hassle. "Thanks, Jonas," I said. "I, uh, I don't know what to say."

"Say goodbye," he replied in an even tone. "Now, I gave you an order. Get moving."

Ruby went to Arthur and kissed him on the cheek. "Thank you," she murmured as she hugged him.

Arthur gave a noncommittal shrug, but he smiled anyway. "You're welcome. See you."

She returned to my side to take my hand, and we backed

through the wall. A minute later, I heard the sound of rotors. Arthur's ride had arrived. He called out, "I'm leaving now. Five minutes from now, the charges will go off."

Obediently, we ran a safe distance from the portal. We heard Arthur yell goodbye once more, and the sound of the helicopter leaving came through. Shortly after, an explosion sounded, the barrier shook, a thin veil of dust sifted down…then the gateway closed, and the wall of stone formed. Would it be forever? I had no idea. Although the pattern was there, our part in this conflict of old versus new was over. I dropped the gun and ammo near the entrance. We wouldn't be needing a weapon here.

Ruby put her arms around my waist and whispered, "Hey, Mr. Goodman, what do we do now?"

It was a good question. We could still leave if we chose to. Someday, another research party might come around to dig out the opening and check. They'd probably see the carving on the cave wall, and maybe they'd try to enter.

If we heard them, then maybe we'd greet them, but we could never return to our old life. If we stayed in the outside world too long, we'd undoubtedly start aging again.

My mind returned to the story of the man who'd sold his soul for immortality. Most things in life come with a price tag attached, with immortality exacting the biggest price of all. Our price for not aging was to stay in our garden, but with Ruby at my side, it was a cost I'd gladly pay a million times over.

And we could still leave if we chose to. Although our bodies were forever linked to this garden world, we could still use another exit in our garden, visit the other caves, and not worry about growing old. Nothing had happened to us on Jerana, so perhaps the magic—or science—still held. We hadn't visited all the caves yet, so we had new worlds to explore.

However, they could wait. We had our garden, we had our lives, and now, we had all the time in the world. "Well, we're here now, now and forever."

Her smile lit up an already bright day. "Yes. Now and forever," she echoed and tugged on my arm. "But you didn't answer my question."

In response, I bent down to kiss her fondly on the lips. "Well, Mrs. Goodman, we can do whatever you want."

Ruby looked around the garden...our garden...and then focused her gaze on me with a devilish grin. "Maybe we should see if our treehouse is still in shape."

We hadn't been gone that long, but then again...oh. "I suppose having a little rest wouldn't hurt."

My wife giggled, and as we set off hand in hand, she heaved a sigh of contentment. "I know it's sort of old-fashioned to say this, but there's no place like home."

She'd said that before, but it was worth hearing it again, and my pulse quickened. "Race you to the treehouse."


The End

# About the Author

J.S. Frankel was born in Toronto, Canada, many moons ago, managing to scrape through school, graduating from the University of Toronto with a BA in Political Science and English Literature.

In 1988, he moved to Japan to teach ESL. In 1997, he married the charming Akiko Koike, and their union produced two sons, Kai and Ray. Frankel and his family make their home in Osaka, where he teaches English by day and writes by night.

He is the author of over seventy novels, all for the young adult set, although many adults enjoy reading his novels as well. Some of his best-known works are the Catnip series, the Titans of Ardana trilogy, Seven Times Unto Eternity, Twisted, Charon Lane, and The Destiny Equation. He continues to write whenever he has free time, and he hopes that everyone will enjoy reading his novels as much as he enjoyed writing them.